SHORT AND SWEET

SHORT AND SWEET

A Collection of Short Romantic Stories

Anna Jacobs

This first world edition published 2011
in Great Britain and in the USA by
SEVERN HOUSE PUBLISHERS LTD of
9–15 High Street, Sutton, Surrey, England, SM1 1DF.
Trade paperback edition first published
in Great Britain and the USA 2012 by
SEVERN HOUSE PUBLISHERS LTD.

British Library Cataloguing in Publication Data

Jacobs, Anna.
  Short and sweet.
  I. Title
  823.9′14–dc22

ISBN-13: 978-0-7278-8106-9 (cased)
ISBN-13: 978-1-84751-401-1 (trade paper)

All Severn House titles are printed on acid-free paper.

Severn House Publishers support The Forest Stewardship Council [FSC],
the leading international forest certification organisation. All our titles that
are printed on Greenpeace-approved FSC-certified paper carry the FSC logo.

Typeset by Palimpsest Book Production Ltd.,
Falkirk, Stirlingshire, Scotland.
Printed and bound in Great Britain by
MPG Books Ltd., Bodmin, Cornwall.

Contents

Kissing Emily Baker

Anna's Notes

This is an updated version of one of the first short stories I ever wrote. I was so thrilled when it was accepted for publication by a major Australian women's magazine. I liked the main character so much, I wrote two other short stories about Emily later.

It was inspired by going to a dance in a tiny country town the year after we came to Australia. I'd never been to a dance where everyone took along a plate of something to eat and their own drinks as well.

When I was a teenager, we used to go to the local dance hall, a paid professional place. There were two of them in my town in those days.

But whatever the venue was like, it didn't stop people having a good time, and it certainly didn't stop the younger ones from meeting people. As my heroine does . . .

Part One

The imaginary town of Beeniup, Western Australia (population 1,533). Quite a few years ago, when Emily was seventeen.

One hot summer night Emily Baker strolled through town with her best friend Vera, on their way to the church hall. 'I don't feel at all like dancing,' she muttered.

'Well, you didn't want to stay home with your father and his new lady friend, either, so you might just as well make the most of it.'

'It'll be the same old crowd. And Bill Nutting will want to dance with you all night.'

Vera smiled. 'I like dancing with Bill.'

Emily sighed. It was clear to everyone that Vera was getting serious about Bill and that he too was rather smitten. Only two years ago, he'd been spotty and thin. Now, suddenly, he was a man, not all that good looking, but kind and with a lovely nature.

She didn't fancy any of the lads in town, which didn't matter because she didn't fancy marriage, either, not after seeing what her mother had gone through. She was going to make a career for herself, be a top secretary, and later she'd go to England to work for a while. She'd got family there: her mother's brother and his two daughters. They'd come out for a visit once, but it hadn't been a success. Her uncle and dad hadn't got on at all. But she'd got on well with her cousin Diana, who was the same age as her, and they still wrote to one another every month, sharing their lives and thoughts.

At the brightly lit hall she and Vera left their plates of food on the supper table, nodded to the married couples sitting at the tables near the entrance and walked past the clusters of younger folk, girls on one side of the room, boys on the other. They always sat in the far corner, near the scratchy three-piece band.

As soon as they took their seats, Vera nudged her friend. 'Hey! There's a new fellow here tonight. I wonder who he is?'

Emily didn't bother to turn round. 'Who cares?'

Vera giggled. 'Go on, have a look. He isn't very good looking, is he? He looks older than the other lads. Wonder why he isn't married?'

Emily turned for a brief glance. The young men were standing in groups, heads together, chatting. Their hair was neatly parted and shiny with brilliantine, their skin showed the ruddy aftermath of a thorough application of soap and water, and their shirts gleamed white against suntanned necks.

The curly ginger hair of the stranger stood out a mile and his skin was covered in freckles. Definitely not worth a second glance.

'How's it going with your father?' Vera asked once they were seated.

Emily scowled. 'It's awful. He's all over that Megs and she spends more time at our house than she does at her own. I don't know where to look sometimes, the way they go on.'

Vera pursed her lips. 'She's not bad looking, for a woman her age, you've got to give her that.'

The music started but Emily ignored it, still thinking about the latest quarrel with her father. There would be two or three married couples dancing, the ones who really fancied themselves. The younger men would take their time about choosing partners, studying them as if they didn't already know the girls they'd been through school with!

A shadow fell across her and a man's voice said, 'May I have the pleasure of this dance?'

Emily looked up to see the new fellow standing beside her and stifled a sigh as she stood up. When she heard his relieved whoosh of breath, she smiled at him briefly and saw his colour start to subside. He had even more freckles when you got close.

'Me name's Tom. Tom Norris. What's yours?'

'Mmm? What? Oh, Emily. Emily Baker.'

She walked on to the floor and allowed herself to be pulled against a strong young body that smelled of peppermint and soap.

They stood poised for a moment on the edge of the floor, then set off in time to the music. Slim Dusty's 'Pub With No Beer' again. She was sick of that song. Waltzes should be romantic, not comic. She looked up into gentle green eyes. He still looked a bit nervous, so she said, 'You're new to town, aren't you?'

'Yes. I've come to work for Sanford's. I'm a brickie.'

'Oh, yes?'

Tom began to tell her about the job he was working on but she couldn't keep her mind focused on what he was saying. Well, if truth be told, she hadn't the slightest interest in him or his bricklaying. She was too worried about whether her father would go as far as marrying the barmaid.

Tom had to stop speaking while he counted aloud the steps in a turn, 'Two *and* three,' then set off on the straight again, mostly keeping time to the music.

He definitely wasn't a good dancer. But then, not many boys in Beeniup were good at these old-fashioned dances the Social Committee insisted on.

'So what do you do to earn a crust, Emily?'

'I work at the Co-op in the fabrics and haberdashery section.'

'Nice job?'

'No.'

Two more fruitless attempts at conversation, four carefully

counted corners, then Tom stopped dead in the middle of the floor and scowled at her.

Emily gasped and looked around. Everyone was staring at them! 'Keep moving!' she hissed.

His lips set in a firm line and he kept his feet where they were.

She tugged at his arm. 'What've you stopped for?'

'It's not much fun dancing with a girl who can't be bothered to talk to you.'

She could feel her face growing hot with guilt. 'I'm sorry. I didn't mean to be rude. I – I've got a few problems at home. It's nothing to do with you, honest.'

She sighed with relief as he took her in his arms and started moving again. From then on she made appropriate responses as he led the discussion carefully through the weather and the latest pop songs, to the lack of rain in the district.

She wished she was anywhere else but here. She'd only come out to get away from the sight of her father and the barmaid cuddling and giggling on the sofa. At their age! Her head was aching and her new shoes were killing her. She should never have bought them, but they'd have to do for best for the next year now, because she couldn't afford another pair.

It seemed ages until the music stopped. 'Thanks for the dance.' Emily made a beeline for Vera without a backward glance at her partner.

Tom watched her cross the floor, wishing he could have kept her by his side. Then he realized in horror that he was standing alone in the middle of the floor, and hurried over to join the group of young men he'd come with.

'What did you stop dancing for?' Bill asked.

Tom shrugged. 'We got talking. I forgot to move me feet.'

Stan, who had been listening unashamedly to their conversation, sniggered. 'Talking's all you'll do with that one, believe me.'

'She's real pretty.' Tom stared across at Emily wistfully. 'I've always liked dark wavy hair. And her eyes are lovely too. Blue's my favourite colour for eyes.'

Stan snorted. 'Well, let me give you some advice, mate: don't waste your time on her.'

'She seemed friendly enough.' Tom's pride was stung. He had

never been a ladies' man, but he wasn't starting off in a new town with a public failure on his record. Besides – he stole another glance across the dance floor – Emily was far and away the prettiest girl here tonight. There was something really special about her.

Stan, who considered himself a bit of a goer with women, spent several minutes explaining the futility of trying to get anywhere at all with Emily Baker. 'And if you think you can do any better, think again.'

'Oh?'

'Yeah. She won't even give a bloke a kiss under the mistletoe, that one.'

'Who says she won't?' demanded Tom, full of Dutch courage from the two beers he'd poured down before the dance.

Stan set his hands on his hips, jaw jutting out dangerously. 'I say she won't!'

Tom squared his shoulders. 'Care to put your money where your mouth is? Or is this just sour grapes because she doesn't fancy you?'

Stan glared at him. 'Sour grapes? About *her*? There's enough trouble in this world without going looking for it. And Emily Baker's trouble with a capital "T". Even at school, when she was in the junior class and we were seniors, she'd snap your nose off as soon as look at you. Too smart for her own good, that one.'

'I don't blame her for snapping *your* nose off,' said Tom. Most of the young blokes in the town were friendly sorts, but Stan was full of spiteful remarks about anything and everything. Tom had taken an instant dislike to him.

'Oh, don't you? Let's see how well *you* do with her, then.' He pulled a banknote out and brandished it in the air. 'Five dollars says you don't get a kiss out of her.'

Tom looked across at Emily, nodded and said quietly, 'You're on. Five dollars it is.'

Stan looked surprised by this ready acceptance, then said with a sneer, 'You don't look like a ladykiller, but you're on. I'll need to see the kiss myself before I pay up, mind.' He folded his arms.

'No trouble,' said Tom airily. 'I'll get her to kiss me right here in this hall.'

Stan pounced. 'Get *her* to kiss you?'

Realizing his error, Tom nearly choked but hid it with a cough. He wasn't going to back down from a challenge. 'Yeah. Make it a bit more interesting, eh?'

Stan's expression said he felt the money was as good as his. 'You're on, mate.'

Tom tried to smile but there was a sinking feeling in his stomach.

'When by?' Stan pressed.

Tom thought rapidly. 'Dunno. Couple of months. Got to get to know her first, haven't I?'

'One month.'

'Two or the bet's off.'

'Oh, all right.'

By this time, all the unattached young men had gathered around them. There was a chorus of guffaws from the group.

'Get to know her!'

'Old Tight-knickers!'

'You'll be lucky.'

Bill Nutting took charge. 'Now, let's get the terms of this bet straight. Tom, you're going to get Emily Baker to kiss you on the lips here in the hall, in front of everyone?'

'Yeah.'

'By the end of two months.'

'Yeah.'

A few dances later, Tom saw Emily sitting in a corner on her own. He took a deep breath and marched across the floor. 'May I have the pleasure again?'

She shrugged and stood up.

He realized suddenly that there were tears in her eyes. She'd been upset earlier on, too. 'Is something wrong?'

'No.' Her voice was tight and false. 'I'm fine really, just a bit tired.' A tear spilled out of one eye and slid down her cheek before she could stop it.

He ached to hold her in his arms and comfort her, but didn't dare touch her. 'How . . .' Nervousness made Tom's voice come out a bit high, so he cleared his throat and started again. 'How about taking a walk outside on the veranda? Bit of fresh air will do us both good. It's far too hot in here. It's the tin roof.'

She stared at the ground, trying to hide her tears. 'Yeah, why not?'

He shepherded her out of the hall, staying between her and the gawking heads in the corner.

'I'm not going past the end of the veranda,' she warned as they walked out into the warm dusty night. 'I don't go down by the creek, not with anyone.'

'Who asked you to?' He made a great play of blowing his nose, while she wiped her eyes surreptitiously.

'Bit childish, that lot.' He jerked his head back at the hall to indicate the group of young men, who were all gawking in their direction.

She looked back listlessly. 'They're about the same age as you.'

'I'm a year or two older, and anyway, I've been on me own since I was sixteen. Me parents died. Car crash. I had to go an' live in a hostel.'

'Oh. I'm sorry.' Bad enough to lose your mum, as she had. Fancy losing both your parents at once. She frowned, not knowing what to make of him. 'So you're working in Beeniup now?'

He nodded. 'Mmm. Like I said, I'm a brickie. Good trade.'

'I'd have gone to work in Perth.'

'I've worked there. I fancied a stay in the country. Easier to get to know people. I'm going back to Perth in a year or so, though. You can find some interesting jobs there if you're a good brickie, and I am.'

She sighed. 'I wish girls could have a trade like boys do. After Mum died, my dad found me a job at the Co-op an' I had to leave school early. He didn't care whether I wanted to work there or not. Any old job would have done as long as I was bringing in money. I wish *I* could be a carpenter or bricklayer.'

Tom guffawed. 'Girls couldn't lay bricks. They're too heavy!'

'And how heavy do you think the rolls of material are in the drapery section, then?' Her eyes glittered at him and she tossed her head. 'You fellows are all alike. Think you're the only ones who can do anything.'

Silence fell. Moths fluttered around them, attracted by the lights. She didn't even seem to notice.

*   *   *

Emily saw Tom open his mouth then shut it again. He was watching her out of the corner of his eye. She didn't want to talk about her problems, least of all to a stranger, wished she could go home now. But she had to wait for her friend Vera. Her dad didn't like her to walk home alone and Vera's parents were the same. As if there was anything to be feared in a sleepy little town like Beeniup.

She turned back towards the hall. 'I've cooled down now.'

He put one hand on her arm to stop her. 'What were you crying for?'

'I wasn't crying.'

'Yes, you were.'

She glared at him, daring him to contradict her. 'I was just hot and tired. That was sweat I was wiping away.'

'Oh, yeah? You'd swear that on a Bible, would you?'

'It's none of your business what I do,' she repeated, tossing her head. 'Now, are we going inside together or do I go back on my own?'

He gave up the struggle and followed her in, admiring her slender figure in the flowery skirt and pale-pink top. Prettiest girl he'd ever met. Never mind the bet, he wanted to get to know her. And he would, too. 'Will you have the next dance with me, then? *Please?*'

She relented. 'Yeah, OK.' At least this one didn't try to paw you or press against you when you danced with him. She hid a smile. Well, he wouldn't. He was too busy counting his steps.

They danced together three more times, but she wouldn't allow him to take her home afterwards. 'No, thank you. I always walk back with my friend Vera. She lives in the next street.' Besides, her dad would kill her if she came home with a strange man.

As the two girls strolled along, enjoying the coolness of the night air after the hot little church hall, Vera chuckled and nudged Emily. 'He's nice, isn't he?'

'Who is?'

'That new lad. Whatisname.'

'Tom Norris, you mean?'

'Yes, him. I think he fancies you. He kept watching you all night. And he didn't ask anyone else to dance.'

Emily shrugged. 'So?'

'Don't you like him? I think he's got a real nice smile. He can't help the freckles.'

'He's all right. Politer than some others I could mention, anyway.' And he'd helped her to hide her tears. That had been kind. It still hit her badly sometimes, the longing to confide in her mother, the feeling of grief.

'We'll have you courting yet, Emily Baker.'

Emily stopped dead in her tracks and glared at her best friend. 'Look, how many times do I have to tell you, Vera Morton: I'm *not* interested in boys. And I'm never, *ever* going to get married. I'm moving to the city as soon as I've enough money saved. In Perth I can train as a secretary and find myself an interesting job.'

'Well, I can't wait to get married, have my own house and start a family. I intend to be well and truly married by the time I'm twenty, and I want to live in Beeniup near my family.'

'If I had a family like yours, I'd want to live near them, too.'

There was silence. They both knew what Emily's dad was like.

As they reached her gate, Vera said, 'Well, I reckon you'll be married by then, too. We'll be able to bring up our children together and we'll stay friends all our lives.'

'I'd like to stay friends and I'll come and visit you often, but I'm still moving to Perth.' Emily was quite determined about that.

The next day her father announced that he was marrying Megs as soon as it could be arranged. 'No reason to wait. She doesn't like where she's living and—'

Emily stared at him in horror. 'How *can* you, so soon after Mum?'

'Your mother's dead and a man needs a wife. Now, I don't want any trouble from you about this, young lady.'

'You'll do what you want to anyway. You don't care about me.'

'I care enough to give you a home.'

'Give me a home! Who had to pay the electricity bill last month?'

'I was a bit short. I'll pay you back after the wedding.'

She knew he wouldn't. Oh, what did it matter? She was moving to Perth as soon as she had enough money. This news only made her more determined. She wasn't buying any new clothes, or spending money on make-up from now on, she would save even harder.

Emily was a bit nervous about going to live on her own in the capital city, which she'd only visited two or three times in her whole life, but if she had some money behind her, she'd be all right. She had to be.

Apart from her father's sister, whom she didn't like, the only relatives she had left that she knew about were her uncle and cousins in England. It had been up to Emily to phone and tell them that her mother had died. Her uncle's wife was ill and he couldn't come to the funeral, but he'd sent a lovely condolences card and letter saying he hoped Emily would come and visit them one day.

Diana had also written to say how sorry she was and to tell her cousin about the lad she was going steady with, who sounded very nice. But Emily wasn't going down that path.

Marriage was not for her.

Part Two

T he wedding wasn't a fancy affair. Emily attended but didn't join the happy couple and their friends at the pub afterwards. And when they got back home, clearly the worse for wear, she stayed in her bedroom.

Megs was friendly enough, but she wasn't good around the house.

Two weeks later, Emily came home after a frustrating day at work, when everything had gone wrong, and lost her temper at the sight of the unwashed breakfast dishes in the kitchen. 'It's not fair, Dad, expecting me to skivvy for you two as well as go out to work. Why can't *she* help clear up? Other people's mothers look after the house.'

Her father smelled of beer already and was unsteady on his feet. 'Don't call your stepmother *she* like that! She has a name, and a pretty one too. Anyway, she didn't marry the house, she married me.' He sniggered at his own joke, he always did.

In fact, Megs had scorned the idea of stopping work. Emily had heard them arguing about the way she let Arthur pay all the bills while keeping her own wages for herself. Every now and then she treated him at the pub to keep him sweet. She was good at managing him, you had to give her that.

Emily sighed. 'All right, then. Why can't *Megs* help more around the house?'

'Because she needs more rest than a young 'un like you, so shut up an' get on with it!'

She knew by the gleam in his eye what kept tiring Megs out. Honestly, the pair of them were worse than Mrs Brown's old tom cat. 'It's not fair,' Emily persisted, determined to make a stand. 'She doesn't leave the house until ten and she hasn't even washed the breakfast things. And she comes home for a rest in the afternoons. I've been working hard all day and there's still the tea to cook for you and me. We were rushed off our feet with the sale and I'm tired out.'

He growled ominously, and when she opened her mouth to continue the argument, he thumped her, something he'd never done before. She stood there willing herself not to cry, but she wanted to. How could he think so little of her? He was her father, he should love her.

He stood there staring, his mouth open, then looked down at his hand and backed away. 'Sorry. I didn't mean to . . . You shouldn't answer me back, though.'

She walked along to her bedroom and slammed the door.

That evening she went round to Vera's and borrowed some make-up to cover the bruise on her cheek.

The following morning over breakfast Arthur took one look at her and complained, 'You're too young to wear that much make-up.'

'I'll wash it off, then.'

When she came back into the room, he swung her round to the light. 'What's that?'

'It's a bruise. *You* gave it to me last night.'

A pause, then he said sulkily, 'You shouldn't be so bloody cheeky. You'd – er – better put that make-up on again.'

'No. I'm too young. You said so.'

Anger rumbled in his throat, but Megs, who had just come

yawning in, leaned against him and jerked her head at her stepdaughter to indicate she should get out quickly.

Emily could hear them arguing as she got ready for work.

'You shouldn't have hit her!' Megs said.

'I didn't mean to, but she's always answering me back.'

'That's because she's grown up now, not a child. Did you tell her you were sorry?'

'Yes.'

'Well, don't do it again. I don't like men who bash young girls.' Megs came along to Emily's bedroom. 'You all right, darl'?'

'Yes.'

'I can lend you some make-up to hide that bruise.'

'No, thank you. I've got to go to work now.'

When her workmates asked her how she'd got the bruise, she told them, 'My dad hit me.' Which caused a sensation.

Later that night, after the hotel closed, Arthur came and threw open her bedroom door without knocking. 'What did you tell people I hit you for?'

'Because you did.'

'Once! I've never laid a finger on you before. And lately, you'd try the patience of a saint.'

She pulled the covers up to her chin and listened to him ranting. At last he went away. There were no embarrassing sounds from the next bedroom that night. She heard him trying to coax Megs and smiled at the sharp refusal.

Bill seemed to have made friends with the newcomer, so Emily had found herself walking behind him and Vera with Tom. He didn't say much, but he smiled a lot. He had a nice, gentle smile, which lit up his face. She didn't mind being with him, not in a group anyway. But she wasn't going steady with anyone and she hoped she'd made that plain to him.

Her heart sank when she found Tom Norris waiting for her outside the Co-op after work. His face lit up at the sight of her and two of her workmates made comments about 'young love'.

Emily hesitated. She could hardly walk past him when it was clear he'd come there specially to meet her, but she hated him to see her with a big ugly bruise on her face. In the end she took a deep breath and moved forward. 'Hello!'

Joan and Connie – both married women – walked on, smiling broadly, which left Emily and Tom standing there together looking like a couple.

'I'll walk home with you,' he said, without so much as a by-your-leave.

'I can get home my own way, thank you very much.' No young man had ever met her after work. The other women would tease her about this for weeks and the whole town would consider her to be going out with Tom. She could feel herself blushing. What must that look like with the bruise?

He ignored her unenthusiastic response, fell into place beside her and said, 'Who hit you?'

'Mind your own business!' She walked on more quickly.

'Tell me who did it!'

'What's it got to do with you?'

'I'm going to thump him, that's what.'

She stopped dead in her tracks. 'Why would you do that?'

He looked sideways at her and she could see anger sparkling in his eyes. 'Because it's not right, hitting girls. Men who hit girls should be taken out and shot, like the mongrels they are.'

She stared at him in amazement. 'But you hardly know me. Why should it bother you whether someone hits me or not?'

He turned bright red, swallowed hard and began walking again, hands thrust deep into his pockets. 'I don't like bullies.'

Emily looked sideways at him. He smelled strongly of soap and had a clean shirt on, so he must have gone home from work to wash and change before meeting her. She could feel herself softening towards him. He wasn't much taller than she was, but he looked strong and healthy. He seemed honest, too, and gentle, in spite of the scowl presently decorating his face.

She patted his arm. 'Look, Tom, it's kind of you to worry about me, but there's no need, really. He won't do it again. Megs saw to that.'

'So it *was* your dad!' Tom digested this for the length of a street. 'What did he hit you for?'

'I cheeked him. I'm fed up of doing all the housework for him an' Megs. It isn't fair.'

'He still shouldn't have hit you. And why do *you* have to do all the housework? Your stepmother should be doing some of it, surely?' He didn't wait for an answer, but shook his head and repeated, 'And anyway, men shouldn't thump women like that!'

She shook her head in exasperation. Once again, Tom Norris was proving more stubborn than she'd expected. 'Look, it's only happened this once and he said he was sorry, so it doesn't matter. Right?'

'It does matter to me.'

'Well, I'm getting away from home next April. I've been saving up – I'll go the minute I've enough money – so just leave things alone.'

Tom stopped walking so she had to stop, too. When he reached out towards her bruised face, the gentle butterfly touch of his fingertips made her feel funny inside. They started walking again, but neither spoke. She was sure people were peeping out of windows at them, sure word would be all round town by the next day that she was going steady with Tom Norris.

She sighed with relief as they reached her gate. 'This is where I live. I have to go in and get Dad's tea.'

'Will you be all right?'

'Yes, of course.'

He swallowed hard and said in a rush, 'Would you come to the pictures with me on Saturday night?'

'Pictures?' She was going to say no, but he was looking so pink and agonized that somehow she couldn't bear to hurt him.

'I might. I'd have to bring my friend, Vera. We always go out together on Saturdays.' Maybe that would stop people getting ideas about her and Tom being a couple.

'Is Vera the girl you were with at the dance?'

'Yes. She's my best friend.'

'All right, then. She can come too. But I'm not paying for her. Only for you.'

Emily jerked back to the present. 'We can pay for ourselves, thank you very much!'

'Not if you come out with me, you can't!' He thrust his hands deep into his trouser pockets and scowled at her. 'If I take you out, I'm the one who's paying.'

'It doesn't matter who pays.'

'It matters to me. I like to do things properly.'

His face was all scrunched up, he was frowning so hard. She

suppressed a sudden urge to giggle. He was such a serious fellow. But nice. 'Oh, very well!' She'd go halves with Vera afterwards on the ticket.

Her dad hadn't come home yet, thank goodness. She changed into an old skirt to keep her work one nice and got on with the housework.

That Tom Norris! What had got into him? She'd have to ask Vera to tell people she wasn't going steady with him.

But would they believe that after seeing her at the pictures with him?

The sooner she got away from here the better.

Beeniup, being the main town of the district, had a proper cinema, not just film showings in the church hall. The programme at the Odeon ran from Tuesdays to Saturdays, with a new film each week, although occasionally a film was brought back a second time – 'by popular demand' it always said in the newspaper. Sometimes plays were put on there, too, by the amateur theatrical group or the school.

Jim Hodson had built the rough little cinema himself on a bit of spare land his family had owned for years and he was there every session, taking the money and rubbing his hands together with pleasure over the clinking coins. His wife ran the refreshment kiosk and his daughter carried round a tray of ice creams in the interval. They were fond of money, the Hodsons.

The young of Beeniup and districts patronized the cinema regularly, whatever the film showing, because there wasn't even a café to sit around in. The only café did meals – mostly roast of the day and two veg – and closed at seven thirty sharp in the evening, and that was that. During the hot summer months, the Memorial Gardens were often full of young folk taking the air and from there they could go and walk along by the creek, where Rotary had put in a nature trail. The creek was reduced to a mere trickle during the hot, dry summer weather but it never stopped flowing, at least.

On the Saturday night Tom escorted Emily into the cinema with a proprietorial air and Vera followed. Bill met them in the foyer, pairing off with Vera straight away.

Tom bought Emily a box of chocolates, which left her speechless. No one had ever bought her a box of chocolates before and it felt – nice. But she couldn't help being aware that they were once again the focus of considerable interest, so she kept her distance from Tom, not giving him a chance even to hold her hand.

During the interval between the shorts and the feature film, Vera stayed inside the cinema, talking and laughing with Bill. So Emily found herself walking outside alone with Tom, who claimed he needed to stretch his legs.

'What's wrong with Stan?' she demanded. 'He kept twisting round to stare at us while the shorts were on and now he's followed us outside, and he's *still* staring.'

'I don't know.'

Tom's face was flaming again. There was something fishy going on here, Emily decided. Perhaps the other lads had dared him to invite her out. He didn't seem the sort to take the initiative without a push. 'Just why did you invite me out tonight, Tom?'

He had to swallow several times before he managed to say hoarsely, 'Because I wanted to.'

'Why? You hardly know me.'

His face was lit up like a packet of Redhead matches. 'Because you – you're pretty.'

She giggled suddenly. He looked so embarrassed, poor thing. He grinned back and the tension eased.

'Sorry.' She patted his hand. 'I shouldn't tease you.'

He beamed at her again.

Vera was right, she decided. He did have a nice smile.

'You can tease me any time you like, Emily,' he managed after much swallowing and wriggling.

Honestly, what could you do with a fellow like him? It'd be like treading on a kitten if you spoke sharply to him.

When they went back inside after the interval, Vera and Bill were cuddled up together, his arm round her shoulders, her head resting against him.

As the film began Tom fidgeted so much that in the end Emily dug him in the ribs and hissed, 'What's the matter?'

'Er – this seat's a bit narrow. Me arm keeps goin' to sleep.'

She grinned in the darkness. Who did he think he was kidding?

Why didn't he just put his arm round her like the other lads did? She wouldn't mind that, not with him.

He cleared his throat and opened his mouth, then shut it again and continued to fidget.

She couldn't stand it any longer. 'Oh, put your arm round my shoulders, Tom Norris. You know that's what you're after. But no monkey business!'

His arm crept around her, though he had some trouble deciding what to do with his hand. She nearly giggled aloud as it twitched to and fro, before settling chastely on her shoulder. But it would have upset him if she'd laughed and she didn't want to do that. He was a nice bloke, Tom Norris. Much nicer than the other lads.

As the film continued, she eyed him sideways. There was no mistaking the happy expression on his face. When he saw her looking at him, he beamed at her. He didn't try anything on, either. Ah, he was just an old softie, this one. She relaxed against him, feeling safe and happy for once.

Afterwards, they all four walked home together. Vera and Bill stopped outside her house, said goodbye and before the others could move off, were clinging to one another in a passionate goodnight kiss. Tom averted his eyes and continued walking along the street with Emily. At her gate, however, he pulled her into his arms before she'd realized what he was doing and gave her a kiss.

And she found herself kissing him back, liking the gentleness of his lips, the way his hand caressed her hair.

As they drew apart she turned and gasped. Oh no! Her father was sitting on the front veranda! And he'd seen them! 'I have to go in!' she gabbled at Tom, fumbling with the gate catch. 'Thanks for taking me out. You'd better go now.'

'Will you let me walk you home after work on Monday?'

'Just go, will you!'

He leaned against the gate post. 'I'll have to have a rest first. It's a long walk back for a disappointed man.' He folded his arms with the air of one prepared to wait until the last trump.

She could see her father scowling at them. 'Oh, very well! Meet me after work, then.' She hurried through the gate.

Her father stood up as she climbed the veranda steps. 'I thought you were going out with Vera!'

'I did!'

'Well, who was that, then?'

'Who was what?'

'None of your cheek. Who was that fellow you were with, the fellow who was kissing you?'

She could smell the beer on his breath, see him swaying from side to side. She hated it when he got drunk. She wondered where Megs was. Her stepmother was usually back from work by now. For the first time, Emily wished Megs was there to distract him.

'Well?' roared Arthur. 'Who the hell is he?'

'His name's Tom. I met him at the church social.'

'You're too young to be walking out with boys. And don't think I didn't see him kissing you.'

'Too young! I'm nearly eighteen! Mum was only eighteen when she married you! You didn't think *she* was too young when you met her in England!'

Her father waggled one finger at her, so close to her face she thought he was going to hit her again. 'Don't answer me back, young lady! No respect nowadays, that's what's wrong wi' the world!'

From nowhere, it seemed, Tom materialized. He pushed himself between Emily and her father. 'You leave her alone, you bully!'

'What the hell . . .?' It took a minute for what had happened to sink into Arthur Baker's beer-clouded brain, then he began to sputter with rage. 'Who do you think you are, you young tyke? Gerroff my veranda before I push you off!'

Emily tugged at Tom's arm. 'Come away! He wasn't going to hit me, honest.' But Tom only unclasped her fingers and turned back to face her father. He had that stubborn look on his face again and her heart sank when she saw it.

'Grown men shouldn't thump young girls,' Tom said slowly and distinctly. 'It's not right.'

Arthur gaped at him. 'It was just the once and she bloody well deserved it, the impudent young madam.'

'Well, if you hit her while I'm around, I'll make you regret it.' Tom squared up to Arthur, fists clenched, jaw jutting out.

The flyscreen door crashed back on its hinges, making everyone jump, and Megs stormed out on to the veranda, all thirteen stones of her. She was wrapped in that dreadful flowery dressing gown, her feet were clacking loudly in high-heeled fluffy pink mules and she had curlers in her hair.

Emily closed her eyes and prayed fervently for lightning to strike her dead on the spot.

Megs shoved Arthur and Tom apart. 'What's the hell's going on here? Can't a lady have a bit of peace in her own home? An' who the hell are *you*?'

'This is Tom Norris,' said Emily hurriedly. 'He walked home from the cinema with me and Vera.'

Tom let his fists drop and nodded politely, holding his hand out. 'Pleased to meet you, Mrs Baker.'

You had to give it to him, thought Emily. He had excellent manners, much better than Bill or that dope Stan. Tom was right: they were only boys while he was a man.

Megs shook Tom's hand and studied him carefully. 'Pleased to meet you, too, Mr Norris.'

'Now, look here—' Arthur began. But the beer had got to his legs and he staggered suddenly backwards, sitting down with a thump on the old veranda couch, burping loudly and looking surprised.

'No, you look here,' said Tom, hands on hips, scowling down at him. 'I'm not having you hitting Emily again, not ever. You hear me?'

Megs looked from one to the other, then nodded her head slowly as her mouth formed an 'Oh' of comprehension. She winked at her stepdaughter. 'Is that what this is about? Nice of you to care, I'm sure, Mr Norris.'

Emily felt impelled to explain Tom's presence. 'I met Tom at the last church social. He's new to town.'

'I think I've seen you in the hotel, but *you* don't stay there all night like some I could mention.' She inclined her head graciously to Tom, magnificently disregarding her curlers and the smear of cold cream on her nose. 'You'll have to excuse my husband, Mr Norris. He's had too much to drink.'

'Well, he still shouldn't hit her.'

'You're quite right there.' Arthur had sworn at Megs a few days previously and demanded a share of her wages, even going so far as to snatch her handbag. She had immediately set about him with the rolling pin, chasing him around the kitchen like an

avenging fury and threatening to kick him in a very tender place
if he so much as waggled a fingertip at her again, let alone touched
her money.

'It's the drink,' she murmured confidentially to Tom. 'He can't
hold it like he used to.'

'Who're you—' began Arthur. He tried to get up, failed and
fell back with a loud trumpeting noise. 'Pardon me for farting!'
He gave a snort of laughter and let out another blast.

Megs didn't even look at him. 'Shut up, you old sot, and mind
your manners when ladies are present!' She patted Tom's arm and
her voice changed into a gentle coo. 'Look, don't worry about
Emily, Mr Norris. I'll see that her father leaves her alone from
now on.' She shot a vicious glance at her husband and added, in
a voice like a squirt of acid, 'Her *and* the beer.'

She led a bemused Tom gently to the gate, inviting him to
come to tea on the Sunday of the following week. When he had
disappeared down the street, she hugged Emily. 'You sly little
sausage! Why didn't you tell me you'd got yourself a young man?'

'I haven't! He's just a friend.'

Megs patted her shoulder and nodded understanding. 'In the
early stages, is it? I'll tread carefully when he comes round, then.'

'But—'

'He seems a nice young fellow. What does he do for a living?'

'He's a brickie.'

Megs nodded. 'Good trade, that. People will always need houses
built.'

'It doesn't matter what he does. He *isn't* my boyfriend!'

Megs had already turned away and was staring down at Arthur.
'Look, Emily, you run along to bed. I'll deal with your father
and then lock up.'

Emily walked numbly to her bedroom, horrified by the idea
of Tom coming to take tea with them. Just as she was falling
asleep, however, she remembered how he had stood up to her
father and a smile crept over her face. Funny sort of knight,
wasn't he, to rescue her from her dragon of a father? All those
freckles. Not to mention the blushes.

Arthur Baker remained outside on the veranda all that night.
When he banged on the locked door of the house and threatened
to break it down if they didn't let him in, Megs banged on the

other side with her rolling pin, threatening his manhood if he set one toe over the threshold before he'd sobered up.

After pleading for entry more humbly, but still in vain, Arthur threw himself back down on the old couch in a huff. Later, when it grew chilly, he pinched the dog's blanket and huddled down under that.

Emily couldn't hide her annoyance when Tom met her on the Monday after work. 'What did you accept the invitation to tea for?' she demanded before they had gone ten yards.

'I thought you'd like it.'

'Like it? *Like it?*' She snorted indignantly. 'It'll be awful! They'll ask you how much you earn and what your prospects are. They'll ask about your family. They'll have us *courting* before we know where we are.'

He avoided her eyes. 'I don't mind.'

She stopped dead in her tracks and sucked in her breath. 'Tom Norris, you'd better understand now that I'm never going to get married! Never, ever!'

'Why not?'

Oh no! He had that stubborn look on his face again.

'What's wrong with marriage?' he demanded when she didn't answer.

'Everything! I've seen what happens to women who get married. I'm not getting lumbered with a husband who spends his life down at the hotel getting drunk while I stay at home and look after the kids. What's more, I'm leaving this one-eyed dump and going up to Perth soon. I can type already and I'll carry on studying at night school till I've learned the other things I need. I'm going to be a secretary in a posh office one day and have my own flat. I'm—'

'Not all men get drunk and spend their evenings at the hotel, Emily. My dad didn't and—'

'Well, he was one in a million, then!'

'And I won't, either. I'll look after my wife properly. She won't have to go out to work. I don't believe in wives working. And she'll have all my wages. Unopened packet every week. That's only fair.'

Emily tried desperately to turn it into a joke. 'You sound almost as if you're proposing. Only there aren't any violins playing.'

'When I propose,' Tom's voice was louder than usual and carried quite clearly to Vera's parents, who were walking past just then, 'I'll do it properly, with flowers and on me knees.' He reached out and grabbed Emily's hand, holding it tightly as if he thought she might try to pull away.

Shock held her motionless, her mouth agape. Mr and Mrs Morton slowed down and when she glanced sideways she saw them watching her.

Tom took full advantage of his moment. 'At present, Emily Baker, we're just going out with each other. And we'll do that properly, too, which is why I'm coming to tea to meet your family.'

'But Tom – we haven't . . . we don't . . . Tom, we hardly know one another.' Her voice wobbled and a little shiver ran down her spine at the determination emanating from him.

'No. We don't. Not yet. But we will.'

'But Tom, I really don't want to get . . .'

Her voice tailed away as the masterful air dropped from him. He put his hands on her shoulders and stared into her eyes with the air of a puppy pleading not to be kicked. 'Won't you even give me a chance, Emily?' His voice was full of raw longing.

'B–but I—'

'I like you, Emily.' Tom swallowed hard and added in a funny gruff voice, 'A lot.'

She could sense how hard it was for a shy man to say those words. And how could she be cruel to someone who had come to her defence against her father?

'It wouldn't hurt to give a bloke a chance,' Tom pleaded softly. 'That's all I'm asking for. Just a chance.'

'Oh, well, I – you see . . .'

He beamed at her, pulled her arm inside his and set off walking again, absolutely radiating happiness.

Oh crikey, he'd thought she meant 'yes'! Stunned, bewildered, Emily allowed him to escort her along the street, convinced everyone was staring at them.

At the corner they met Stan Bowler. The expression of shock on his face was more than she could deal with in her present state. She could feel herself blushing and clung for dear life to her only support in a bewildering world – Tom's arm.

Stan stopped dead in his tracks, mouth open. She watched as Tom grinned triumphantly at him and slowed down to give her a quick hug. Then he started walking again, whistling cheerfully. She was about to ask what was going on between him and Stan when they arrived at her house.

At the gate they stopped, and Tom's hand tightened on hers as he raised it to his chest and pulled her closer. He had to swallow twice before he could get the words out, and even then his voice was rough and choky-sounding. 'You're the prettiest girl I've ever met, Emily Baker. Ever.'

'I–I bet you say that to all the girls, Tom Norris,' she quavered, making a last-ditch attempt to lighten the atmosphere.

'No, I don't. I couldn't. Just to you, Em.'

His eyes were a clear green and his expression was serious and loving. She gulped and looked down at his hand. Square-tipped fingers, scrubbed nails, little scratches. It felt strong and warm and comforting. She felt a funny little ache start in her chest; to think that a man should be so gone on her.

He released her hand and smiled. 'You'd better go inside now, Em. We don't want your father getting upset at me again.'

'Yes.' She couldn't even voice her usual protest at the shortening of her name, she felt so strange and wobbly.

She watched Tom stride away. Maybe it wouldn't hurt to give this bloke a chance. It'd be nice to have someone to go out with. Most of the other girls her age were paired off. That didn't mean she was courting, or intending to get married. No way. But she did like him. They could just be friends. No harm in that.

Part Three

Three weeks later, however, Emily found out about the bet. She had never been so furious in her whole life, not even when her father hit her.

Vera, who had told her about it over a shared lunch in the Memorial Gardens, looked at her anxiously. 'I thought you ought to know.'

'I'll kill him!' Emily raged. 'How dare he bet on me like that? Just wait till I see that Tom Norris!'

'Keep your voice down. Mrs Lukas is coming.'

Emily bit down on her fury and tried to smile.

Mrs Lukas, who had probably been coming to ask for their help at the church fête, as usual, took one look at Emily's flushed angry face, made a smart left turn and walked away.

Vera patted her friend's arm. 'You shouldn't get mad at him. He only did it because he fell for you. Bill told me Tom took one look at you at the social and he was gone.' She sighed enviously.

'One look and he was ready to make a laughing stock of me. I *will* kill him!'

'Bill says Stan was making all sorts of nasty remarks about you that night, an' Tom stuck up for you.'

Emily opened her mouth to say something scathing, shut it and then asked hesitantly, 'He stuck up for me? Even before he knew me?'

'Mmm. Bill says he's never seen anything to beat it. Love at first sight. Don't be mad at Tom. He's absolutely crazy about you.'

It was nice to know someone was crazy about her, but still the bet rankled. 'Yes, well, we'll see what he has to say for himself.' It must be a mistake. Tom wouldn't bet on something like that. Bill had probably got it all wrong.

Tom could tell that there was something wrong the minute he saw Emily that evening. She was waiting for him at the corner near the Co-op, arms folded across her chest, foot tapping impatiently. Every line of her body looked tight and angry.

'You're late. And I can smell the beer on your breath from here, Tom Norris.'

'It was just the one. It's been a scorcher today. I was thirsty.'

'Well, you can flipping well go back to the hotel and stay there. I don't want to be taken home by a man who drinks.'

'I do not drink.'

'You've just had a beer. You admitted it.'

'That was one lousy beer.' He grabbed her arm and swung her round. 'What's really wrong, Emily?'

She breathed deeply, then the words burst out, 'I've heard about it.'

'About what?'

'About your bet.'

Her voice was so loud, her expression so furious that a group of women from the Co-op stopped to watch. Tom glanced around in panic, then dragged her across to the Memorial Gardens.

She let him pull her as far as the flower beds and then stopped to confront him, hands on hips. 'I don't want to see you again, Tom Norris. And I'll never, *ever* forgive you for that bet.'

He froze for one moment, then reached for her.

'Let go of me! I'll scream if you don't.'

But he didn't let go.

And she didn't scream.

Although she made a half-hearted attempt to struggle, he didn't even seem to notice and pulled her right into his arms, kissing her long and hard – not as a shy lad, but as a man kissing the woman he loves.

And when he stopped, she felt so dizzy, so bewildered, she let him hold her close and explain what had happened.

'I'm sorry about the bet, Em. Really sorry. I don't care two hoots about it. I'll give Stan his money and he can crow all he wants about winning. It's you I care about.'

She stared at him, bemused.

'I'm *not* letting you go. I'm not. I love you, Emily Baker. I want to marry you. I'm *going* to marry you.'

'But—'

'I know it's a bit soon to be talking of marriage, but when you meet someone who's so,' for the first time his voice faltered, 'so right in every way,' his voice became firm again, 'you don't let them walk away.'

'But Tom, I—'

He stopped her protest with another heart-stopping kiss, then he drew her over to one of the park benches. 'Oh, Em, don't finish with me! I couldn't bear it if you did that.'

Her protest died unborn. The look in his eyes made something turn to jelly inside her. His hand seemed to have left a warm print on her arm. Not since her mother died had anyone shown such deep feeling about her. Vera was right. It was just like in films. Tom Norris really had fallen madly in love with her.

And she loved him, too!

She stared at him open-mouthed as that realization sank in. How had that happened when she'd vowed never to get married?

She saw how anxiously he was looking at her and shook her head at him. 'Oh, you are a fool.'

It was as if he sensed the change in her, because he smiled as he leaned forward and left a trail of little kisses across her face.

'An absolute fool,' she breathed in his ear as she kissed him back, not caring now whether anyone saw them or not.

Vera, walking home with Bill, paused for a moment to watch her friend's enthusiastic embrace. 'I knew she was getting fond of him,' she said softly, then hurried Bill past before he could call out or whistle and destroy the moment.

'It's so romantic!' she sighed as she looked back over her shoulder to see them still sitting there, Emily's head on Tom's shoulder. 'He was looking at her as if she was the sun in the sky.'

'Other fellows can be just as romantic,' Bill growled.

'Oh?' She looked at him challengingly.

But for the life of him, he couldn't find the courage to kiss her right there on the main street with friends of his parents watching them from their shop doorway.

Vera set a cracking pace home, nose in the air.

Bill trailed along by her side, and when they got away from the main street, he pulled her into his arms and kissed her. But he knew it wasn't as good as the sizzling kisses Tom and Emily had been exchanging in full view of the whole town.

Tom Norris won his bet two weeks later, but only because Emily couldn't bear to see that slimy Stan Bowler win five whole dollars off him.

At the next church social she hissed, 'Now!' and kissed him – on the lips – in front of everyone.

And only he heard the words she muttered afterwards, 'Don't you *dare* make such a bet again, Tom Norris!'

She was a bit huffy with him for days afterwards, in spite of the big bunch of flowers he bought her. It had taken a lot for her to kiss him like that in front of everyone. He understood that and bore her wrath meekly. She was a wonderful girl, his Em was. She still hadn't agreed to marry him, but it was only a matter of time before she did.

They both knew that.

Dance With Me

Anna's Notes

*I've enjoyed visits to small country towns so I like to set my stories
there.*

*I didn't experience a Bachelors and Spinsters Ball at first hand,
because I was happily married before we came to Australia, but it seems
a great idea.*

*After I'd watched a documentary about one on TV, the old 'what
ifs' started popping up in my imagination, and here's the result.*

Jodie hummed as she drove along the highway. Her friend Marissa
had moved to the outback the previous year, and though they'd
kept in touch by email and phone, they'd not managed a
get-together for a while. But this weekend she was going to stay
with Marissa, who was eight months pregnant. And when the
baby was born, she was going to be its godmother. How cool
was that?

The road was almost hypnotic, tugging her on past farms, horse
studs, and only occasionally through a tiny cluster of twenty or
so buildings. Jodie smiled. Country towns were sometimes tiny,
but they were still called towns not villages.

She didn't stop anywhere, was in a hurry to get there.

As she got close, she could see how different everything looked
from her last visit. She'd read about the drought, but this trip
really brought it home to her. The grass was bleached beige and
cars were dusty, apart from the windscreens. Well, who would
waste precious water washing a car?

Feast or famine, that was Australia.

As she turned on to the sandy track that led to the farm, a
plume of dust rose into the air behind her car, signalling her
arrival. Marissa must have been watching out, because she rushed

out to hug her and show her to her bedroom. It was the same little sleepout as last time; an enclosed corner of the veranda which they used as a guest bedroom.

In the evening Pete left the two of them to chat and went into town to have a beer with his mates.

After they'd caught up on all the news, Marissa began fiddling with the arm of her chair.

Jodie knew the signs. Well, they'd been flatmates for three years, hadn't they? 'Spit it out, Marissa. What's the matter?'

'I – do you mind going to the dance tomorrow?'

'A dance? I've not brought anything but jeans. Why didn't you tell me about it before I left?'

'We weren't sure about it. You can borrow my blue dress. I don't fit into it any more. I was wearing it when I met Pete. It's a lucky dress, that one.'

It wasn't till they were driving into town for the dance that Marissa blurted out suddenly, 'I didn't explain everything about tonight.'

'Oh?'

'It's a Bachelors and Spinsters Ball.'

Jodie looked at her in puzzlement.

'The dance – it's only for singles. Happens every year. People come from miles around. It's very popular. Half the town met their husband or wife there.'

'But you two are married, so you can't go now and . . .' Jodie's voice tailed away and she looked accusingly at her friend.

Marissa avoided her eyes.

'You haven't!'

Silence.

Jodie's heart sank. 'No way am I going to this ball on my own. Anyway, I'm a city girl. What would I want with a husband who's a farmer?'

'I told you not to do it,' Pete said.

Marissa began to cry.

Jodie wasn't going to fall for that. 'I'm sorry to upset your plans, but I'm definitely not going.'

'Why not? You always said you wanted to get married one day. If someone hadn't pushed me into going, I'd not have met Pete.'

Jodie heard Marissa's breath catch on a sob and felt mean.

'You don't have to go, Jodie,' Pete said. 'I told Marissa not to do it. We'll take you to the hotel for a meal instead. They can easily fit another place at our table.'

'We were going to wait at our friends' house and pick you up again at midnight – well, unless you phoned to say you'd met someone.'

'How kind of you!'

'I've arranged for you to sit with some friends of mine,' Marissa said. 'You'll really like Kate and Pam, even if you never dance a single dance.'

'What part of "*no*" don't you understand?'

They reached the town then. It was a bit bigger than some of the ones she'd driven through, with one wide main street, a few shops with verandas and a couple of hotels – one did meals, the other only sold drinks.

'Oh, look!' Marissa waved wildly. 'Kate and Pam are waiting for you outside the Country Women's Association hall.'

Muttering something, Pete pulled up there.

The two young women were dressed in shimmering black and vivid red, all glammed up for a night out, with hair and make-up perfect. They rushed over to the car, bubbling with enthusiasm, and Jodie had to admit they seemed fun.

Marissa sent her a pleading glance, one hand on her stomach, tears in her eyes.

Jodie tried to hold out and failed. 'Oh, all right. I'll go. But don't expect me to come back with a man. I'm a career woman. And make sure you keep your mobile switched on.'

The hall was a wooden structure at the end of the main street, quite large and overflowing with people. It was surrounded by a sea of vehicles, mainly four-wheel drives. People were strolling across a nearby field from their cars, talking and laughing.

Jodie followed her new friends inside the big double doors. Their progress was slowed by stops to greet friends and introduce her. They seemed to know just about everyone.

She chose a seat at the rear of their table, feeling overwhelmed by the noise. The guys were eyeing the girls as if they were on a shopping spree. Though actually, the girls on her table were eyeing the guys just as openly.

A meat market, that's what it was.

And is a club in the city any different? a voice inside her head asked. She didn't answer that question. She was here for three hours maximum. She could do it. And she'd kill Marissa tomorrow!

The lights dimmed a little, a group of musicians began to play. They were good and soon had people up dancing. One by one her companions were claimed and taken on to the central floor.

When she was left alone, Jodie held her head up and tried to keep a pleasant expression on her face. It was a bit embarrassing to be the only one left sitting at the table.

She was so busy watching the dancers and tapping her fingers on the table in time to the easy-going country music that she didn't realize someone was standing next to her till a deep voice asked, 'Would you like to dance?'

She looked up . . . and up. He was tall, dark, not exactly handsome but definitely nice looking. Anything was better than being a wallflower, so she pushed her chair back. 'Thank you. Yes.'

They circled the floor and he said almost nothing. Strong silent type, obviously.

'So . . . what do you do for a living?' she asked brightly.

'Grow flowers.'

She blinked. 'I thought this was farming country.'

'Diversification.'

It was like drawing teeth getting him to speak. 'What sort of flowers?'

'All sorts. Lilies do well, chrysanths, whatever's in season. Native flowers, too.'

They circled the floor three times more in silence and to her relief the dance ended. He had the good manners to escort her back to the table, then nodded and walked away.

They played one of her favourite songs next. Her foot started tapping almost of its own accord. 'Don't you girls ever get up and dance together?'

'Not at the B and S, we don't,' one girl said. 'We're here to meet guys. Look, there's that guy I met at the last rodeo.'

Rodeo, for heaven's sake, Jodie thought. It's like the Wild West.

She danced with one guy after another. Shoes were kicked off,

She realized she was holding John's hand and smiled. How had that happened?

As she looked sideways, their eyes met and he swung her into his arms for a kiss. She was so surprised she didn't protest, even more surprised to find herself enjoying his kiss, not wanting it to end.

He let her go and smiled down at her. Why had she ever thought he wasn't good looking? He was gorgeous. She pulled his head down and gave him another kiss out of sheer curiosity. Hmm. Definitely not a trace of frog in this one.

He pulled back a little. 'This wasn't meant to happen.'

'Nothing much has happened yet.'

His frown changed into a wry smile. 'It will if we don't watch out. I've thought about you all year. You're even prettier than I'd remembered.'

He set his hands on her shoulders and looked her straight in the eyes. 'Either you run away now or we give this a chance . . .'

She didn't run away.

John was not only attractive, he was fun, in a quiet understated way. And she didn't want to die a childless spinster.

Of course Marissa didn't stop crowing about it for years.

Jodie didn't care. She loved growing flowers and three children seemed like just the right number, especially when they were John's children.

Dolphins at Dawn

S ara fell in love with the house at first sight. Who wouldn't? A town house with its own small jetty on a waterfront block. She'd lived in several parts of the world, but Western Australia would always be home and, after the accident, she'd moved back here to the holiday town of Mandurah.

The sale went through quickly, though not quickly enough for her.

The day she moved in, her neighbour was just getting out of his car in the next carport. He stopped to nod politely and would have turned away if she hadn't moved forward and held out her hand.

'I'm Sara King, coming to live next door.'

'John Barraby.' He shook her hand, nodded again and went indoors.

So much for getting on with the neighbours. He clearly wanted nothing to do with her.

She could see a little girl watching them through the window of the house. When Sara smiled and waved to her, the child's face brightened and she lifted one hand.

The man called out, his voice carrying clearly through the open windows, and the child vanished from sight.

Miserable fellow! Would it have hurt him to crack a smile?

Then the removal men arrived with her furniture and she

forgot all about her neighbour as she directed them where to put it. There wasn't much, but she'd buy other bits and pieces as she needed them.

That evening Sara went to sit on her jetty, tired after unpacking her boxes. Below her dangling feet the clear water lapped against the piles. She stared down at it, mesmerized by the fractured patterns of light and the little fishes darting around in groups.

A pelican flew past. A cormorant sat on the next jetty, long neck hunched into its body.

She sighed blissfully. She was going to enjoy living here.

It was the dolphins who brought her and her young neighbour together. The first morning Sara saw them, she rushed outside, entranced. They were swimming in the canal right next to her block, several adults and two babies. The babies were playing together in the middle of the canal, rolling around in the water like puppies.

Joy filled her as the adults moved past, their bodies leaving smooth circles in the surface of the water when they dived. One came up with a fish in its mouth. Another splashed her as it twisted in the water, and she could swear it'd been looking up at her.

'They often come past at this time. I like to watch them.'

Sara turned and smiled as she saw the child sitting on the next jetty. 'I do, too.'

Not until the last grey dolphin had vanished from sight did she turn and limp into the house.

'Have you hurt your leg?' the child called.

'Yes. I was in a car accident in England.'

'Kerry! Come back inside this minute.'

'Daddy doesn't like me to pester the neighbours,' the child whispered, hurrying off.

The next morning Sara watched the dolphins on her own. When she turned to stare at the house next door, she saw a face at the upstairs window and a hand waved briefly, so she put up one hand to fiddle with her hair, afraid if she waved back openly the child would get into trouble.

A few evenings later there was a frantic knocking on Sara's front door.

When she opened it, Kerry was there, tears streaming down her face. 'Come quickly! My dad's fallen downstairs and hurt his leg.'

Sara found her neighbour lying at the foot of the stairs unconscious, blood trickling from a cut on his lip, a bruise already staining his forehead. One leg was twisted at an unnatural angle.

'We need to call the ambulance. And don't touch that leg. Where's the phone?'

'In the kitchen.'

'Stay with him. If he wakes up, tell him I'm calling for help.' But when she went back into the hall, the man hadn't stirred.

'He's not dead is he?' the girl sobbed.

Sara put an arm round her. 'No, he's not, just knocked out. I think his leg might be broken, though. The ambulance will be here soon to take him to hospital.'

Kerry clung to her, sobbing.

'Could I call anyone to help you, your mother perhaps?'

'Mummy's gone to live in America.'

'Any other relatives or close friends?'

'No, just me and Daddy.'

There was a flashing blue light outside and Sara ran to open the door.

After one of the paramedics had examined John, who was now half-conscious, he looked at Sara. 'I'm afraid we'll have to take your husband to hospital.'

She limped across to join them.

'Are you hurt, too?' the ambulance officer asked.

'No. It's an old injury.' Before she could correct them about her relationship to John, one had hurried out to get the gurney, and then they were both occupied in lifting him on to it and wheeling him out.

As she closed the rear doors of the ambulance, the paramedic called to Sara, 'See you at the hospital. Go to the Emergency Department.'

Kerry tugged at Sara's hand. 'Will you take me?'

'Yes, of course. Let's make sure this house is locked up and you have some keys.'

Once that was done, Kerry went to the door, her eyes beseeching Sara to hurry.

'I'll just fetch my bag and car keys, and lock my place up.'

She stood for a moment next to her car, apprehension churning through her. She hadn't driven at night since the accident. But Kerry was looking at her so trustingly, she swallowed hard, summoned up her courage and got in.

All the way to the hospital, the little girl sat hunched in a tight ball. 'He won't die, will he?' she asked once as they stopped at some traffic lights.

'No, of course he won't. It's only a broken leg and concussion.'

'Are you sure?'

'Pretty sure.'

'Can't you go any faster?'

'No.' Sara swallowed. 'It's not safe to drive fast at night.'

Her husband had been speeding when the accident happened. Killed instantly, they'd told her afterwards, as if that would be a comfort. But she wished he'd lingered for a while, wished she'd had time to say goodbye to him.

When they arrived at the hospital, reaction set in and after she'd parked, she buried her head in her shaking hands.

'Are you all right?'

She forced herself to smile at the child. 'I'm fine. It's just a long time since I've driven at night. I was . . . a bit nervous.'

In casualty they told her that Mr Barraby needed an operation for his broken leg. 'When did he last eat?'

Sara turned to Kerry. 'You were the only one with him.'

'Dad didn't have any tea,' she said, wrinkling her brow. 'But he had a sandwich at lunchtime and a cup of tea about two o'clock.'

'Are you sure about that? Maybe he had a bar of chocolate or a biscuit?'

Kerry shook her head. 'No. He doesn't like chocolate. And we forgot to buy some biscuits last week. He's been working at his computer all day. It was a rush job.'

That probably meant that Kerry hadn't had any tea, either, so Sara bought them something to eat from the hospital café. After that they went back to the waiting area.

It seemed a long time until a nurse came to tell them the operation had been successful. 'But he won't be properly awake for hours yet,' she added. 'You'd be better taking your daughter home, Mrs Barraby.'

Sara tried to explain that she was only the neighbour but the nurse had hurried off again. She looked down at the anxious child. 'I suppose I'd better take you home with me. Or perhaps you'd rather I found a social worker and—'

Kerry looked terrified. 'Please don't do that! If you let me stay with you, I'll be really good, I promise.'

Not until they got into the car did she add, 'Daddy and me don't like social workers. When my mummy married again she went to America and she wanted to take me with her. Only I wouldn't go. The social workers said I could try living with Daddy but they're still watching us.'

Sara nodded. That explained John Barraby's wariness. 'Well then, you can definitely come home with me. I'll give the hospital my phone number.'

As she was tucking Kerry up in bed, the little girl put her arms round Sara's neck and gave her a hug. 'Thank you for letting me stay. Can we watch the dolphins together in the morning? They always make me feel better.'

'Yes, of course. I like watching them too.'

It was a long time before Sara got to sleep. She wasn't at all sure her neighbour would approve of her looking after his daughter, but there was no one else and there were still two or three weeks to go before school started again after the summer holidays.

She smiled as it occurred to her that the hospital staff still thought she was his wife. She'd correct that the next day, or he would. In fact, he'd probably have sorted it all out. But if he was wary of getting tangled up with social workers, who knew what he'd have said. She'd better be careful till they compared stories.

In the morning Sara and Kerry got up early and stood on the jetty together. The water was choppy, but not from boats passing. Several sleek grey shapes were curving in and out of the water and the two baby dolphins were back playing together.

Water slapped gently against the two jetties and seagulls circled, hoping to snatch something from the dolphins. Their cries were so much harsher than the ones in Europe.

'Aren't the dolphins lovely?' the child asked, taking her hand and smiling.

They watched the dolphins herd the fish to the canal wall. Silver shapes twisted and leaped out of the water, trying to avoid being caught, while a pelican hovered nearby, ready to snatch any stunned fish that came close enough.

Sara rang the hospital at eight o'clock and the nurse said, 'Ah, yes. Mr Barraby is awake and asking for you to bring in his daughter. Shall I transfer you?'

She didn't want to risk being overheard. 'No. Just tell him Kerry's fine and we'll both be there in an hour or so.'

He was in a private room and she hesitated by the door as Kerry ran across to hug him. He still looked pale and when he thanked Sara for looking after his daughter, it was obviously an effort.

She remembered from her own accident how the anaesthetic lingered and how dopey she'd felt.

A nurse came up to them. 'Ah, your wife is here.' He didn't bother to explain that she wasn't his wife and when Sara looked at him in puzzlement, he put one finger to his lips and looked at her pleadingly.

Not till the nurse had left them did he say, 'I wonder if I can ask you to look after Kerry for a day or two, Ms King, just until I can hire someone to housekeep for us while I'm incapacitated?'

'Of course.'

As he hesitated, his daughter said, 'I've told Sara about Mum and the social workers.'

'Ah.' He looked at her anxiously.

'I quite understand your position and it doesn't make any difference to me. I'd love to have her. She's been no trouble and I'm enjoying having company.' Sara saw him relax visibly.

'Thank you, Ms King. Um – you don't go out to work?'

'Do call me Sara. Like you, I work from home. I'm an editor.'

She didn't take offence at him asking a few more questions. It was only natural he'd be worried about his daughter living with a stranger.

After a few minutes, however, she could see him getting drowsy, so she took Kerry away, promising to return that evening.

Sara quickly realized that Kerry was older than her years; used to being with adults; quiet in her play. They visited the hospital for the next two days and when John was ready to come home, they made him up a bed in her living room for the first few days.

'I can get up the stairs at my place if I take my time,' he protested. 'You've done enough, looking after Kerry.'

'I've enjoyed her company. I've been on my own for a while now.'

But as soon as he could, he moved back, hiring a housekeeper to come in every morning.

She missed them when they moved back into their own home, but the housekeeper didn't do shopping and, once again, he was wary of asking help from any government service.

'Oh, for heaven's sake!' she said in the end. 'I'll do the shopping, with Kerry's help. How hard is that? I have to go shopping for myself, you know.'

'Oh. Well. Thank you very much.' His stiffness vanished and he gave her a genuine smile. 'I'm so grateful. I don't know what I'd have done without your help.'

'That's all right. People helped me a lot after the accident. It's good to pay something back to the universe.'

She enjoyed the shopping expeditions, which were punctuated by Kerry's instructions.

No, Daddy hates that cereal!

Oh, but we always have this sort.

He never eats bananas. They're too squishy.

Because John was still on crutches, Sara had to drive them to the shops to buy the school uniform and other equipment for Kerry. And since the child had clearly grown a lot recently, they had to buy some casual clothes too.

She found herself advising the little girl about clothes and hair, smiling at John about Kerry's strong views on what was cool and what wasn't.

They felt almost like a family. She'd once hoped for a family. She liked children. But it hadn't happened.

He felt more like a friend now, had relaxed enough to share a drink on the patio, or bring her a fish he'd caught.

She couldn't help wishing . . . wishing for more. But she didn't dare wish for too much because he was still holding back a little, still acting only as a friend and neighbour.

Pity.

Then one day there was a knock on the door and she found John there, leaning on his crutches. She made him a cup of coffee and carried it out for him as they went to sit by the water.

'I wonder if you'd help me and Kerry again.' He fiddled with his cup before adding, 'I have no right to ask, but . . . I've been notified that they're sending someone to check up on me. My wife's lawyer is making another fuss about who looks after Kerry.'

'Were Kerry and her mother close?'

He shook his head. 'No. Jen wasn't a very hands-on sort of parent at all. But she does like to win, and she regards not getting custody as losing.'

When he didn't continue, Sara prompted, 'So . . . how can I help?'

He took a deep breath. 'Could you pretend to be engaged to me? That'd make it look so much better – and you *do* get on well with Kerry. It shows when you're together.'

She was so surprised for a moment that she could only stare at him, then she smiled. 'I wasn't even sure you liked me.'

He closed his eyes for a moment, then stared at her. 'I like you too much. I didn't think I ought to get mixed up with anyone when I have so many hassles in my life. So I held back. But fate keeps bringing the three of us together.'

'It's nice to have good neighbours,' she said carefully.

'We're more than that, I hope. I'd really like to get to know you better.'

'I'm happy to pretend to be engaged, if that will help, John. I'm really fond of Kerry. And I'd like to get to know you better too.'

His voice grew gentler. 'Why don't we give it a try, then?'

She nodded. She knew what she hoped for and she rather thought he felt the same way, but there was no need to hurry.

He was still wary and she wasn't going to push him into something he wasn't sure about. Let him find his own way.

Anyway, living next door made it simple to take things easy as they got to know one another better.

Just then a dolphin swam past, swishing its tail and looking as if it was smiling at them in approval. She smiled back.

Suddenly, she felt sure it would all work out as she wished.

The Pelican Affair

Anna's Notes

This is based on another personal experience. In my little seaside town, pelicans really do mug tourists. They're big birds.

When we first moved here, they used to try to get inside the houses. They knew where the catches were for the doors, but those huge beaks are no use for opening them. Thank goodness.

We have stood outside watching the sunset, though, and been joined by a pelican, who stood with the circle of people, quite at ease. He (or she) was as tall as my shoulder.

The West Australian sun shone down brightly and seemed to be winking at her, telling her to stick to her decision. Sarah Lawson took a deep breath and tried to recapture the tone that used to make her daughters do as they were told.

'You won't change my mind, Jan. I'm going to hire a holiday flat for a week and give you and your family a bit of a break.' She just had to get away from her kind but bossy daughter for a while, if they were to stay friends.

'But Mum, there's no need. We love having you here. I've been wanting you to visit us in Australia ever since Dad died.'

'Two months is far too long for any guest. You and Tony could drive me down to Mandurah, though. Or no – perhaps I should hire a car.'

'No need for that. It's a small seaside town. You can walk everywhere you need to if you get a place near the Foreshore. We'll drive you down and see you safe.'

What did they think was going to happen to her in a rented holiday flat, for heaven's sake? She'd been living on her own in England ever since Bill died, and managing very well, if she said so herself.

But Jan, dear fussy Jan, was treating her like a third child, one who needed watching and guiding every moment. The trouble was, Australia was a long way to come from England for only a short stay. But a week was long enough for any guest to stay, and she should have known better, should have planned a visit to Sydney for a week or two in the middle, perhaps.

The drive to the small holiday town passed in a tense silence. But the flat was lovely, with a balcony overlooking the water.

When Jan had stopped fussing and left, Sarah sat in the living area of the flat, relishing the silence. She loved her grandsons, but they were a noisy pair.

Now to make herself more comfortable and get into a holiday mood. She'd seen a liquor store at the end of the road and decided to buy herself some wine.

She chuckled as she left the flat, feeling like a rebellious teenager. Not looking where she was going, she bumped into someone and ricocheted back against the wall. 'Oh, sorry. My fault. I was miles away.'

The man smiled at her. 'I was too. You look happy. I hope you enjoy your holiday.'

'I intend to make the most of every blessed minute.' She continued down the stairs, humming an old Abba song that had been running through her head for two days, ever since she'd heard it on the wireless. She didn't care if she was old-fashioned, she'd always loved that song.

After a short walk, she found the liquor store, bought two bottles of Chardonnay and a bar of chocolate, and carried them home in triumph.

When she opened the fridge to chill the wine, she saw the casserole Jan had insisted on making for her. 'It'll last two days, Mum, save you money.'

It wasn't going to last even one day. Jan's cooking hadn't improved over the years and because the children were small, she made everything very bland. Not feeling even slightly guilty, Sarah scraped it into the rubbish bin.

She went out again for a walk along the foreshore, looking for somewhere to eat. This was such a lovely little town, built along the sides of an estuary.

She found a Chinese restaurant and had a delicious meal, then, since it was getting dark, strolled back to the flat. Sitting on the balcony she sipped her wine, now nicely chilled, and watched the town's lights reflected in the water. She didn't even switch on the TV.

The following day she went for a ride round the canals in a large tourist boat, looking at the houses of rich people – to her anyone who owned a large house right on the water was rich. She envied them the beautiful views, but it was no use longing for what was out of reach, so she'd just borrow their scenery while she was here then go home to her small English terraced house.

When the boat returned, edging slowly into place alongside a jetty right in the town centre, she wondered what to do with herself next. She saw some people sitting by the water, eating chicken and chips out of boxes, and suddenly she was hungry. OK, it was junk food, but there was no harm in having it occasionally. She joined the queue.

She took her box further along the foreshore and sat down to eat, opening it and sniffing in appreciation.

Suddenly something large and soft landed on the grass next to her. She let out a squeak of shock, then realized it was a pelican. It didn't seem at all aggressive, just stood watching her. She forgot her food, entranced by being so close to an exotic bird. When she was sitting down, it was the same height as her.

It edged slowly forward and she sat still, not wanting to frighten it away. Then suddenly it lunged at her and before she could move, it snatched her box of food.

Fleeing in a clumsy run, it jumped off the walkway and lifted up into the air, crossing the water, still carrying the box.

'Are you all right? It didn't hurt you?'

It was the man she'd bumped into at the flats.

She burst out laughing. 'Oh, they'll never believe me when I go back to England. I've been mugged by a pelican.' The more she thought about it, the more she laughed, and he did too.

Then her stomach rumbled and reminded her of why she was sitting there. 'I'd better go and get something else to eat. I'm ravenous.'

'Since you're a visitor to our town and a resident has stolen your lunch, would you allow another resident to buy you a replacement?' He swept a bow. 'James Brennan at your service.'

'Oh. Well, that's very kind. But there's no need.'

His disappointment showed clearly. 'I'd enjoy some company, but I'll not impose myself on you.' He turned to leave.

'No, wait! I'd enjoy some company too. But I'll buy my own meal.'

She felt a bit shy as they walked back to the café strip, but the sun was shining and he had an infectious smile.

'Let's eat indoors,' he said. 'You've caught the sun a bit today.'

'That's because I haven't got my daughter here to tell me off and nag me into the shade. I do love to feel the sun on my face.'

'Are you staying with your daughter?'

'I have been. She lives up in Perth. It's the first time I've been abroad since my husband died. Do you really live here in Mandurah all the time? How wonderful that must be.'

'I love it. Look, this is a good café. I'm a regular here and I promise you their chicken is much nicer than the fast food stuff.'

He took her to a table by the window, from which they could see the estuary and the boats going up and down it: big ones, little ones, and suddenly a group of fins.

'Dolphins!' she exclaimed, leaning forward. 'Oh, how wonderful! Dolphins *and* pelicans in one day.'

They lingered over the meal, finding they had a lot in common: films, music, a love of the sea. When they eventually left the restaurant he hesitated. 'I've really enjoyed your company. May I see you again?'

She felt suddenly shy. It'd been nearly forty years since a man had asked her for a date – and that man had become her husband. She was so out of practice at what to reply, she settled for the plain, unvarnished truth. 'I'd like that. I've enjoyed your company too.'

'I'll walk you back to the flats. How about a trip out for lunch at a restaurant up the river tomorrow?'

She beamed at him. Even Jan couldn't say that was unsafe as a first date, if she ever told her daughter, which she probably wouldn't. 'I'd love to do that.'

'I'll pick you up at ten o'clock.' He pulled a card out. 'Here's my phone number and address.'

'I've got a mobile. My daughter bought it for me, just a very basic one. I'll give you my number, too, in case you change your mind.'

'I won't.'

His smile made her feel breathless.

That evening Sarah sat on the balcony again, sipping her wine, then went inside and tried to read a book of Jan's that she'd borrowed. But it was a dreary tale, even if it had won a literary prize. Thank goodness for the magazines someone else had left in the flat. She settled down to a crossword.

When her mobile phone rang, she saw it was Jan and nearly didn't answer. But if she didn't, her daughter might come rushing down to check on her, so she picked it up.

She loved Jan dearly, but she and her husband were so earnest about life. They stared at her sometimes when she laughed at things.

The next day was even hotter. Sarah wore a light summer dress. She didn't even think of taking a cardigan because there wasn't a single cloud in the blue sky.

There was a knock on her door at ten o'clock and she opened it to James's smiling face.

'We can walk to the jetty if those pretty sandals are comfortable enough,' he said.

'They are and I love walking.'

The boat was large, capable of taking about a hundred people, but it was only half full. They sat on the upper deck and James pointed. 'Look, some of your friends.'

Sarah shaded her eyes with her hand and watched four pelicans riding a thermal current in the sky above some more waterside houses. 'It's amazing to think that such huge birds can be so graceful.'

The boat took them down one of the residential canals and stopped. 'Ladies and gentleman, a shoal of fish must be up here today, because there's a group of cormorants fishing and if you watch very carefully, you'll see some pirates attack them.'

Sarah looked at James in puzzlement. 'Pirates?'

He grinned. 'You'll see.'

Suddenly several pelicans landed and pushed into the group of diving cormorants. One took hold of a cormorant by the neck and shook it till it dropped its fish.

Sarah gasped. 'I wouldn't have believed it if I hadn't seen it with my own eyes!'

James chuckled. 'They don't only mug humans, they mug other birds as well.'

'And here was me thinking how romantic it was to see them.'

The boat set off again, stopping at a waterside restaurant, where they had lunch.

'I'll never eat again,' she said as she pushed her empty plate aside. 'It was so kind of you to buy me crayfish. Such a luxury.'

On the way back she said, 'Do you live in one of the flats, or were you just visiting someone when I bumped into you.'

He hesitated.

'You don't have to answer if I'm being too nosy.'

'No, it's all right. Only don't let it put you off me. I own the block of flats, actually. I was just checking that some repairs had been finished properly.'

So he was rich. Well, he was by her standards, which put him way beyond her reach. And wasn't she silly even thinking that sort of thing about a man she'd only just met?

'You looked a bit sad then. Are you all right?'

She forced a smile. 'Yes, of course.'

When they got off the boat, he walked back to the flats with her and hesitated. 'Would you come and have dinner at my house tomorrow? I've got to go up to Perth during the day but I'll be back by five.'

'Are you sure?'

'Certain. I'm quite a good cook, actually. Is there anything you can't eat?'

She hesitated. So far she'd managed to hide it, because some people got upset when they found you were a coeliac. She explained that she couldn't eat wheat and was lactose intolerant, and he nodded.

'A friend of mine's the same. I'm used to catering for that.'

The evening seemed too quiet after her lovely day so she put the television on. But she spent more time daydreaming about James than watching the programme.

★   ★   ★

The following day as five o'clock approached, she got ready, determined to enjoy this brief holiday flirtation. She wondered what James's house was like. He hadn't told her anything about it.

The knock came just before five and there he was, beaming at her. He had such lovely brown eyes. 'Are you ready?'

'Yes.'

His car wasn't large but it was luxurious. Her son-in-law would have known what make it was, but she hadn't a clue.

'This is the most comfortable car I've ever ridden in.'

'That's exactly why I bought it.'

He stopped at a large house, a strange-looking place, with a garage and high walls being the main street features. It was like a miniature fortress. The garage door lifted up and he drove in.

When they went into the house she couldn't help exclaiming as she realized it was on the water. 'This is one of the houses we sailed past!'

'I'm afraid so. Don't hold that against me. Let's go and have a cocktail on the patio.'

'Nothing too strong.'

'OK. I'll do a strawberry surprise. Help yourself to some nibbles.' He pulled a platter out of the fridge and set it on a low table outdoors, right on the edge of the water.

The only thing wrong with the evening was that James didn't kiss her. She'd have liked to have Prince Charming kiss her, even if this was only a holiday flirtation.

He kissed her the next night, though, and the one after that. And very good kisses they were, too.

When the last evening came, she entertained him to a meal, insisting on repaying his hospitality.

'I wish you weren't going back to Perth,' he said wistfully.

'So do I.'

'You could stay another week.'

'My daughter would have a fit. And there probably isn't a flat free.'

'There is, actually. Or you could be my guest?'

She hesitated. 'Do we know each other well enough for that?'

'Not yet. But we will. So you'll stay in the flat?'

Did she dare? Of course she did. This was . . . important. Or it might be. She hoped it would be. 'Yes. And thank you.'

Jan did have a fit when she phoned, and they insisted on coming down on the Sunday to check that she was all right.

The next day she went round to James's beautiful house for lunch and wandered on to his jetty as he was getting the meal ready.

There was a thump behind her and another pelican landed. This one had a malformed foot and it stumbled, bumping into her and sending her flying into the water.

She let out a yell of shock and by the time she surfaced, James was there on the jetty. Without hesitation, he dived in and came up spluttering next to her.

She bobbed about in the water, laughing at him. 'I didn't actually need rescuing. I used to be a good swimmer.'

He grinned at her, water streaming down his face. 'Don't say that. I've always wanted to be Sir Galahad and save a fair damsel in distress.'

'Is that what I am?'

'Oh, yes. A very fair damsel.' He pulled her to him in the water.

This time his kiss was very different, full of passion. When they clambered out of the water, he held her hand as they dripped their way into the house.

In the guest bedroom, she changed out of her wet clothes into his silk dressing gown and came out looking like a drowned rat, she thought.

He was waiting for her with a tender smile on his face. 'Dear Sarah, you seem as if you belong here. Would it be too soon to ask you to stay with me tonight?'

She gave up fighting the attraction. 'No. Definitely not too soon. In fact, it's perfect timing.'

'And would it be too soon to ask you to stay on here with me, with a view to making that permanent?'

Joy flooded through her and she gave up fighting her own feelings for him. 'No. Not too soon for that, either. If you're sure, James?'

'I'm very sure, Sarah darling. I've felt happy with you since the first time we had lunch.'

'I've felt the same.'

'It's amazing, isn't it, how two strangers can suddenly feel attracted. I thought I was past all that, but I'm not.'

She gestured around her to the magnificent house. 'I feel like Cinderella, only I'm staying at the palace, not going home.'

'In that case, you'd better marry the prince. It's the obligatory ending to the story, you know.'

She couldn't help chuckling. 'Strange kind of fairy godmother, a pelican.'

'I shall never think badly of them again.' He drew her into his arms, gentle as ever, and it felt so right she pulled his head down and kissed him rather less than gently.

Take A Chance

Anna's Notes

I'm not a big gambler, but I do like to buy a Lotto ticket every now and then. I once won $700, and as this came at a time when we were a bit short of money, it was very exciting.

I enjoyed giving my heroine a much bigger win, and this story led to me writing my book Licence to Dream.

I love writing about happy ever afters and fantasies that lift people's lives out of the ordinary.

Louise got herself a cup of coffee and sat cradling it in her hands, staring into space. Thirty-eight! No husband, no family, nothing she'd once hoped for. She was just good old Auntie Louise. She sighed and opened the Sunday paper.

As usual, she checked the Lotto results last. She liked to dream about winning for as long as possible. It was the only thing she ever gambled on. She was definitely not the sort of person to take chances. But one dream a week wasn't much to ask. She picked up a pencil and a minute later it dropped from her trembling hand.

'It can't be true!' she whispered. She checked the numbers again. A whole line of them. She'd won the first division! She was − she might be − rich.

The day passed in a blur after that. She lived alone and didn't want to ring her elder sister Rosemary, who would come over and start telling her what to do with the money. Of course, it might not be a lot of money. You didn't find out until the next day whether it was shared among several people.

She didn't tell anyone at work, but when she phoned the Lotto office and discovered that she'd won just over a million dollars, she pleaded a headache and left work quickly.

Two days later, she walked into her boss's office. 'I'd like to hand in my resignation.'

He gaped at her. 'But Louise, you've been with us for ten years! What's wrong?'

'There's nothing wrong. I just need a change.'

Her whole life needed changing because time was running out and her biological clock was ticking. Now she had the money to do something different, get away from her sister and her sensible ways, take a chance or two. Even, perhaps, meet someone who . . . no, that would be wishing for too much.

Although if you could win Lotto, maybe you could win the other things that gave you the chance of a happy life . . . like a husband and a family. And if that made her old-fashioned, so be it.

She was going to have a go.

In the end Louise told her family she was taking a holiday because she felt rundown. She ended up in the south-west, in the wine country. She'd always loved that part of Western Australia: the forests and beaches, the clean tangy air, the vineyards, the winding tree-lined country roads.

She had enough money now to manage without working, if she was careful, but she couldn't imagine sitting around all day. She needed to do something that would let her meet people.

With the help of a friendly real-estate agent she investigated several businesses, and ended up buying a run-down café just outside the holiday town of Margaret River.

She still hadn't told her sister about her win and didn't intend to do so until after she'd signed the contract to buy the café.

She took the coward's way out and rang Rosemary. 'I'm back in Perth, but only temporarily.'

'Oh? Have you found a job somewhere else? I think you were very foolish giving up your job like that.'

'No. I've bought myself a business near Margaret River.'

Silence. Then, 'What sort of business? You surely haven't cashed in your superannuation?'

'It's a café with the chance of putting a B and B behind it.'

'How can you afford that?'

Here it came. 'I won Lotto.'

'Ha! Ha! Very funny.'

'I really did.'

Dead silence. 'When?'

'A few weeks ago.' She listened to a tirade from Rosemary, and when her sister ran out of words, said simply, 'It's what I want to do, and it's too late to change, even if I wanted to, and I don't.'

To her relief, Rosemary and her husband were about to go away on a trip to Europe, and once Louise moved down to Margaret River, she was three hours' drive away. And, actually, there was nothing Rosemary could do to interfere.

Her sister knew that too. So she sulked.

Louise sometimes wondered what she would have been like without Rosemary. Would she have been quite so sensible? Or would she have let her sense of humour loose occasionally and had a bit more fun?

The day after Louise moved into the run-down café, there was a knock on the door. She opened it to find a man clutching a bloodstained hand.

'I'm your neighbour. I'm sorry to trouble you, but I've cut myself pretty badly.'

She drew him inside and examined it. 'It needs stitches.'

'Oh.' He looked at it doubtfully. 'I don't think I can drive. Could you possibly—'

'Take you to a doctor? Of course.'

'My name's Richard, by the way.'

'Louise.'

She had him in the nearest doctor's surgery in ten minutes flat. 'I'll wait and drive you back.'

'I'm really grateful.' He smiled at her.

He had a lovely smile. It lifted his face from ordinary to attractive. She found herself responding to it and for a moment the two of them just stood there, smiling. Then the nurse came to take him into the small operating theatre.

A little later the receptionist came across. 'The doctor wants to tell you how to look after your husband's hand.'

'He's not my . . .' But the woman was already leading the way back.

The doctor looked exhausted. 'Ah, Mrs Crossley!' He then

proceeded to explain rapidly how to look after the hand. He had
gone off to see the next patient before either of them could
correct the misunderstanding.

Richard grimaced at her. 'Sorry about that. I tried to explain,
but no one would listen. They've had a bit of a busy day, I gather.'

Louise shrugged. 'It doesn't matter. I'm happy to help you.
That's what neighbours are for, isn't it?'

'I'm your nearest neighbour, actually. I have a two-acre block
next to yours.'

As she parked she noticed that the gardens were stunningly
beautiful, but the house had an unloved air.

'It's a bit messy,' he said apologetically when she took him inside.

'Never mind that. Come and sit down. You look as white as
a sheet. I'll make you a cup of tea.'

'I prefer coffee, actually.'

'So do I. Where's your percolator?'

'I haven't got one, only instant. Will you join me anyway?'

Good coffee was her biggest weakness. She tried not to pull
a face at the thought of instant coffee, but he looked so pale he
didn't like to leave him alone yet. Anyway, he seemed a nice man
and it always paid to get on good terms with your neighbours.

As she made the coffee, she lectured herself. *Stop trying to be
sensible, Louise. You like him. You want to get to know him. Admit
it.* It was the smile that had done it. And the long, lean lines of
his body. Attractive. She'd always liked tall men.

He sipped the brown liquid. 'Aaah! I can never get it to taste
like that. But then, you're a trained cook, aren't you?'

She shook her head. 'No. But I do love cooking.' It had been
her secret passion for years. Luckily she was the sort who stayed
slim, because she was famous for her chocolate cake.

'If your prices aren't too steep, I'll probably come next door
quite often for my meals.' He gestured towards the window. 'I'm
addicted to gardening, but I don't often bother to cook for myself.'

Within two weeks, Louise had the café open. Not for fancy
meals, just snacks. Her own beefburger recipe; fresh salads; crusty
bread; home-made cakes. It wasn't hard to organize. She'd been
working out her business plan ever since she signed the contract
for the house.

She soon grew accustomed to seeing Richard every evening and began to look forward to it. He was her last customer, he always joked, there to help eat the leftovers.

It was lovely to have someone to talk over the day with, to laugh with over the absurdities of the customers, many of them from the holiday rentals just down the road, or passing traffic from cars. She and Richard had a similar sense of humour, as well as their mutual addiction to coffee and chocolate cake.

And when his body brushed against hers accidentally, well, he couldn't tell how her pulse speeded up, could he?

When his hand was better, Richard asked, 'What about the gardens?'

She was thinking out a new sandwich list. 'Mmm? What?'

'The gardens here. What are you going to do about them?'

She stared out of the window. 'I'll have to hire someone. I hate gardening, but I can't leave it like that, I know.'

'Can I apply for the job?'

'You?'

He looked at her with that steady expression on his face. 'Yes. Me.'

'I can't pay much.'

He grinned. 'I'm fairly self-sufficient financially. I was thinking more of payment in kind. Meals. You're a very good cook, Louise.'

'Oh.' And why she should start blushing, she didn't know. For heaven's sake, she told herself as she fussed over one of the displays. *What's got into you, woman? He's only interested in your cooking.*

When the colour in her cheeks had died down, she turned back to him. 'Sounds like a good idea. We'll give it a try.'

After that, Richard seemed to be popping in at all times of day. It was nice. It was . . . neighbourly. He put in some fast-growing border plants and the gardens quickly began to look better.

The next time she went into town, she took the opportunity to buy herself some new clothes, younger styles, more attractive. She had a good figure, after all. Why had she not made more of it before? Because she'd been brought up to wear sensible clothes that lasted.

The change was nothing to do with Richard, it was just – well, you had to look smart when you were meeting the public, didn't you?

★　　★　　★

Three months after Louise took over the café, her sister got back from Europe and came to visit within a couple of days. Until now, Louise had been free to do what she liked and it had been wonderful not to receive those sharp phone calls, not to hear Rosemary's strident voice telling her what to do.

Typical of her sister! thought Louise, fuming. No warning. Turned up right in the middle of the busiest time, with her two teenage daughters in tow. And she expected Louise's instant attention.

'Lovely to see you,' she said, showing them to the only empty table. 'Can't stop to talk till I've finished serving this family.'

She came back a few minutes later. 'Sorry about that. Do you want a cup of something?'

'The coffee smells heavenly.'

When she went into her kitchen, Louise leaned her head against a cupboard and thumped the wall with her fist.

'Is something wrong?'

Two strong arms turned her round and Richard peered at her anxiously. 'Are you all right?'

She leaned against him for a moment and it felt good. His body was every bit as firm as she had fantasized. Fool! She told herself. He's just being kind to you. Will you never learn that men don't think of you like that? You're an eternal sister as far as they're concerned. But she didn't move away, because it felt so good to be held like that.

'It's my sister and nieces, actually,' she confessed. 'They've just turned up out of the blue and I'm rushed off my feet. Kerry couldn't come in today. I think I'm going to have to hire a more reliable part-time waitress.' The café was doing quite well, better than she'd expected at this stage.

'Can I apply for the job?' His voice was as gentle as ever, his brown eyes soft with concern.

'Only if you'll let me pay you. Could you manage a few hours at the weekend?'

He gave her a quick hug that sent her heart tangoing round inside her chest. It was a moment before she could speak and then her voice sounded softer than usual, but she couldn't help it. 'You're hired, Mr Crossley.'

'That's great. It'll give me plenty of time to see to the gardens during the week. Now, you get some coffee ready and I'll take it out to your sister. Which one is she?'

They peered through the glass porthole together. His arm was still round her shoulders, and his body was still close to hers. *Stop it!* she told her imagination. *Stop it right now!* She pointed. 'That's her.'

His breath fanned her cheek as he spoke. 'She looks a bossy sort.'

'She is. People think I'm bad, but she's worse.'

He grinned. 'You're not bossy, just efficient. I love to watch you work. You're so neat about everything and you move gracefully.'

It was a long time since a man had given her a compliment. Any sort of compliment. Two compliments at once made her blush bright pink.

He chuckled and touched her cheek with his fingertip, painting a trail of liquid fire down it that had her gasping for breath. 'And I like a woman who can blush, too.'

Bemused, she watched him carry the tray into the café. Was it possible? Was it really possible?

When the café was empty, Louise stood in the kitchen, reluctant to go out and talk to her sister. Richard seemed to understand. He stopped stacking plates in the dishwasher and came across to give her another hug. 'Want me to stay around, in case you need help with the dragon lady?'

Louise nodded. 'Please. I'm such a – a coward where she's concerned.'

'Family can be more difficult to deal with than anyone. Wait till you meet my Aunt Jennifer.'

'Here I go, then.' Louise drew in a deep breath, squared her shoulders and went to face Rosemary, grateful for his presence behind the scenes.

'Ah, there you are at last, Louise. Who is he?'

'I beg your pardon?'

'Who's the man? We all thought you'd gone mad when you bought this place, but I can see there's more to it. Who is he?'

'Shh!' Louise looked round, worried that Richard would overhear. Rosemary's voice had such a carrying tone to it. 'He's just a neighbour.'

The two girls snickered and exchanged knowing glances.

'What does he do for a living?' Rosemary demanded, picking up the last little cake and taking a greedy snapping bite at it.

'He does the garden for me. And serves in the café occasionally. Apart from that – I don't know.'

Rosemary stiffened. 'He's after your money, then. I knew we shouldn't have let you do this.' She made no attempt to lower her voice.

Louise winced.

The door banged open and Richard came striding out of the kitchen, his expression very determined.

Louise stared at him in panic. He'd heard! Oh, heavens, he'd never speak to her again!

He walked across the café with a firm tread, winked at her when Rosemary couldn't see and put an arm round her waist.

He wasn't angry, then. Louise leaned against him gratefully. She had never been able to cope with Rosemary in this sort of mood.

'Why don't you introduce me, darling?' he said in his deep velvet voice.

Darling! What did he mean by darling? Louise turned her head and Richard grinned at her mischievously. Biting off a protest, she played along, her spirits lifting.

Rosemary's expression registered shock and the nieces looked like two baby birds, mouths open, waiting to be fed.

'Didn't Louise tell you?' Richard said, easy and smiling. 'We're engaged. I'm Richard Crossley, by the way.'

'No. She didn't tell me. She didn't tell me anything.' Rosemary stared at him, eyes narrowed suspiciously. 'This is all very sudden, isn't it?'

'That's how it happens,' he said. 'You see a person and you fall madly in love.' He nudged Louise. 'Don't you agree, darling?'

'Yes,' Louise said faintly. 'Darling.'

Rosemary looked down at Louise's hand. 'Where's the ring?'

Louise pulled herself together. She was not going to let Richard down. 'We're going to get it after the weekend rush. We want to take our time, find something really pretty.' Suddenly she was dying to laugh. For the first time ever, she wasn't afraid of her elder sister. Filled with mischief of her own, she stretched up to kiss Richard's cheek.

He stared at her and, for a moment, the two of them seemed to be alone in the café, and though her sister said something, Louise couldn't tell what it was.

Then he pulled her closer and kissed her back, a long, soft communion that was far better than any of her dreams. When he moved his head away, he mouthed, 'All right?' and she said the first thing that came into her head.

'Wonderful.'

There was the sound of a throat being cleared, a sound that Louise had always dreaded. Now, it was nothing. She turned back to Rosemary. 'We'll let you know when we name the day. For the moment, we're not rushing anything.' She put her arm round Richard's waist and leaned there while Rosemary talked at them.

A little later, as Louise escorted her sister and nieces out to the car, Rosemary asked, 'Are you sleeping with him?'

'None of your business.'

'He's rather nice,' Kathy said suddenly. 'For an old man.'

Louise glared at her niece. 'Old? He's not old!'

Her other niece smiled. 'And I love your new clothes. Much more trendy. Good on you, Auntie Louise.'

'Well, I think those clothes are far too young for you, but now you've bought them, I suppose you may as well get the wear out of them.' Rosemary scowled sideways.

Louise chuckled. 'Oh, I'll definitely continue to wear them. Richard likes them, you see.'

When the car had driven away, she felt suddenly shy about facing him. But there was no avoiding it, so she turned and walked back into the café.

He was sitting at one of the empty tables. He gestured to a steaming cup of coffee. 'I thought you'd need this after your encounter with the dragon lady.'

She sank into a chair. 'I do.' She raised her eyes resolutely to his. 'I'm grateful to you for – for intervening. Rosemary is – she's like a tank rolling over you sometimes. Mind you, her heart is in the right place. She'd do anything for her family.' She realized she was gabbling and shut her mouth, stirring her coffee very carefully.

'So you didn't mind me saying we were engaged?'

'Of course not.' A smile creased her face at the memory of Rosemary's shock. 'Actually, it was fun.'

'My ex-wife used to hate my sense of humour.'

'I like it.' Oh, no, what had she said? She sounded as if she were encouraging him!

Now it was his turn to stir his coffee too carefully. 'We could try it, if you like.'

'Try what?'

'Try being engaged.'

'What?' Louise goggled at him.

He looked at her with a quizzical grin. 'Is that "yes" or "no"?'

'Why?'

He didn't pretend not to understand. 'Because I like you, Louise. A lot.'

'But I'm not – not pretty. And I'm too . . . brisk and managing.'

'Only in the little things. And you are pretty. Especially now that you're doing your hair like that and wearing more flattering clothes.' He leaned closer. 'I really do like you, Louise. Very much. I think it could develop into something permanent. What do you say we take a chance and find out?'

For a moment the room whirled around her, then she looked at Richard's smiling face and took the biggest chance of her whole life. 'I'd like to try it. I really would. Because – I like you, too. Very much indeed.'

His kiss only reinforced the rightness of her decision.

Then he held her at arm's length and said, 'We've both skated round the word, but what I really mean is, I love you. I vowed I'd never say it to a woman again, but that was stupid. I do love you, Louise.'

'I didn't take any vows about saying the word; I just didn't meet someone to love. Till now. I do love you, Richard, but I didn't realize how much until today.'

Possibilities

Anna's Notes

OK, I confess. I love looking at the personal columns in the newspapers and trying to work out what the people are like who advertise.

I always think 'Good for them!' It's too easy to sit at home on your own and feel lonely.

I've known several people who've found partners and friends that way.

Of course, the results of advertising may not always be as people expect. This one wasn't!

Sara tossed the newspaper away. It fell off the chair – well, it had been that sort of a day. The pages scattered all over the floor and the one that settled near her foot said '*POSSIBILITIES*' at the top in large black letters.

She kicked it aside. 'Ha!' She had given up on men, absolutely given up, and even if she hadn't, no way would she advertise for a date like that. Never! You had to be desperate.

The following morning her mother rang her up at work. 'Um – are you busy tonight, love? Want to have tea with me?'

'Love to.' Since her father's divorce and removal to Sydney, Sara tried to see her mother a couple of times a week.

The minute she entered the house she realized her mother had been up to something. Well, you couldn't mistake the bright mischief in her eyes. If Beth Greenby lived to be a hundred, she'd still have young eyes. Mind, at fifty, she wasn't doing badly. Trim figure, russet hair only lightly threaded with grey. Sara just hoped she'd look as good as that when she grew older.

'What are you plotting, Mum?'

'Oh. Well – as it happens I've put an advert in that *POSSIBILITIES* thing in the paper.'

'*What?*' Sara forced a smile. Just because it was something she wouldn't do herself, it didn't mean she should make her mother feel bad. After all, her father had been gone for three years now. 'You old devil. Feeling like a bit of masculine company?'

'Not for me – for you.'

Sara lost all desire to smile.

'It'll be fun.'

'No, it won't, and I'm not doing it.'

But her mother was very determined and by the end of the evening, Sara had agreed to look at the replies.

Only as she was getting into bed did she realize she hadn't asked exactly what her mother had put in the ad. 'I'll phone her tomorrow,' she decided.

But work was crazy with the new project taking off, so she forgot all about the stupid advert until a week later, when she was summoned to inspect the replies.

'There are seven.' Beth waved a bunch of envelopes triumphantly.

Three were disgusting and went straight into the bin.

'These two sound lonely.' Beth sighed. 'Poor things.'

'Well, they can just stay lonely. What would I look like going out with a guy that much shorter than me? And I've never liked blond men.'

'Which leaves two possibles. What does yours say?'

'This is an advert for a dating agency.'

'You open the last one.' Her mother passed the letter across.

Sara felt more like ripping it into tiny pieces. Still, with a bit of luck, it'd be some no-hoper and she'd make sure her mother never did this to her again.

They studied it together. *'I'm thirty, looking for an intelligent female with a sense of humour. Loved your advert. How about we meet? Mark.'* There was a phone number.

Sara frowned. 'I don't think I want to phone a complete stranger. And he doesn't say much about himself. He could be five foot one and bald, for all I know.'

'Where's your sense of adventure?'

'Gone on holiday.'

'Please, dear. Just give it a try. After all, he contacted you first. And you haven't met anyone interesting for ages. What have you got to lose?'

Sara sighed, but with her mother's steady gaze on her, she took the phone being held out to her and keyed in the number. A voice answered, a lovely deep, velvety voice. 'Hello?'

Suddenly she was nervous. 'Um – you answered my advert in *POSSIBILITIES*.'

'You're twenty-seven with glorious hair and a wicked sense of humour?'

Sara's mouth fell open and she turned to stare accusingly at her mother. 'Um – I suppose I am. Do you often look through those ads?'

'No. Someone else pointed yours out to me. It certainly caught our – my interest.'

His voice *was* rather attractive. And he had a good sense of humour. With her mother nodding encouragingly, Sara told him her first name, agreeing to meet this Mark fellow in town at a café she knew.

Putting the phone down, she gave her mother a basilisk stare. 'Show me the advert!'

'I–I—'

'Show me!'

It was the longest in the whole column. It detailed her interests as well as her appearance. Sara felt cruelly exposed. 'Oh, Mum! Promise me faithfully you won't do this again.'

'I hope there'll be no need. I have a feeling about this.'

'Promise!'

'Oh, very well.'

Of course, that was the week Sara met Bill. A friend introduced them and they clicked immediately. After two dates on two consecutive evenings, she knew she didn't need or want to meet Mark. She rang her mother.

'Mum! I left the phone number of the guy from *POSSIBILITIES* at your place. I need to cancel.'

'Oh, Sara! He sounded so nice.'

'Well, I've met someone else and he's pretty nice, too. Gorgeous, in fact.' Her pager started beeping. 'Look, could you give Mark a ring and tell him it's off. I have to go. There's a crisis here. It's like a madhouse.'

★　　★　　★

Beth put down the phone and stared at it. Why had she ever started this? Her husband had always said she was too impetuous and that was one of the things that had driven him mad. Well, he'd had a few faults too.

Taking a deep breath, she dialled Mark's number. She tried several times that day and couldn't get an answer.

After two days of fruitless efforts she rang her daughter, but could get no answer there, either. The evening of the date arrived and she couldn't bear to think of a nice young man sitting alone waiting in the café. It was all her fault, so it was up to her to put things straight.

She dressed with care to give herself confidence. When she looked in the mirror she smiled. 'Not bad for an oldie.'

But as she sat in the taxi going into town, butterflies fluttered in her stomach. She was carrying a newspaper, wearing a pink carnation, as agreed – oh, what a stupid idea this was! She should just turn round and go back home.

But once again the image of a lonely young man feeling rejected rose before her and just – but only just – overcame her nervousness.

The café was full of young people. No one else was wearing a pink carnation. She sat at a corner table and ordered a cappuccino, but couldn't swallow a sip, just stirred the froth around. She shouldn't have come. He'd be furious when she told him.

'Sara?'

Beth turned round. 'Oh – er – no – that is, yes – well, sort of.'

He was tall and certainly good-looking, but he was as old as she was. Indignation surged through her. 'How dare you say you're thirty! You're closer to my age!'

Her voice was so loud people turned round to stare.

'Shh!' He sat down, scowling at her. 'You're no spring chicken, either. Why did you advertise for a younger man?'

Furious, she jumped to her feet and tried to walk out, but tripped on the chair leg and nearly fell over. He caught her and they stood chest to chest, staring at one another. Noises bounced around them and she sat down – well, collapsed actually – telling herself she'd just rest for a moment till she'd pulled herself together, then ask them to call her a taxi.

'I didn't advertise for me,' she muttered as the silence grew uncomfortable. 'My daughter can't make it. I didn't want this poor young man sitting waiting.'

'Oh.' He eyed Beth's cup with longing. 'Look, do you mind if I order a coffee while we sort this out? It's been a long, hard day and my throat's parched.'

She shrugged.

'Your *poor young man* was called to the States on business and only remembered this date after he got there. I'm his father and I'm here – reluctantly I might add! – to stop your *poor little daughter* feeling let down.' He held out his hand. 'My name's Jeff, by the way. Jeff Bairnes.'

'Beth Greenby.' She took the hand, finding it firm and warm. He had a friendlier look in his eyes now. The chorus line of butterflies inside her stomach began to subside into a soft shoe shuffle.

By the time his coffee was plonked on the table, she'd taken a few surreptitious glances at him. Well-dressed, a nice tie and a really classy suit, the sort she'd always wanted her husband to wear and he'd refused to buy because he hated suits, period.

She caught Jeff studying her just as closely and blushed. 'I – it was all my fault, I'm afraid. This mix-up, I mean. I put the advert in without telling my daughter. I was so worried about her, you see . . .'

When she had finished explaining, he smiled and patted her hand. 'I'm to blame as well. I like reading the *POSSIBILITIES* column, and nagged my son into answering your daughter's advert.'

'Why?'

'It was so fresh and appealing. She sounded delightful.'

'She is.'

By the time they'd finished their coffees, the place was full of young people, loud music was throbbing out, and the waitress had twice asked them if they wanted anything else.

'Let's get out of here,' he said with a grimace.

As they stood outside in the late evening sunshine, he asked hesitantly, 'Would you care to have dinner with me? Not if you don't want to – I'm not trying to force myself on you, heaven forbid.'

It was the uncertainty in his voice and face that did it. 'Why not?'

Over dinner they got talking about their children again.

'It wasn't fair of your daughter to dump this on you,' he said. 'You put yourself at risk tonight. I could have been anyone.'

'Well, your son wasn't much better,' she countered. 'He completely forgot about his date.'

'In fact, it'd serve the pair of them right if . . .' he hesitated.

He has a cheeky little boy's grin, she thought. I do like him! 'If what?' she asked, intrigued.

'Well, I just thought . . .'

Sara rang up on the Sunday evening. 'Sorry I haven't been in touch all week, Mum. I've met this fabulous guy. I won't be over till next weekend, I'm afraid. Bill's – well, he's rather special.'

'No worries. I've been a bit busy myself. In fact –' Beth took a deep breath – 'I've met someone, too.'

'*What?*'

'Yes. You remember the young man you were supposed to meet, the one from *POSSIBILITIES*? Well, I went to the café for you and – we had dinner – and I'm seeing him again.'

'Mum, you can't be! Mum, he's far too young for you!'

'I'm not *that* old. We're meeting in the same café on Friday night.' She remembered the speech she and Jeff had worked out and launched into it. 'I don't think age differences matter all that much, actually. Not when two people get on well.'

'But Mum—'

'I can't chat any more now. I'm just on my way out.'

She put the phone down and fled, ignoring it when it started ringing.

'I did it!' she said breathlessly to Jeff the following evening when he came to pick her up.

He put his arms round her and waltzed her round the coffee table. 'So did I. I phoned my son this morning. He's very worried that I've got myself tangled up with a young woman who's after me for my money.'

'What other reason would anyone go out with an old fogey like you for?' she teased.

'Same reason someone would go out with an old biddy like you,' he retorted, his eyes so warm and admiring she felt a thrill run through her.

★   ★   ★

When they were sitting in the café on the Friday evening, however, Beth felt nervous. 'Do you think they'll turn up?'

'Sure to.' He chuckled. 'I'm looking forward to seeing their faces when they realize they've been had.' He picked up her hand and brought it to his lips. 'Can we go on meeting, Beth? Afterwards, I mean. I'm really enjoying your company.'

She tried to ignore the blush that crept up her face. 'I'd like that. Very much indeed.'

And when he leaned across to kiss her cheek, she didn't even notice how the two people by the door were staring at them, how they bumped into one another as they both tried to push their way between tables.

'Mum!'

'Dad!'

Beth and Jeff turned as one, then exchanged quick smiles. 'I'd forgotten about them,' she whispered.

'So had I.' He gave her hand a squeeze and grinned at his son. 'Something wrong?'

Three months later, Sara split up with Bill. At the wedding she sat next to Mark and it was obvious they got on like a house on fire.

Their newly-wed parents exchanged smiles as they both gave speeches, then Beth whispered to her new husband, 'I think this has distinct possibilities for those two, don't you?'

Remaking Emily Baker

'I'm forty-six today,' Emily told her reflection. She pulled a face at the mirror but something made her linger in front of it. After a few moments more of scrutinizing herself, she sighed and added, 'And I look it, too.' Her hair needed cutting and her body looked shapeless in that baggy old tee shirt.

It's time I pulled myself together, she decided, drawing herself up. She still missed Tom dreadfully, always would, but nothing would bring him back again, so she'd better get on with making a new life for herself. Other widows did it and so would she.

That thought sent a tiny trickle of excitement through her veins – quickly followed by guilt.

Stop that, she told herself sternly. You can't feel guilty every time you enjoy yourself, my girl. You could have another thirty or forty years to live, if you watch how you go.

The phone rang.

'Happy birthday, Mum!'

'Hello, Katie darling.'

'Don't forget you're coming to tea with us tonight. Do you want Don to pick you up?'

'Goodness, no. What do you think I've got my own car for?'

'All right. And there's no need to dress up. It's just family and we don't mind what you look like.'

Emily stiffened.

'Are you all right, Mum? You've gone quiet.'

'Yes, love. I'm fine.' Emily glared at her reflection in the mirror. It was merciless, that mirror. It told her she wasn't fine. She was a mess.

'I'll see you later, then, Mum. I must dash now or I'll never get everything done.'

Emily put the phone down. '*They* might not mind what I look like,' she told the mirror, 'but *I* do. I mind very much.'

Crossing to the wardrobe she pulled out her favourite blue dress, scowled at it and put it back, then flicked along the whole rack of clothes. They were old-fashioned or nondescript, and many of them were faded. For how long had she been dressing like that? Why had no one told her she was so shabby?

Not even her Greenie friends had said anything. She smiled at that thought. Well, they wouldn't. They weren't the sort to care about dressing up or plump Anisha wouldn't keep wearing those baggy trousers in shockingly bright colours.

'Just about everything I own is old-fashioned!' she told the half-empty wardrobe, which still looked strange without her husband's clothes. Poor Tom! He hadn't had much to boast about, either. She hadn't even liked to give his clothes to the charity shop, except for his best suit, and had thrown most of his things into the rubbish bin out of shame. Well, bricklayers weren't paid to look smart, were they?

At the end of the row of hangers was the new black dress. She took it out of its polythene dust bag, stroking the soft crêpe reverently. She would wear this tonight. It was the only smart thing she had. She and Katie had nipped into town to buy something for the funeral and for once, she hadn't even looked at the price. She'd needed to look her best in order to face all the fuss without making a fool of herself by bawling her eyes out.

'I can afford a bit of a spend-up now, though,' she said, thinking aloud. Did all widows talk to themselves? She'd spoken to herself at the supermarket the other day while she was loading shelves and young Karen had stared at her as if she was going senile.

The thought of the supermarket didn't please Emily, either. It had been interesting at first, going out to work and meeting people – not to mention wonderful to have her own money. But the novelty had soon worn off. The job at the supermarket was boring, the manager treated you like dirt and she was fed up to the back teeth of it. Perhaps she'd get herself another job. Yes, that'd be somewhere to start with in her new life – finding a more interesting job.

She went downstairs and opened the newspaper to scan the columns of 'Job Opportunities'. But it didn't take her long to realize she didn't have any of the skills they needed. She could use a computer now, and do emails, but she couldn't do anything fancy on it. She'd even forgotten how to touch-type, it was so long ago that she'd studied typing.

With a sigh she turned to 'Domestic Help Sought' and the advert nearly jumped out at her. *Housekeeper required for senior executive and family. Must be competent cook.* She was qualified for housekeeping all right. She'd spent her whole life keeping her house nice. And she was a good cook, even though she hadn't had much chance to practise the fancier dishes she'd learned about at night school.

She got as far as the hall, but there was another mirror over the phone and it was just as unkind as the one upstairs. This executive and his family would take one look at her and say, 'No, thank you.' She knew they would.

Setting the receiver down, she walked back into the lounge and switched on the television.

'Job search!' announced a bright-eyed young woman with an impossibly thin body.

Like a walking skeleton, she is! Emily thought, but for some reason she continued to watch.

Good jobs were scarce, it seemed.

'Tell me about it!'

Dozens of applicants for each one, so you had to make a really good first impression.

'I'd never impress anyone, not in a million years.'

Qualifications were important.

'That lets me right out.'

You had to write everything about yourself in a résumé. Tears filled Emily's eyes. Her information wouldn't even fill a page. Housewife. Mother. Grandmother. Circumstances kept remaking her life, but always as an attachment to other people. Not as a teacher or chef or scientist – or even as a secretary, which had once been her ambition.

She got angry with herself and switched off the TV, picking up the weekend magazine. The advert leaped off the page at her.

'*Do you need a makeover?*' Ha! She certainly did!

'BEFORE' showed a young woman with frizzy hair and an unhappy expression. 'AFTER' showed the same young woman, barely recognizable with a new hairstyle and subtle make-up. She looked gorgeous.

Emily stared at it, then began to nibble her thumb. Why not do it and try for a more glamorous look? Well no, not glamorous. She didn't think she could manage that, but perhaps smart. She could manage smart if she tried, she was sure she could.

She read the advert again.

Should she? Did she dare?

Of course she should! What was she hesitating for? What had she to lose?

Going back into the hall she dialled the number in the advert, then panicked and put the phone down as soon as it started ringing. What if they really could work miracles? How would it be if she looked too different? People might laugh at her, call her mutton dressed as lamb.

Or – they might look at her with more respect.

Coward! she thought. You've turned into a coward as well as a frump, Emily Baker. She stopped in shock. More and more she was calling herself by her maiden name, she didn't understand why. She had to stop and try to understand that. Perhaps it was because that was the last time she'd been herself. Not Tom's wife. Not Gavin and Katie's mother.

Taking a deep breath, she dialled again.

'Beauty International. How may we help you?' cooed a young woman's voice.

'Do you do those makeovers on older women?' Emily demanded. 'I'm forty-six and I look a right old mess.'

'Of course, madam. Our service can help anyone.'

'How much do you charge?'

'Three hundred dollars for a complete makeover, madam.'

Emily gasped and couldn't speak for a minute, so shocked was she at the amount.

The voice became husky and confidential. 'I know it sounds a lot, madam, but just think what you get. A hairstyle by Mr Benjamin himself – and he's the best hairstylist in Perth, I do assure you – and a facial and remake by our Mrs Wentworth. She used to be in films, you know. She's done the stars, she has. There's no one to touch her for make-up, I promise you. And finally our Miss Dashley will take you shopping for a new outfit. She has a real eye for what suits people and she knows all the best places.'

Emily found herself smiling. Well, they'd certainly earn their three hundred dollars with her! They'd have an impossible job making someone like her look glamorous. Oh, why not? With all that insurance money just lying in the bank she could easily afford to spend a bit on herself.

She'd had no idea that her Tom had taken out such massive life insurance, but then, he'd always tried to look after her.

'Are you still there, madam?'

'Yes. I'm thinking about it. It's a lot of money to spend – well, it is for me, anyway. What if I don't like the makeover?'

The voice became haughty. 'I can assure you, madam, that no one has *ever* been dissatisfied with one of *our* makeovers.'

'There's always a first time.' Emily prided herself on being practical. 'Go on. Tell me what happens if I don't like it.'

'In that case, madam, our watertight guarantee comes into operation. You may either have your money back – *in full* – or you may have another makeover, entirely at our expense.'

'Hmm. Well, that sounds fair enough. Book me in for one.'

She did the best she could for her birthday tea at Katie's, but in the end she couldn't bring herself to wear the black dress with sticky young fingers around.

On the way out she paused in the hall. 'You wait!' she told that mirror. 'Two more days and you won't recognize me.'

She hoped.

By the time Emily arrived at Beauty International two days

later, she had a million butterflies practising for the Olympics in her stomach. She'd never even been into a beauty salon before and hadn't told Katie or the girls at work what she was doing. Well, the young ones would laugh at the idea of someone her age going to a beauty salon and the older ones would wonder if she had a new man in view.

Beauty International was in one of the top city hotels. Emily had never even been anywhere which oozed luxury as this place did. She and Tom had always rented holiday flats when they went away, and she'd done the cooking, with perhaps one or two meals out, for a treat.

When a doorman in a top hat flourished her a bow as he held the door open she inclined her head in thanks, unable to speak for nervousness.

She paused just inside the foyer. She hadn't realized it would be so big. Where did she go now?

Away in the distance, across a mile of thick carpet patterned with pastel leaves and flowers (she was glad she didn't have the cleaning of that!) there was a sign saying 'RECEPTION'.

As she made her way over to it, she felt sure everyone was staring at her, wondering what such a scruffy person was doing in a place like this. She hadn't liked to wear the black crêpe just to get her hair cut and her face made-up, but if she went on like this, that dress would never come out of the wardrobe again.

An elegant young thing smiled at her from behind the reception desk. 'May I help you, madam?'

'I'm looking for Beauty International,' said Emily, wishing her voice didn't always become gruff when she was nervous.

She shouldn't have done this, she really shouldn't. Just because she had some spare money, there was no need to waste it. Of all the foolish ideas, fancy trying to do something with a face like hers and with unruly hair which would never do as she wanted!

'Take the lift to the first floor, madam, and turn left when you get out. Beauty International is the last shop in the row.' The girl gestured with one perfectly manicured hand.

Emily saw a sign saying 'LIFTS'. First hurdle over. 'Thank you,' she managed, because it was unthinkable not to be polite. She'd always drilled it into the children. Manners cost you nothing. A beggar can be as polite as a king.

Her son seemed to have forgotten about that nowadays, though. Gavin had come down briefly from the north for his father's funeral, said very little and gone back to work again. He'd hardly said a word to her, let alone asked her what she was going to do now.

She was going to have to do something about her lazy son, she definitely was.

She came out of the lift into a world of palest pink walls, more thick carpets, dusky pink this time – how impractical could you get? – and subdued lighting. Flowers cascaded out of huge bowls on little gilt tables, looking so perfect she had to touch one to check if it was real. And it was.

Soft-toned paintings in ornate gold frames graced the walls and she paused in front of one of them, two children in 1920s dress playing with a little dog while their mother looked on smiling. It was beautiful, every detail perfect.

Emily swallowed hard and turned left, staring into the shop windows in amazement. Dresses that cost as much as she spent on clothes in a year. Shoes that cost four hundred dollars for two little straps. Jewellery, perfumes, all the luxury goods you could imagine. It was like another world. It *was* another world to her.

When she saw the outside of Beauty International, she paused as if to look in the window, then sucked in a deep breath and took herself by surprise, sweeping through the door before she could change her mind and run away.

She had never run from anything in her life and she *bloody well* wasn't going to start now. She didn't normally swear, didn't believe in it. But then, she didn't normally visit beauty salons in posh hotels.

'Good morning, madam.'

It was the same cooing voice she'd dealt with on the phone. Emily looked at its owner and took heart. The young woman might be ultra-smart but she had a really nice smile. You could tell a lot about people from their smiles. Emily peered at the badge on her chest. 'Good morning, Rachel.'

'How may we help you?'

'I'm booked in for a makeover.'

'Mrs Norris?'

'Yes.'

'Please come this way, madam.'

Grimly determined, Emily followed Rachel into a perfumed world of discreet lights and soft music.

The young woman looked sideways at her and winked. 'Birthday present, is it?'

Emily relaxed a little. 'No. Just a present to myself to cheer me up.'

'You won't regret it. They work miracles here, honest they do.'

'They'll have to, with me.'

There was the sound of a door opening and the young woman's voice changed back to its formal tones. 'Our beauty team will be with you in a moment. Please take a seat, Mrs Norris.'

Emily walked over to an ultra-modern chrome and leather chair and sat down on the edge of it, clutching her handbag. Smart, but uncomfortable, that chair. All show and no go, her stepmother would have said. Poor Megs. She hadn't lived to make old bones. Sixty-two was nothing nowadays.

Emily's parents hadn't made old bones either. She was going to do her best not to follow their example, had learned about nutrition when the children were young from a book she'd picked up in the library.

All around her were mirrors and lights. She avoided looking at her reflection and picked up a glossy magazine.

'Mrs Norris?'

A tall young fellow with long blond hair tied back in a pony tail and tight black leather trousers minced across the room towards her and extended a languid hand. 'I'm Benjamin. I do the hair.'

As he let go of her hand, he looked at her head as if he had seen a maggot crawling out of an apple he was eating. 'Hmm, yes. I see.'

Emily wondered whether to get up and leave now, to save further embarrassment, but before she could move, a middle-aged lady with red hair (definitely dyed), wearing a floating pink overall over black trousers and top, marched forward and also extended a hand, this time one embellished with dark red nails. 'I'm Alice Wentworth. Make-up.' She scrutinized Emily's face. 'You came without today. Very sensible.'

Emily gathered her courage together. 'I don't usually wear any.'

'Really? How brave of you!'

Emily felt her courage shrivel into a small tight ball in the pit of her belly.

Miss Dashley, the last to greet her, was of indeterminate age and extremely thin. Her sleek hair, in a shade neither blonde nor grey, was tied back with a huge velvet bow at the nape of her neck and she was so elegantly clad that you'd think she'd just come back from taking tea with the Governor-General of Australia. She didn't bother to shake hands or speak but stood there looking thoughtfully at her new customer. And Emily didn't need telling what she was thinking.

Giving her an unexpectedly warm smile, Mrs Wentworth took charge. 'You've been told the price?'

Emily's back stiffened. Did they think she couldn't pay? 'Yes.'

'We could offer you a discount if you'd allow us to photograph you before and after. Fifty per cent off.' Her eyes were alight with fervour. 'We haven't had a lot of older women using our services. It would make a very telling advertisement.'

'*No, thank you!*' Emily might be stupid enough to waste her money on a makeover, but she wasn't stupid enough to tell the world about it.

'Are you sure? Half price,' Mrs Wentworth added coaxingly.

'I'd rather keep this private, thank you very much.' Fed up of them looking at her like that, Emily demanded, 'So, what happens now?'

'First, I'll cut your hair and restyle it.' Mr Benjamin held up one strand in disdainful fingers. 'You have strong hair, for your age, but it's been badly cut. You must never go back to the butcher who did this to you.' He shuddered artistically. '*Never!* They've destroyed all the natural bounce.'

Emily's courage did not extend to arguing with him. Besides, the proof of the pudding was in the eating. Let him prove he could do something better. Mavis at the local salon had been in a hurry and cut it a bit raggedly last time.

Mrs Wentworth went on with her explanation, 'After Mr Benjamin has finished, I shall give you a facial and teach you how to use make-up.'

'I don't really like make-up,' Emily ventured. What would Katie say if her mother walked around all dolled up like an actress on opening night?

'Our make-up is very unobtrusive. We do *not* believe in plas-
tering thick colour on our faces,' declared Mrs Wentworth,
elevating her nose and using the royal plural as if she had a right
to it. She relented, to add, 'You'll be amazed at the difference a
little subtle colour can make, though, Mrs Norris. Amazed. They
always are.'

With that she drifted out. Miss Dashley had already left.

Emily stared warily at Mr Benjamin. He snapped his fingers
and a slender young woman in a pink jumpsuit appeared.

'This is Angel. Angel, will you get Mrs Norris ready for her
cut?' He picked up a strand of Emily's hair again. 'You haven't
coloured it?'

'No.'

'It's holding its colour quite well, then, really, considering your
age. I don't think we'll touch that this time. Wash and condition,
Angel. Lotion number five, I think. Then bring her through to
me. I'll see you shortly, Mrs Norris.'

Emily gave herself up to the luxury of letting Angel wash and
massage her head, pat her and push her, swathe her head in a
soft, warmed towel, then escort her through to Mr Benjamin.
By then she was feeling somewhat more relaxed. There was
nothing like being pampered. Mavis's towels weren't half as soft.

Mr Benjamin didn't even ask her what she wanted doing, but
talked over the top of her head to Angel, who was, it turned
out, some sort of apprentice.

The first snip of the scissors sent terror slithering down Emily's
spine, but by then it was too late. A large chunk of hair at the
front had vanished. In the end she simply closed her eyes and let
the gentle fingers move her head around.

Half an hour later, as the apprentice put the blow-dryer away
for Mr Benjamin, Emily stared into the mirror in amazement.
Jaw-length hair, cut square across the bottom, gleamed and
bounced around her face. She looked years younger already.
Tears welled in her eyes and she had to wipe them away on the
corner of the pink wrap that covered her body. 'It's beautiful,'
she said, her voice turning gruff again. 'I never expected this.
Thank you.'

In front of her Mr Benjamin's reflection preened itself in the
mirror. 'It is rather you,' he said modestly. With a regal inclination

of the head – this lot could give the Queen of England lessons! – he drifted out.

'If you'll come this way, madam,' said Angel, 'I'll take you through to Mrs Wentworth.'

With one more surreptitious glance at her reflection Emily followed, eager now for more miracles.

'Oh, yes,' said the make-up artiste, head on one side, studying Emily. 'Ye-es, it really suits you. He's a clever lad, our Benjamin is.'

Emily nodded. For the second time that day, she sat stiff and suspicious in a cubicle, this time surrounded by bottles and make-up tubes of all shapes and sizes.

Once Angel had left them, however, Mrs Wentworth unbent. She winked at Emily in the mirror. 'I'm not going to murder you, you know.'

'I'm just – I'm not used to make-up and – and all these things.' In a burst of honesty Emily added, 'I've never even been inside a beauty salon before.'

'Really? Well, you don't know what you've been missing. I like to let someone else spoil me from time to time. Let me just put the neck support in and then this band round your forehead, so that we don't mess up your hair. There you are. Comfy?' A flick of Mrs Wentworth's fingertips sent the chair into a reclining position.

Emily clutched the armrests and reminded herself how well her hair had turned out.

'Close your eyes. I'm going to give you a facial first. You aren't using enough moisturizer, you know. Women of our age need to cherish their skin and protect it from the weather. It's ruinous to let it get dry, absolutely ruinous. You wouldn't believe the amount of money I spend on my moisturizers, but they're worth every cent.'

A gentle monologue was accompanied by the slapping on of lotions and the massaging of Emily's face. A faint perfume drifted into her nostrils. An astringent lotion made her skin tingle. When, after what seemed ages, the last one had been wiped off, her skin felt cool and fresh. She put up one hand to touch it.

'Feels good, doesn't it?'

'It feels wonderful.'

'I'll teach you how to do it at home. I have it all written down.'

After the facial, Mrs Wentworth let Emily try dozens of creams and smears of make-up on the back of her hand, and they studied them together. Then she frowned at Emily's expression. 'It's no use me giving you the works, love. You won't use most of these, will you?'

Emily blushed. Mrs Wentworth had read her correctly.

'How about we concentrate on the eyes, then? You've got nice eyes, you know, but you don't show them off to best advantage. We'll give you a facial moisturizer with a hint of colour in it, and a dash of lipstick. Not too dark. That wouldn't suit you.' She chuckled at the relief on Emily's face. 'You're thinking of stage make-up, love. We want you able to face the world with confidence, not sing in the back line of the opera.'

When Mrs Wentworth had finished, Emily sat silent in front of the mirror. Her hair bounced nicely around her face. Her complexion had always been good, but somehow it seemed better now. And her eyes. They looked big – and had they always been so bright a blue? 'It's wonderful!' she breathed. 'Just – absolutely – wonderful!'

'Yes, I have done rather a good job on you, if I say so myself. Your skin's not bad, for a woman your age. Now, if I were you, Mrs Baker, I'd get my eyeliner tattooed in.'

Emily jerked upright in shock. 'Tattooed!'

'It's only semi-permanent. Look at my eyes. Never think that line was tattooed on, would you?'

Emily stared at Mrs Wentworth's eyes. 'Tattooed?' she repeated faintly. Whatever would people think of next?

'Well, love, I don't know how your eyesight's going, but I can't see to draw those fine lines on myself nowadays, not when I take my glasses off, I can't. So I had them tattooed on instead. Marvellous, aren't they? If I were you, I'd get yours done. Not thick lines, just delicate ones. I can tell you where to go for it.'

'I'm not sure about that.'

'I am. You can face anyone if your eyes look good, even if you've no other make-up on at all. Now, let me call Angel to get you a nice cup of tea and then we'll turn you over to our Miss Dashley.'

She leaned forward to whisper confidentially, 'Don't be put off by her coolness. She wouldn't get excited if a bomb went off under her, that one, but she knows more about clothes than anyone I've ever met before, far more than those women on the telly. I always take her out with me when I want something special.'

By six o'clock that evening, Miss Dashley had helped Emily to spend over two thousand dollars and Emily didn't begrudge a cent of it. When she got home, she sat on the bed, surrounded by her new clothes – casual, everyday and smart, the basics for every occasion. She stared at herself in the mirror, a smile curving her lips. She'd never looked this good – well, not for a long time, anyway.

She'd been quite pretty as a girl, she remembered now, looking at a face that seemed to have grown younger. At least, Tom had once thought she was pretty; had fallen in love with her at first sight.

She sat there for ages and it was only the phone ringing that made her realize she hadn't even put the new clothes away.

'Mum?'

'Oh, it's you, Katie.'

'Mum, are you busy tonight?'

'No, dear.'

'Can I come round and see you, then? I have something to tell you.'

'Of course you can, dear. It's good news, I hope.'

'Er, yes – well, sort of.'

'Let their father put those young terrors of yours to bed. You can have your tea with me.'

As she put the phone down, Emily smiled at the thought of how surprised Katie would be when she saw the makeover and the new clothes. Then she picked up the magazine she had found at Beauty International. They'd been very nice about letting her take it away with her. She opened it at the back, where there were adverts for all sorts of things.

WANTED: SUPERIOR HOUSEKEEPERS
FOR TOP CLIENTS
EXCELLENT SALARY FOR THE RIGHT PEOPLE
TRAVEL ROUND THE WORLD – LIVE IN LUXURY
MUST BE UTTERLY RELIABLE AND
SUPER COMPETENT

This advert had caught Emily's eye immediately. Going through an agency sounded a better approach than answering advertisements in the paper and not being sure what you were getting yourself into. She had to confess that she liked the sound of this sort of job. She looked at herself in the mirror and beamed at what she saw. If she could look like this, she could . . . why, she could do anything.

She'd give the agency a ring tomorrow and find out how to set about becoming that sort of housekeeper. She was going to do it, oh, yes, she was – get away from everything, spread her wings, do something with her life.

Still clutching the magazine, she sat and dreamed for a while of faraway places and living a more interesting life, then thought about Katie and began to worry. What would her daughter think of all this? Katie relied on her to babysit, turned to her in emergencies. She'd think her mother had gone mad. How was Emily going to tell her that she hadn't gone mad, but that, just for once, she needed to do something for herself?

When she was a girl she'd longed to travel. She'd never managed to get her husband out of Western Australia, even for a holiday, so she'd never left it herself. She'd read lots of travel books from the library. She'd gone to classes to learn to cook different types of food, pretending to herself that she was going to the various countries for holidays.

Now she would go forth and see some of the world, she really would.

And she'd get herself one of those fancy housekeeper jobs, too. Well, she'd have a good old try at it, anyway. If she failed at that, she'd do something else, but at least she'd have had a go.

Her final thought had been hovering for a few days and she'd kept pushing it away. Now, when it settled at the forefront of her mind, she let it. She was going to revert to her maiden name. Emily Baker.

She didn't know what the children would say. But even they weren't going to make her change her mind. The name change was symbolic, somehow, of the changes she was making to her life. It was the outward sign of a promise to herself.

It'd have hurt Tom dreadfully. But he wasn't here any longer and the children had their own lives. They'd soon get over it.

I'm remaking Emily Baker, she told herself, and smiled.

She wasn't even applying for a passport until she'd done that. How did you change your name officially?

Yet another thing to learn. Life was full of new things to try. She sighed happily and let herself dream some more.

Katie rang to say her husband was going to be late. She'd grab something to eat and wouldn't arrive till nearly eight o'clock.

She bounced into the house, stopped dead at the sight of Emily, then shrieked, 'Mum! What have you *done* to yourself?'

'I've had a makeover at a beauty parlour in Perth. You . . . don't think I've overdone things, do you?'

'Oh, no. Mum, you look lovely! Just lovely! Dare I touch you?'

'Come here and give me a hug this minute!'

But after Katie had studied the new hairdo, tried the expensive moisturizer and enthused over the clothes, she fell silent.

Emily watched. Her daughter had other things on her mind, easy to tell that. 'Best come straight out with it. What's the matter?'

Katie looked across at her. 'It's Don. The new job. Oh, Mum, we have to move to Sydney. I'll be so far away from you. Over four hours by plane.' She flung herself into Emily's arms and burst into tears.

It took a while to calm Katie down again. 'So what's the problem about that?' Emily asked, as if she didn't know.

'I don't want to leave you. Especially now you're on your own.'

'You think I can't look after myself, eh?'

'It's not that. You know it's not that. It's me as well as you. I've never lived anywhere but Perth and – oh, I'm going to miss you so.'

'Is it a good job?'

'Oh, yes. When Don finished the first training course, they said he had management potential. But he needs experience, which means working all over Australia, starting in Sydney. They rent houses for you and they pay the removal costs, so we'll be all right there, but – we'll have to keep moving for a while, every year or two at least.'

Katie's mouth wobbled and Emily could see that tears were still close to the surface, so she spoke firmly. 'Well, if your man's done so well, you can't let him down by being a coward, can you?'

'No-o. But what about you?'

'What about me? I'm a grown woman, Katie. I don't need wet-nursing. Besides – I've been thinking of getting a job myself, going overseas as well. I want to see a bit of the world. Your dad – well, you know what he was like. I used to read books from the library about other countries and long to visit them.'

Katie's eyes were wide with astonishment. 'I remember that. You never got him to go to Bali, even.'

'What was the point? At first I couldn't afford to go, and later he used to get so tired.' Emily chuckled suddenly.

'What are you laughing at?'

She patted Katie's shoulder, then hugged her for good measure. 'It's quite funny, really. I've been worrying about how to tell you that I'm going to travel a bit, maybe get a job somewhere else. And here you are worrying about leaving me alone. So it's all turned out for the best. It was meant to be.'

She hesitated. 'And I'm changing my name, too.'

'Changing your name?'

'Yes. Back to Emily Baker.'

'Why?'

She tried to explain, but gave up after a while. Her daughter didn't really understand this need to be herself. Katie was in the throes of being part of a family group and would be for a long time yet.

A little while later, Katie said thoughtfully, 'What'll you do about Gavin?'

'What I should have done years ago. Tell him to move out.'

'He won't be pleased about that.'

'No, but he'll just have to lump it.' Emily grinned. 'Or find some girl to look after him, as your father did.'

'Who'd have Gavin? He's a right old chauvinist, thanks to Dad.'

Emily frowned. It upset her to have a son who only regarded women in such a limited way, but that wasn't down to Tom, who had respected women. 'I don't think it's your dad. It's these fellows Gavin's been working with up north.'

'I must say I don't much like his friends. But he'll be useless at looking after himself.'

'Well, he can learn, can't he? He's a grown man and I've done my best for him. This is my time of life and I'm going to make the most of it.'

Katie got up and gave Emily a long hug, rocking her to and fro. 'You're wonderful, Mum,' she said huskily. 'No one could have a better mother than you, no one! I'm going to miss you dreadfully. I don't know how I'll ever manage without you. And just wait till I tell Don about how glamorous you've become.'

As she got ready for bed that night, Emily looked at herself in the mirror, the same mirror that had started it all off. This time it seemed pleased with what it saw.

'Well, my girl,' she said aloud. 'Here's your chance. Don't blow it!'

She shook out the new nightdress, a filmy thing of blue lace, the sort of lingerie she'd always hungered for but which hadn't seemed practical. There was no one to see it except her now, but still, she'd wanted it. She smoothed it against her body. It made her look – desirable. She blushed at the thought and hurried through the rest of her preparations.

I mustn't make a mess of this, she decided. It'll need very careful planning. And courage. Well, she'd find that from some-where. She wasn't going to sit in this house till she died.

She looked round the room and her hand hesitated over the switch of the bedside lamp. The house was old, well cared for but small and badly designed. They were pulling this sort of place down nowadays and building two or three villas instead on these quarter acre blocks. If she sold the place to someone like that, she would buy a villa or flat for herself, so that she had some-where to come back to.

She stared across the bedroom. 'When I sell this house,' she told the speckled old mirror, 'I'm definitely not taking you with me.'

She switched off the light and as she snuggled down she stroked the lace yoke of her beautiful nightdress and smiled.

The Christmas Spirit

Anna's Notes

This story was much shorter when I first wrote it, but I liked the characters so much I had to extend it before I put it in this collection. That's the trouble with short stories. They're tantalizing. I always want to go more deeply into what happened, not to mention working out what happened next.

The idea for this story came from my own irritation with the commercialization of Christmas. It starts in October now, for heaven's sake! Buy, buy, buy is not my idea of the spirit of Christmas.

Part One

Bianca shuddered as she entered the shopping mall. Christmas again! Acres of tinsel and tasteless decorations in all the shops. They were making very sure you couldn't avoid the Christmas spirit, even though here in Australia December was the middle of summer and the weather was usually hot.

A fat man dressed as Santa Claus strolled by, looking very pink and sweaty in his extra layers of clothing. He wished her 'Merry Christmas!' in a booming voice and followed it up with a mirthless 'Ho, ho, ho!' When she glared at him, he blinked in surprise and moved on quickly.

'I hate Christmas!' she muttered. She knew why, of course. Being Italian, her family threw lots of parties at this time of year, and her mother used them all as excuses for matchmaking. In fact, her mother kept producing second cousins and neighbours' sons one after the other, like rabbits out of hats, and it was driving Bianca mad, because it was so obvious!

She sighed as she stared round at the fake snow and sleighs.

One year she was going to find a cave deep in a forest and hide
in it for the whole of December. It was her favourite Christmas
fantasy, a cool dream for hot nights.

She whizzed round the supermarket at top speed, refusing to
be tempted by overpriced delicacies or seasonal luxuries. When
she got home, she carted the shopping bags inside and sighed in
relief. In spite of her car's air conditioning, she felt like a limp
lettuce.

After throwing the fresh stuff into the fridge, she showered
and put on her bikini, smiling now. She loved living in this villa,
which she'd bought last year after her divorce. It was well worth
the residents' fees to have a swimming pool always available, a
pool that someone else had to clean – not to mention the high
fences and regular security patrols round the whole complex.

As she was getting a towel for her swim she heard a noise from
the back garden and glanced out of the bedroom window. A man
was climbing over the fence from next door. *A burglar!* It must
be. The next villa had been empty for three months.

Briefly she considered calling the security guard, but held off
to watch for a minute because the man wasn't making any
attempt to break into her house. Instead, he was standing peering
through the slits in the fence, looking at something in the garden
next door.

Intrigued, she moved closer to the open window to watch.

She couldn't help noticing how good-looking he was, with
dark hair, and a lean, lightly muscled body. He was dressed only
in denim shorts and his feet were bare, so he kept hopping to
and fro on the hot paving.

She frowned in puzzlement as he continued to stand there.
Burglars didn't usually creep around half-naked and barefoot when
they wanted to break into houses.

He shook his head as if upset and heaved a sigh so loud it
echoed through her open window. His shoulders were sagging,
too.

By now she just had to find out what was going on. What on
earth was he watching so intently? Even standing on tiptoe, she
couldn't see next door. And why did he keep sighing?

Perhaps he was a stalker? Perhaps someone had moved in next
door and he'd nearly been caught?

She felt anger rise at the mere thought. She'd had a prowler soon after she moved into a flat on her own – her ex-husband. She'd had security screens fitted, but he'd smashed the windows anyway.

She'd spent three long months living in fear. Then she'd got so angry she'd attended a self-defence course and bought herself a baseball bat. She'd had to prove to Roger that she would use it, though. And take out a restraining order against him.

So she'd moved into this new development, which had monitored alarm systems in all the villas and a security guard on duty who did regular patrols of the grounds. She got a silent number, and the phone calls and harassment had stopped.

She found out later from a mutual acquaintance that Roger had met someone else and they'd moved in together. Heaven help the poor woman!

Well, if the man in her backyard was a prowler, she'd show him a trick or two that would shock her mother. But before she went out to confront him, just to be safe, she hung the alarm pendant round her neck so that she could summon help with one press of the button.

Women's voices floated over the fence, loud and strident, but all she saw was their shadows bobbing along the back wall of the other house. Someone must definitely have moved in. It'd be nice to have neighbours again, though not noisy ones, she hoped. Most people were very friendly and considerate in this miniature village. That was yet another bonus of living here.

'He's not in.' A voice carried clearly through the still air, sounding like an older woman.

'But that's his car, Jen!'

'He must have gone out. Fancy leaving the front door unlocked like that! I'll scribble him a note. I can't wait any longer. I've got half my Christmas shopping to do yet.'

As the voices faded, Bianca saw the man move to and fro again to ease his feet on the hot paving and his frown vanished. He had black curly hair, cut short, and his grin was infectious, even when you could only see half of it. She found herself smiling in sympathy. She was pretty sure now that he wasn't a prowler.

Impulsively she went outside, crossing the three metres of patio space without him even noticing her. When she cleared her throat and said, 'Hello. Can I help you?' he jerked in shock and spun round, his mouth opening in alarm.

The same older woman's voice immediately called from inside the house next door, 'Did you hear something, Rita? I'm sure I heard a voice.'

He gasped and looked from side to side as if he wanted to flee for his life.

Bianca tried again. 'What are you—?'

He cast a desperate glance over his shoulder, and as the voice said, 'I'll just look outside again,' he grabbed Bianca and pulled her towards him, covering her mouth with his and muffling the rest of her words with a kiss.

She ought to have been afraid, but she wasn't. In fact, she forgot all fear, not to mention self-defence strategies, as her hormones kicked suddenly into action. It had been nearly two years since the divorce and she hadn't been seeing anyone seriously since.

She hadn't really missed having a man in her life, either. Now, for some weird reason, her body was responding to a stranger's kiss, and she was relishing the sheer maleness of his body against hers.

Words of protest died to a gurgle in her throat as his lips moved on hers. For a moment or two she found herself returning the kiss.

Then he moved away, but was still so close she could feel his soft breath against her skin. She stared up into his eyes, beautiful blue eyes fringed with long lashes, and every thought left her head but one: *he's gorgeous!*

She wasn't aware how long she stood there in his arms, but at the sound of a car pulling away from the central roadway between the units, she came abruptly to her senses and began to push at him.

This time he made no attempt to hold her, but stepped back with his arms spread wide in a gesture of surrender. 'I'm sorry for that. I was desperate to keep you quiet.' Then he smiled, a curl-your-toes sort of smile. 'Mind you, I also plead guilty to enjoying it.'

She sucked in air frantically. She'd enjoyed it, too. Fancy enjoying kissing a stranger! 'Who are you?'

'I'm your new neighbour.' He stuck out a hand. 'Hal Crawford at your service.'

She was still feeling disoriented and couldn't manage more than, 'Oh. Well. I'm Bianca. Bianca Marella. And – um, this is my unit.'

He pumped her hand. 'Pleased to meet you. And I do apologize for kissing you like that. I wasn't trying to harass you, I just had to stop you making a noise and it – well, got a bit out of hand. Thank you for going along with it.'

Going along with it? She'd not been able to think or move.

She was suddenly aware that she was only wearing a skimpy bikini that showed a lot more than it concealed. It was the heat that was making her so slow to react. It must be. She tried to speak sharply, in the tone which usually shrivelled men up and made them turn away to find softer, easier females to conquer, only the words didn't come out sharply this time. 'I didn't have much choice about the kiss, actually.'

As she watched, he blushed. He actually blushed. Bright red. She could feel herself softening. How could you stay angry with a guy who blushed like that?

'It was an emergency,' he pleaded. 'My mother and aunt aren't sure whether I'm actually living here yet. I told them I was going away on business for a few days, but trust them to come round and check that out.'

Bianca watched him run one hand through his hair, setting the curls springing about in glorious disarray. He *must* be a male model! she decided.

He glanced towards the front of the house. 'That damned car is such a giveaway and somehow I've got to hide out from them for five more days.'

Now she was utterly fascinated. If this was a pitch, it was a good one. But she didn't think he was trying to chat her up. He looked genuinely worried. 'Could I ask what exactly you're hiding from?'

'Christmas.'

She blinked.

He stared at her with a challenging expression. 'I hate Christmas. It's nothing but commercialism. There's no real Christmas spirit left. But most of all, I hate big family parties with all the old aunts trotted out and kids screaming everywhere – not to mention the women my mother finds and parades in front of me because she's desperate for grandchildren. Tall ones, short ones, pretty ones, even ugly ones. I don't know where she finds them, but there's always a new one waiting for me whenever there's a family gathering.'

She could relate to that. Oh, boy, she could certainly relate to that. 'Tell me about it!'

She groaned as her own troubles resurfaced. 'My mother is just the same. I've not answered the phone for days without checking first who it is on the answering machine. But she's sure to come round and catch me in one day.' She grinned at him. 'And actually, I hate Christmas, too.'

'You're a neighbour after my own heart, then. You'll not be deafening me with carols or wrapping tinsel round the palm trees or having loud parties.'

'I most certainly won't.'

They stood smiling foolishly at one another for a few moments, then his smile faded and the worried expression reappeared. 'My family are determined to get me over there for dinner on Christmas Day, and if I know my mother she'll set up a roster of cousins and sisters to keep coming round until they catch me in.'

She nodded and couldn't help sighing. 'I've got two sisters, both married with children. It makes my mother twitchy about me. They keep trying to find me another man.'

'Another?'

'I'm divorced.'

'Ah. You have all my sympathy, then. I've not got any sisters, but I have about a million cousins, who all keep producing friends I just have to meet. The thing is, I don't want to get married. I never have. It's simply not my scene. Well, not yet, perhaps never. I'm having a great life without it.'

Sympathy flooded through her. 'Don't let them persuade you into anything you're not sure about. I escaped from a nasty marriage two years ago, and I wouldn't recommend it unless you find Miss Perfection – and even then you should think twice.' She realized how thirsty she was and without thinking, asked, 'Would you like a nice cool beer?'

'I'd kill for one. I've been moving boxes all day and taking delivery of furniture, and I haven't had time to go out and stock up on booze yet.'

Just as they were going inside, the phone rang. Bianca froze. On the answering machine, her mother's voice called out brightly, 'I know you're there, Bianca, and I'm warning you – if you don't turn up on Christmas Day, we'll come over and get you!' There was the sound of a phone being put down.

Bianca stood staring at the answering machine in dismay. 'They will, too,' she whispered.

He patted her shoulder sympathetically. 'My family do things like that, too. They'll send someone round to winkle me out on Christmas Day, I just know they will. This is my first Christmas in Western Australia for years and I'm out of practice at avoidance tactics.'

He straightened up and a determined expression settled on his face. 'That settles it. I'll have to book into a hotel under a false name for a few days.'

By that time they were inside, so she went to the fridge, took out two beers and handed her fellow sufferer one. She popped hers and took a long cooling gulp from the can, then realized he was staring at her.

'No fancy glasses or holders?'

'I don't let anything come between me and a cold beer on a hot day,' she retorted.

'You're a woman after my own heart.' He gulped down some of his beer with a blissful expression.

For a few minutes they sat in the air-conditioned coolness, not talking, just relaxing.

'What do you do for a living?' he asked after a while.

'I'm self-employed,' she told him. She was very proud of that. Roger had jeered at her when she'd broached the idea of starting her own business. He'd said she'd never make it, but she was doing really well. 'I'm in IT. I train people to use software packages, small business people mainly. And I run workshops about the various software programs for small to medium companies.'

'Hey, I'm in computers, too, but I design and build linked systems, the hardware. I'm a company man, work for a multinational.' He grinned. 'Well, a company bright boy, actually, so I don't have to conform to suits and ties and that sort of stuff. I produce such lovely gizmos they put up with my little quirks. And they pay me rather well, too.'

'What are you doing in sleepy old Perth, then? The centre of the universe it is not.'

'We're just opening up an office in Western Australia and a new research unit as well. I was going to settle down here for a while, but now I'm having second thoughts about that. I may have to arrange for a sudden transfer to Sydney or London.'

They spent a few minutes discussing computers, then he finished the beer and stood up. 'I'm keeping you from your swim and I still have some boxes to unpack.'

'It was nice to meet you, Hal. See you around.'

His smile faded. 'Not until after Christmas, you won't. Hell, what am I going to do? I'm sick to death of hotels. They're full of the Christmas spirit, too.'

It was then that the idea began to blossom, a really neat idea. Smiling, she stretched out one hand to stop him leaving. 'Wait a minute. I have an idea.'

'Oh?'

'About Christmas – and our mutual problems.'

'You have?' His eyes lit to an incandescent blue and he took an eager step towards her.

She backed off a prudent yard or two. Being close to that gorgeous body scrambled her brain. 'This is rough thinking at the moment, right? But what gave you away was your car. And what'll give me away is my car. So—'

He said it for her, 'Why don't we park in each other's carports? We're round the corner from each other, so the cars should stay fairly well hidden.'

She nodded.

'Brilliant.' Then his shoulders sagged and he shook his head. 'They'll knock on the door if they see any sign of life at all, trying to find out where I am. And if I leave the door unlocked again, they'll be inside before you can blink. My mother's pestering me for keys now, so that she can drop meals off for me. As if I haven't learned to cook for myself after eight years away from home.'

'My mother's just as bad. She'd love to be able to pop in, but I told her it's a rule of this place that we don't give people keys – because of the security angle.'

'Good one. I must tell mine the same thing.' Then he grabbed her arm. 'Hold on! I've just had another idea.'

'What?' Her question was more of a gasp than a word, what with his naked chest so close and his hand warm on her bare flesh.

'Well, when we see someone coming, we could nip through the back gardens and answer each other's door.'

She was beginning to nod approval, seeing what he was getting at, and without thinking she finished the idea for him. 'We could say we're friends, house-sitting for the holidays while the owner is away.'

For a moment, they were both silent, contemplating the blissful image this raised.

'Or if the other is out, we could just sort of hide next door,' he added. 'They can't see the rear patios from the street.'

'Oooh, don't tempt me.'

'Why shouldn't we do it? I'm talking survival here.'

There was silence as they both thought this through.

'Why not indeed?' she said at last. 'I've no training jobs on at this time of year, so I'll be around most of the time.'

'I could rig up a buzzer to call for help.' He smiled modestly. 'That'd be simple. As I said, I'm a whizz with electronic gizmos.'

It was the thought of her elderly Aunt Maria that did the trick. The old lady kept questioning her publicly, in the overloud voice of someone who was hard of hearing, asking when she was going to find herself another husband.

Or worse still, her mother producing yet another 'lovely young man' and saying things like 'You two have got so much in common, I'm sure you're going to get on like a house on fire.'

'Let's do it!' Bianca breathed.

'Do you think it'll work?'

'We can only try.'

Part Two

For the first time in years Bianca faced Christmas without fear of her mother's matchmaking. She told her family she was going down to the country with a group of friends, while another friend house sat for her. She invented several fictitious people and casually offered the information that they included a man she was interested in.

'Oh? Tell me about him. What's he called? How did you meet him? How old is he?'

Her mind went blank and she could only think of, 'His name's Hal.' But hey, he'd understand that if anyone would.

'Hal who? And you haven't answered my other questions. What's wrong with him that you can't bring him round to meet your family? He isn't another Roger, is he? I never did like that husband of yours.'

Bianca knew her mother wouldn't let the matter drop without some information. 'He's called Hal Crawford and he's in IT, like me. And I'm not bringing him round yet because Aunt Maria would be giving him the third degree about what his intentions are and – you know, I don't want to put him off.'

'All right. Remember, you're not getting any younger, thirty-two next year. I don't like you going away for Christmas, though. It's a *family* time. Still, if you've got a young man, just this once I'll forgive you.'

Bianca's cousin Paola rang up the next day 'for a chat'.

'I'm looking forward to getting together on Christmas Day.'

'I'm going away with friends this year.'

Seething, Bianca put down the phone. Paola hadn't rung her for months. It had to be her mother checking up on her again!

But on Christmas Eve her anger about the festive season and her interfering but well-meaning family faded as she carried in her shopping and prepared for a siege. Outwitting them was going to be fun.

Just as she was unpacking the fruit and salad, the buzzer went.

For a moment, she couldn't think what it was, then remembered and rushed out to the back in time to see Hal climbing over the fence.

'My aunt's here!' he hissed.

'Right.' Bianca set one foot on the pole supporting the fence. With a mutter of impatience, he put his arms round her waist and lifted her up. That took the air from her lungs. What was there about his touch that did this to her? She didn't want to react so strongly to a man. She was enjoying her freedom. Intended to go on enjoying it.

Breathing rather rapidly, she rushed into his house.

Someone was knocking at the front door and rattling it. 'I know you're there, Hal,' a voice called, 'and I'm not going away till you let me in.'

Bianca snatched a towel from the bathroom and wound it round her head as if she'd just washed her hair. Smoothing her top down over her midriff, she opened the door. 'Can I help you?' she asked, hiding her amusement at the look of shock on the woman's face.

'I'd like to see Hal. I'm his Aunt Naomi.'

'Oh, sorry. He's gone away for the holidays. I'm house-sitting for him.' Bianca realized suddenly that she didn't know exactly what tale he had spun to his mother and clamped her mouth shut, making a play of looking at her watch. 'Look, I'm rather busy. Can I give him a message when he gets back?'

'When exactly is he returning?'

'After Christmas.' Damn! They really should have synchronized stories better.

'Then tell him we're all expecting to see him on New Year's Eve. *Without fail!*'

As she closed the door, Bianca sagged against it in relief. Phew! His family must be as bad as hers. No wonder Hal was taking serious avoidance tactics.

Two hours later it was her turn to use the buzzer to summon help. By that time, they'd spent a hilarious hour synchronizing stories, so Hal was able to get rid of her Cousin Gina without blowing their cover.

'This is fun!' she said as they met at the fence on the way back to their own houses.

'You're right, Bianca.' He helped her climb over, paused for a moment before he let her go, then shook his head and stepped quickly backwards.

Oooh! she thought as she went indoors. Men didn't come in any more tempting packages. Good job she was now fireproof against them.

Well, sort of fireproof. Just because she didn't want to get married again didn't mean she had to stay celibate, did it? Then she frowned. She'd never been into casual sex and she wasn't going to start now. It had to mean something.

So did marriage. More than it had to Roger, that was sure, the rat!

Thinking of him dampened her reactions down. It always did.

Christmas Day dawned with a weather forecast of a 'century', a hundred degrees Fahrenheit, old style. Hot sun beat down from another cloudless sky. Bianca went for an early swim then took cover inside her house. At ten o'clock the buzzer sounded and a minute later Hal climbed over the fence, a harassed look on his face.

When she got back from sending one of his cousins away – boy, his mother must be the suspicious type! – he was sprawled in one of her patio chairs looking as if he belonged there.

Temptation whispered in her ear and she gave in to it. 'What are you doing for a meal today?'

He shrugged. 'I've bought a steak.'

'Do you want to bring it over and join me in a barbecue? Nothing fancy, but I'm obviously not going to dare set foot outside today.'

He gave her a long cool glance, then smiled. 'I'd really like that. I confess I wasn't looking forward to being totally alone. I've got a bottle of very good champagne and a box of decadent home-made chocolates that are just meant to be shared with a friend.'

When he named the brand of chocolates, she licked her lips. Her favourites. 'I'm your slave for life! Why don't you come round about twelve?'

'That would be perfect.'

As he climbed back over the fence, she stood and admired the play of taut muscles, then hurriedly turned away before he could catch her staring.

Humming, she went into the bedroom to put on the new summery dress she'd bought a couple of weeks ago. She'd been looking for an excuse to wear it.

He turned up dressed in casual navy shorts and a white top, which looked brilliant with his tanned skin.

The day just got better from then on. As they both worked in the same industry, they found a lot to talk about. But more importantly, they chatted like old friends, enjoying comfortable silences as well as lively exchanges of opinions.

Later, they watched TV together. She enjoyed his sharp mind and his gentle wit, and they even liked the same sorts of programmes.

She had never felt such instant rapport with anyone. And that was beginning to worry her, so she made sure he left at ten o'clock by claiming to be tired.

He didn't try to argue or kiss her, but looked at her shrewdly and nodded. 'Very sensible.'

They didn't see each other again till after Christmas, because they were both spending Boxing Day with friends.

And a good thing, too!

Wasn't it?

On the day before New Year's Eve, she bumped into Hal at the local supermarket. 'Hi there! How's it going?' she asked brightly, determined to keep the conversation brief.

He shrugged. 'Christmas was fine, but my mother's insisting on my going round tomorrow to the family party. Big fuss if I don't. And if only she'd lay off the matchmaking, I'd love to catch up with everyone. But she won't. My cousin's already warned me that she's found a new female to toss at me – a librarian who goes to her church.' He sighed.

Her heart went out to him. 'My mother's the same. Only with her it's New Year's Day. If I don't turn up then, they'll murder me. And she's got a cousin with an eligible son visiting from Italy. She has too many cousins, my mother does.'

They pushed their trolleys along in single file for the length of an aisle, both stopping at the fruit displays.

He picked up a bunch of bananas, studied it intently, then shot a quick glance sideways at her. 'You – um – wouldn't consider coming with me tomorrow night, would you? My mother puts on a great feast and I think you'd enjoy yourself. And you'd be excellent protection. I'll do the same for you the day after, if you like.'

'Hmm.' It was dangerous. He was too attractive. But she wasn't looking forward to spending New Year's Eve on her own, so in the end she shrugged. 'Why not?'

'You mean, you will come?' His face brightened instantly.

'I said so, didn't I?'

They finished shopping. 'You'd better come round and tell me the details!' she called as they stopped at her car. 'I'll put the kettle on.'

'You're an angel.' He walked off whistling.

He came over the back fence again. She was getting used to seeing him do that. Far too used to it.

He looked at her over the rim of his coffee mug. 'There's just one thing. I was thinking as I unpacked the groceries – would you mind – um, pretending to be – well, pretending that we're seeing one another? In love, even. It might give me a few months' grace afterwards.'

His blush was back. She was a sucker, but she still couldn't resist him when he blushed. 'No, I wouldn't mind. As long as that's all it is, just pretending. I meant what I said about not wanting another relationship.'

'Your marriage was that bad?' he asked gently.

She stared down into her mug. 'Worse than bad. Roger turned out to be violent.' She had never told anyone else the details. 'I was stupid at first, kept giving him another chance, because in between he could be really nice. But it didn't work. He kept promising to get therapy and not following through, though I made enquiries and they said they could help him.'

She sipped more coffee, then said it aloud for the first time, 'When I decided to leave, he came home and caught me moving out. He thumped me.' She swallowed hard. She'd thought he was going to murder her but he'd stepped back and, for no reason that she could figure, had left the house.

Hal gave a long, low whistle, and for a moment his hand covered hers. 'I'm sorry.'

She clung to his hand for a moment or two more, then let go and told him the rest, 'He stalked me for a while. They didn't manage to catch him. Then he found himself a new woman.

'I've not seen him since, but it's left me a bit – nervous. Which is why I love living in this gated development.'

Silence drifted around them for a few moments, then he said, 'I moved in here because of my equipment. It's insured, of course, but I can't bear the thought of some thieving burglar getting his hands on it.'

Another silence, then he added gently, 'Thank you for your help. And for your confidences. I won't take advantage of your goodwill gesture, I promise. I'm definitely not looking for a permanent relationship.' He got up, put the mug on the sink and went out of the back.

She didn't know whether to be glad or sorry about that last statement.

Glad! Of course she was glad! She didn't want anything permanent either. She didn't dare.

Bianca stared at herself in the mirror, twitching the skirt down a little, but of course it shot up again. Was it too short? You could wear any length you liked these days, but did she really want to show so much leg? What would his family think of her? No, she'd better change into her long blue skirt.

The doorbell rang just then and she nearly panicked at the thought of him seeing her like this, but she took a deep breath and told herself not to be stupid. They had an agreement, right? No involvements.

She went to open the door and slammed it in her ex-husband's face so quickly that she managed to push his foot out again before he could jam the door open. Without thinking, she rushed for the buzzer and pressed it to call Hal. Then she realized she should be pressing the alarm button and let go of Hal's home-made buzzer to press for security.

A siren began to ring and a blue light flashed outside her house. A figure came running round the front of the villa and for a moment she tensed, then realized it was Hal. He grabbed hold of Roger, who was still banging on her door.

She rushed to open the door. 'It's my ex.'

The two men stared at one another, then Roger shoved Hal away and ran off.

'Are you all right.'

When he pulled her to him, she went readily, leaning against him and shuddering.

His voice was soft, anxious. 'Bianca? Did he hurt you?'

'No, but he tried to – to push his way inside.' She couldn't help shivering at the thought of what might have happened if he'd succeeded.

A car squealed to a halt outside and she moved back from Hal. 'Sorry. I meant to press the security alarm, but pressed your buzzer first by mistake. This is none of your business.'

'I'm there if you need me. That's what friends are for.'

'You all right, Miss Marella?' The security guard was eyeing Hal suspiciously.

'I am now. My neighbour came to my aid.' But she was still shaking.

'Shall we go inside?'

She nodded and held the door open.

As he entered the house, the security officer asked quietly, for her ears only, 'Is Mr Crawford here with your permission?'

'Yes. I – he's a good friend.'

'Perhaps you should sit down and tell me what happened?'

She explained and then found them a photograph of her ex so that they'd be able to keep an eye open for him.

'Will you be all right now, Miss Marella?'

'Yes. Hal and I are going out soon. And I always leave the alarm system on.'

When he'd left, Hal drew her close and simply held her again, which was just what she needed. She allowed herself to cling to him for a minute or two longer.

'That must have been a dreadful shock.'

'It was. I was so – unprepared to see him again.' She managed a shaky smile. 'I thought I'd got over that – the fear, I mean. I even took self-defence classes.'

'How about a brandy?'

She nodded, sipped it and found it comforting. 'I feel a fool. Why don't you join me?'

'I'm driving. And you're definitely not a fool. But I will have a lemonade.'

It was half an hour before she declared herself ready to leave. She double-checked that the windows were locked and set the alarm, stepping into Hal's car, relieved to be getting away.

Then she clutched his arm. 'Oops! I forgot the chocolates for your mother!'

'There's no need.'

She shook her head. 'I can't go empty-handed the first time.'

'My family has that custom, too.'

His smile curled her toes and she was the one to blush this time. It was a relief to dive out of the car and go back into the house, where she stood for a moment, with her hands pressed against her burning cheeks.

'Heavens, he's so good-looking when he smiles,' she muttered. 'I've got to be careful here.'

Hal's mother eyed the chocolates in approval and kissed Bianca's cheek. 'Thank you, dear. That was kind of you.' The look she gave their linked hands was so knowing that alarm bells rang in Bianca's head and Hal took her away quickly to get a drink.

His father was behind the makeshift bar. 'For a lovely young woman like this, it must be champagne,' he announced loudly.

Everyone nearby turned round to stare at Bianca. She pressed closer to Hal for moral support. He put his arm round her.

The faces all smiled at them in a sentimental way.

'I'd forgotten how they stare,' he muttered. 'Sorry about that.'

'It is a bit unnerving. But my relatives will be as bad.'

'Here you are!' Mr Crawford pressed a glass of champagne into Bianca's hand and clinked his own against it. 'I'm delighted to meet you, my dear. Delighted. It's about time Hal brought someone home.' He winked at her.

She didn't know what to do, so gulped down some champagne.

Brandy plus champagne made her feel very relaxed, she found. She decided it was good to be surrounded by people on New Year's Eve and she might as well enjoy herself. She was grateful to Hal for helping her, and what did it matter if she went along with the fiction that they were in love? It was just a game – a very pleasant game, too.

She went across to join him. 'Stare into my eyes, lover boy! Let's give them something to talk about.'

As they gazed into one another's eyes, he whispered, 'Could you bear to let me kiss you, Bianca? Only, my mother's still determined to introduce me to the new girl – just in case. We have to prove that we're together beyond all reasonable doubt.'

She nodded. 'Go ahead.'

He took the champagne glass out of her hand and set it down carefully next to his orange juice. As she lifted her lips to his, it seemed as if there were only the two of them in the whole universe. Slowly he bent towards her.

When their lips met, it was even better than she'd expected, far better than that other kiss when they first met.

The kiss deepened and his hand came up to cradle the back of her head. When he moved his lips away, she heard herself murmur a protest, then realized what she was doing and moved quickly back. She took a long, slow breath and told her heart to slow down. It didn't.

He was also taking a deep breath and staring at her as if he'd never seen her before.

This had to stop.

Part Three

Hal's mother's voice broke the spell and Bianca jerked away from him, suddenly remembering that she and her handsome neighbour were at his family's New Year's Eve party, pretending to be in love.

'Hardly the place for that sort of thing, Hal,' Mrs Crawford said disapprovingly. 'There are children around, you know.'

'Sorry. It – um, kind of took us by surprise.'

She gave them a fond, understanding smile and gestured to the young woman beside her. 'I wanted to introduce my friend's daughter. She's a librarian. Rosemary, this is my son, Hal. He wasn't here when you arrived. And this,' her glance was speculative but not unfriendly, 'is Bianca. I thought you young people might enjoy a chat, Hal. Rosemary must be fed up of us older ones and our talk of grandchildren.' She turned and walked away.

Rosemary grinned at them both impartially. 'Nice to meet you, Hal, Bianca. And I'm really sorry we interrupted you. Actually, you don't need to worry about keeping me entertained. I know what matchmaking relatives are like. I met a rather dishy guy last week and I've arranged to meet him later.' She wandered off, smiling.

Hal's flush was fading. 'I don't usually kiss women in front of my family.' He looked across the room, saw his mother still watching them and turned red again.

Bianca followed his glance and linked her arm in his. 'Don't worry. I know just what it's like. And actually, your mother is very like mine, so you'll probably face the same sort of thing tomorrow. Come and dance with me.'

'You are . . .' he hesitated, then finished, 'the best of good friends.'

But she wondered if he'd been going to say something else.

It wasn't till midnight that Bianca realized she'd had more drinks than she'd intended. She wasn't drunk, but she was a bit unsteady. That was why she was holding Hal so tightly.

As the old year ended, everyone counted down from ten to zero, then cheered the new year in, Hal pulled her close again, moved until they were standing behind a potted palm and kissed her till her toes curled.

He was definitely the best kisser she'd ever met. The best everything. Why couldn't she have met someone like him the first time round? Before she'd been spoiled for marriage.

When he said they'd better leave, she was feeling so happy she insisted on dancing down the front path. In the car, she sang 'Auld Lang Syne' to him and he harmonized in a rich baritone. Then she lay back and let the lights whirl past . . .

She woke up in her own bed the next morning, with her clothes still on but her shoes placed neatly on the floor next to her. When she raised her head too sharply she groaned and stood up slowly and carefully.

In the living room she squeaked in shock and Hal jerked upright on the sofa, where he'd been asleep.

'What are you doing here?' she gasped.

'I was worried about you. You were – um, a bit tight last night. I didn't want you leaving any windows open, letting anyone in.'

She went over to the sofa and gave in to the temptation to ruffle his wild curls still more. 'You're a wonderful friend, Hal Crawford. Let me show my gratitude by cooking you breakfast.'

'I'll just nip home and shower first, if you don't mind.' He glanced at the clock. 'And it's brunch, really.'

She gasped and looked at her watch. 'Oh, no! We're supposed to be at my mother's in an hour.'

'Oh, hell! I'd forgotten that.'

She wasn't going to let him off the hook. She needed him beside her if she was to face her family. 'Go and change. I'll do the same, then I'll make some toast. And Hal –' he halted by the door – 'I'll drive this time, so you can have a drink or two.' She grimaced. 'I don't usually drink so much and I've got a bit of a headache. Don't forget your bathers. My parents have a big swimming pool.'

While he was away the phone rang. She picked it up without thinking.

'Bianca—'

She slammed it down. How had Roger got hold of her phone number? Heart pounding, she went round to check all the doors and windows before diving into the shower.

When footsteps crossed the back patio, she glanced out, relieved to see Hal, skin flushed from his shower, curls still damp. Her heart did a little skip. He really was a beautiful man.

'It's just chemistry,' she said aloud. That was it. Chemistry. Could happen to anyone. They were both young and fancy free, after all, so why not make the most of it? She rushed to open the back door.

'Wow, you look stunning.' He stared at her as if he'd never seen her before.

'Um – so do you.'

'I'm – having trouble feeling platonic about you.'

'I'm having the same trouble.' She could feel herself swaying towards him, see his arms reaching out for her.

The phone rang. That jerked her out of the weakness. She

turned round and slowly approached it, making no attempt to pick it up.

Her husband's voice came over the answerphone. 'Bianca, please get back to me. It's important.' He reeled off a phone number.

She shuddered and moved closer to Hal. 'It's my ex. That's the second time he's rung this morning.'

He put an arm round her. 'Well, you don't have to call back, do you? And you can change your phone number tomorrow.'

'I know. But I have to admit it does make me feel shaky to hear from Roger. I can't think how he got my address and phone number.'

Hal guided her into the kitchen. 'Toast,' he demanded. 'I'm very hungry.' His eyes said he was hungry for other things than food.

Toast was safer. She stared at him for a moment, then pulled herself together. 'Toast it is. With honey.'

He rolled his eyes in mock ecstasy. 'I loooove,' he lingered on the word with a wicked grin on his face, 'honey.'

She rushed to put the bread in the toaster and clattered around the kitchen, offering him a piece of fruit till it was ready. It was safer to keep away from close contact.

She would never have believed that eating could be such a sensual experience, but as they ate the hot toast, which she'd slathered with honey, sticky streams of it trickled down their fingers.

He licked his fingertips slowly and carefully, clearly enjoying every drop, and she watched him, entranced. He looked up, caught her eyes on him. 'Shades of *Tom Jones*, isn't it?'

'Do you like that old film, too?'

'Love it.'

He took another bite then ran his tongue over his lips in an exaggerated gesture.

She picked up her toast and bit into it with a snap.

He put his remaining piece of toast into his mouth very slowly.

She couldn't keep it up any longer and giggled.

They both burst out laughing.

'I don't know how the actors kept their faces straight,' she said. 'I didn't realize eating toast could be so much fun.'

'You're always fun.' He began to fiddle with the handle of his coffee mug. 'Look, I think we're going to have to rethink our relationship. Would you . . . mind?'

She couldn't lie to him, not with those clear blue eyes fixed on her. 'No. As long as we take it slowly. I don't believe in falling into bed with anyone.'

'Neither do I. It'll be your call on how fast we go,' he assured her.

That thought was terrifying and exhilarating at the same time. She stood up and became very brisk, getting them both out of the house in five minutes flat on the pretext that they were already late.

He did as she asked, but his eyes lingered on her more than once, and his hand lingered on her shoulder for a moment as they walked towards her car.

There were vehicles parked all round her mother's house. Bianca stopped and drew a deep breath, then looked at him and asked in a voice which came out rather husky, 'Ready for the fray?'

'I'm completely at your service.'

She led the way in and Hal followed, clutching a bottle of grappa for her father and a bunch of orchids for her mother. It was nice that he had the same feelings about not going to a new house empty-handed the first time. It was nice that they agreed about so many things.

And it might be nice to get to know him better. But she was not diving head first into any relationship again. Definitely not.

On the other hand, she was only thirty-one and she wasn't made of stone.

Her mother came forward with raised eyebrows, made a fuss about the beauty of the orchids and did not for one second stop studying Hal. 'So. How long have you known my daughter?'

He raised one eyebrow at Bianca. 'How long is it, darling? To me it seems for ever.'

'Mama, you can stop grilling him right now!' she exclaimed.

Her mother made a puffing noise, waving her fingers in a gesture of dismissal. 'He calls you "darling", so I got a right to ask, hey?'

'We've known each other a while, but we're taking things easy,'

he informed her, putting his arm round Bianca. 'It's understand-
able that she'll not rush into another marriage, don't you think?'

Bianca's mother nodded. 'You're much nicer than him. Better
looking, too.'

Hal blushed.

Face also red, Bianca tugged him away, muttering, 'You don't
have to play up to my matchmaking mama quite so much.'

With the bottle of grappa still clutched in his hand, Hal followed
her round the edge of the garage to the back patio where dancers
of all ages were gyrating more or less in time to the music under
the shade of the big awning. He put down the bottle and held
out his arms.

She walked into them without hesitation. Their steps matched
perfectly, their bodies fitted neatly together.

When the music stopped, it took Bianca a minute or two to
catch her breath again. 'You're quite some dancer,' she muttered.

'You're quite some everything.'

Someone cleared their throat behind them and she turned to
see her father. 'Papa!'

He enveloped her in his usual bear hug, then waited to be
introduced to Hal, who was retrieving the bottle. Papa accepted
the grappa with a murmur of thanks, scrutinizing her young man
carefully but not embarrassing her as her mother had.

'Your cousins are in the pool.'

She felt reluctant to take her clothes off, or let her female cousins
see how handsome Hal looked in his swim shorts. 'Maybe later.'

'Come and get a drink, then.'

The day passed smoothly. After a while she forgot about her
mother and allowed herself to enjoy Hal's company.

They left early.

When they arrived at the gate to their development, a figure
stepped out of the shadows and knocked on her car window.

'Oh, no! It's Roger.'

'I've had enough of this.' Hal swung out of the car. 'Look,
you—'

Another figure stepped forward to join them, a woman. 'He's
not trying to hurt her; he's trying to apologize.'

Bianca got out of the car and moved close to Hal. Her ex was
clutching the woman's hand but looking at her pleadingly.

'Kylie's right. I am trying to apologize, but I seem to be making a mess of it. I've been having counselling. I think – no – I'm sure I'm cured. But it won't feel right till you forgive me. Bianca, I'm so sorry I hurt you.'

She felt tears of relief rise in her eyes. 'I'm so glad you did something about it at last.'

'It was the only way Kylie would have me. And I *am* sorry. Truly sorry.'

'Good.' She felt a load slip from her shoulders.

'Be happy.' He stepped back and got into his car.

'Well, who'd have believed it?' she said. 'It'll be great not to be looking over my shoulder all the time.'

'I'd not have let him hurt you,' Hal said quietly.

He said goodbye to her at the door. His kiss left her tingling right down to her toes. They looked at one another and he muttered, 'We're taking it slowly, right?'

She nodded, not trusting her voice. But he looked disappointed.

She woke that night worrying about herself and Hal. Things were going too smoothly – and far too quickly. Was she going to allow that to happen?

The decision was taken out of her hands. The following day she came home to find a note in her letter box.

> *Had to fly over to LA. Big fuss and they need me to sort something out. I'll be back in a few days.*
> *Hal*

She missed him dreadfully and got angry about that. But though she kept busy, and gave herself several lectures, she grew very despondent when she didn't hear from him.

She was annoyed that her heart skipped a beat when she saw him returning one evening, because she'd decided to have nothing more to do with him unless he had a very good explanation for his lack of communication.

She waited for him to come round, and when he didn't, she was devastated. Had he just been playing her for a fool? Or had he met someone in LA?

What was going on here?

Just as she was going to bed, the doorbell rang. She crept down the hall in the dark and used the peephole. The security lighting was bright enough to show that it was Hal. Should she open the door or not?

She'd done it before her mind got control of her hands. 'I suppose you'd better come in.'

He marched into her living area and glared at her. She stared at him in shock. What was wrong?

'It's no good,' he said. 'I can't pretend any more.'

'Pretend about what?'

'About you and me.'

'Oh, well. Sorry. I won't trouble you again and—'

He grabbed her arm and pulled her close, his voice softening. 'That's not what I meant.'

She looked up at him from the circle of his arms. 'What did you mean, Hal?'

'I can't pretend not to care for you. I can't take it slowly. I've fallen madly in love with you. And if there's no chance of you loving me back, I'll have to move away, because I can't bear to see you every day and not—'

With a laugh that was almost a sob, she pulled his head down and kissed him. This time she welcomed it when the world began to spin round them, and she could have sworn there was music playing somewhere. When she pulled away, she said softly, 'Don't move out.'

He looked at her. 'And that means?'

'I've fallen in love with you, too, you big fool. I've missed you every hour of every day you were away. Why didn't you phone me or email?'

'I didn't dare in case I said something that upset you.'

She squeaked when he lifted her up and carried her across to the sofa. He set her down then knelt in front of her. 'Bianca, it's so bad between us that I'm going to do something I've always vowed I'd not do.'

'What's that?'

'I'm going to ask you to marry me. You will, won't you?'

She surprised herself. 'Of course I will.'

With a cheer, he tugged her to her feet and danced her round the room, then sighed and looked at her pleadingly. 'My family will make a big fuss. Can you bear that?'

'Only if you'll put up with my family. They'll be even worse.'

'Should we run away and get married? Would that be easier?'

She shook her head. 'That's what I did last time. It hurt them. We'll just have to put up with the fuss.'

'How soon can we do the dreadful deed?'

'One month and a day is the notice you have to give.'

They sat down on the sofa, holding hands.

'I want children,' he said. 'I hope you do, too.'

'Yes. Not more than two or three, though.'

'That's all right by me.' He scowled. 'There's just one thing.'

'What?'

'I refuse, absolutely and categorically refuse, to spend Christmas with either of our families from now on. I still don't like Christmas.'

'I was about to make the same stipulation.'

'No wonder I fell in love with you, woman. We have so much in common.'

'We'll work something out.'

The trouble was, every year they had so much fun finding ways to escape their families that Christmas lost its sting. Even their three children got into the spirit of the game as soon as they were old enough to understand what was going on and voted the getaway Christmases cool.

And one year, they really did find a cottage in a forest with a cave nearby. They all sat inside the cave with a huge box of their favourite chocolates and solemnly toasted one another with champagne and lemonade.

'Here's to Christmas!'

'I just *love* Christmas!' little Jenny sighed ecstatically, and couldn't understand why her parents fell about laughing.

A Sticky Affair

Anna's Notes

I wrote this story nearly twenty years ago, and could never forget the char-
acters in it. One day, when I was sitting looking at a little lake in Wiltshire,
England, I suddenly saw the story taking place there, instead of Australia.

We'd been looking round a village full of old houses that week, and
as the old stone houses in Wiltshire are often stunningly lovely, it seemed
natural to put a very old stone farmhouse into the tale. And how can
you have a farmhouse hundreds of years old without a resident ghost?

My heroine's daughter came about because my niece has two delightful,
intelligent children who sadly have SMA3, Spinal Muscular Atrophy,
which makes their back muscles weak and could lead to them using
wheelchairs as they grew older. I checked with her that she'd not mind
me using this as the background for my new heroine's daughter and she
was pleased, because people don't understand that, apart from the spinal
weakness, such children are just . . . normal children.

As it turned out my husband felt that the child character was the
star of the book! She was certainly fun to write.

The result was the novel Saving Willowbrook. *And it all started*
because a story would keep coming back to nag me to tell more. If you've
read Saving Willowbrook *you may be interested to see how it all began.*

Tacie parked her station wagon in the back street, among the
mud-spattered utes and station wagons. Her thoughts were
miles away, anger at the bank delays still simmering within her.

'Oof!' The breath whooshed out of her as she collided with
someone at the corner, bouncing back so hard that she would
have fallen if he hadn't grabbed her.

She realized that she was gaping at him like an idiot and pulled
herself together. 'Sorry! Thanks for catching me.'

'My pleasure.' His eyes flickered over her slim body and

shoulder-length auburn hair, not offensively but with definite approval. He wasn't tall, just a little taller than she was, but he was muscular and looked confident, as if he knew how to take care of himself. His short brown hair was burnished into near-gold by the sun and his eyes were very blue and direct.

As he walked on, he looked back over his shoulder at her and those eyes said he wished he could pursue their acquaintance.

She stared openly as he drove away in a gleaming white Mercedes convertible, a car as incongruous in a small West Australian country town as he was, in his dark business suit.

As she turned to enter the minimart, she sucked in her breath in surprise. She'd forgotten how desire could flare at a glance. Since she and Richard had separated and divorced three years ago, she'd steered clear of men. Why her body should spring suddenly to life at the touch of a stranger whom she would never see again, she couldn't imagine, however good-looking he was. A distraction like that was the last thing she needed at the moment. The very last.

She bought her groceries, then went to fill the car with petrol, facing yet again the problem of Matt Harding, who seemed to think himself God's gift to women. If only there was another petrol station in town!

Twenty minutes later, she turned into her gateway, stopped to pick up the letters from the road mailbox, then bumped along the two hundred metres of driveway to the house, her mind already on what she'd need to do today.

She braked to an abrupt halt when she saw the white Mercedes parked outside, its owner lounging on her veranda steps as if he belonged there. What on earth was he doing here?

He stood up, his eyes widening in surprise. 'Ms Johnson?'

Reluctantly Tacie took his outstretched hand. Currents immediately started playing along her nerves and she could still feel the firmness and warmth of his fingers after he'd released her. She concentrated on breathing slowly and carefully through her nose.

'I'm Daniel Gregory. I'm here on behalf of the bank, about your request for a second mortgage.'

Disappointment coursed through her. Fool, she thought! How could a man like him possibly be interested in you? She led the way into the house, determined to remain calm and polite, whatever he said about the loan. 'Would you care for a cup of coffee?'

'If it's no trouble.' He followed her into the kitchen, but stopped just inside the doorway, whistling in surprise. 'What a beautiful room!'

'Yes. It's my favourite. I like to look out at the lake as I prepare the food.' The mere thought of living anywhere else made the anger against Richard surge up again. How many promises had her ex broken now?

She led the way out on to the veranda and sat with Mr Gregory at a table. Be businesslike, she reminded herself. Crisp and businesslike. It's your only chance.

Daniel Gregory stirred the coffee. 'I gather that your ex-husband now wishes to withdraw all his money from your business, as part of the divorce finalization.'

'Yes.' Trust Richard to stick the boot in just at the time of year when the tourist trade slowed down.

'I believe you've received a good offer for the property from a developer.' He gestured towards the windows. 'A hundred acres of scenic land with its own trout lake and tourist cabins is a very marketable asset.'

'I didn't put the property on the market. My ex did! That offer came as a complete surprise to me, and I have no intention of selling this place willingly.'

'It's always wise to consider every option.'

'Selling my home is not an option! You can tell the bank they'll have to evict me to get me out, and I'll scream every inch of the way! This is my home, for heaven's sake!'

'I'm only here to assess the situation in general, not approve or deny loans.'

Despair twisted inside her. Whatever he said, they would probably veto an increase in the mortgage. Banks still didn't trust women, especially women under thirty. She lifted her coffee cup and took a bitter sip.

He put his cup down and gave her a wry smile.

He had such beautiful blue eyes she was betrayed into smiling back. She needed to watch herself here. She didn't dare lower her defences, however charming this man was.

'I'd like to rent one of your cabins for a few days while we

look into things, if I may, Ms Johnson. I lunched at the hotel in
town and found it very noisy. You have the only alternative
accommodation, I'm told.'

'Very well.' Business was business, after all. Money coming in
was always welcome.

She showed him to cabin Number Six. It was the prettiest by
far, set on the very edge of the lake, looking across to the natural
bush reserve on the other side. As she turned to leave, he said
casually, 'I believe you also provide meals? I'd appreciate dinner
tonight, if that's possible.'

She managed to keep her voice calm. 'Certainly. Meals are
served in the veranda dining room. Will seven o'clock suit
you?'

'It'll be perfect.'

Tacie left him to settle in and walked slowly back to the house,
wishing there were other guests staying. It was going to be difficult
staying businesslike with her pulse rate accelerating every time
Daniel Gregory even brushed against her. She had to remember
that he wasn't on her side. Why was that so hard?

As she prepared the meal, she watched a group of kangaroos
hop swiftly through the bush on the far side of the lake, one
with a joey poking out of its pouch, and she listened to a kookaburra shrieking with laughter. How would she ever bear living
in a town?

Just before seven o'clock there was a knock on the kitchen
door. 'Come in!' She turned, expecting Daniel Gregory, and saw
Matt Harding from the garage instead.

'Thought you might be lonely tonight.'

He was swaying on his feet and she could smell his beery
breath from across the room. 'Well, I'm not lonely. And I'm busy.
Go away!'

'I'm a ver' lonely man, Tacie.'

She kept the table in between them, furious. 'I'm not surprised
you're lonely if you make a habit of getting drunk. Just go home
and sleep it off!'

Instead, he shoved the table hard, so that it banged into her
thighs and pushed her backwards.

'Ouch! Stop that!'

He chuckled hoarsely. 'I c'n give you a good time, Tacie.' He thrust against the table again. 'It's been three years since Richard left. You must be missing it. Don't you get lonely at nights?'

She picked up the nearest implement, which happened to be a meat tenderizing mallet. 'If you don't get out of here, Matt Harding, I'll whack you over the head!'

Another thrust trapped her between the table and the sink. For the first time, fear crept in behind her anger. 'I'll call the police! This is sexual harassment!'

'Only your word against mine.'

'Not quite!' snapped a voice behind him.

Tacie took advantage of Matt's astonishment to shove the table into him as hard as she could. He yelled as it caught his legs and turned back to her, cursing. She hefted the mallet and started moving round the table, rage filling her.

'I'll deal with this.' Daniel grabbed Matt's shoulders, spinning him round, away from Tacie and the mallet. When Matt made a flailing attempt to punch him, Daniel countered the blow easily and then twisted Matt's arm behind his back, frogmarching him to the door.

Tacie put the mallet down, feeling cheated out of a treat.

At the door there was a further scuffle which degenerated into a brief punch-up on the front veranda, then Matt stumbled across to his dusty ute and drove away so hard the canvas that covered the rear tray was flapping madly.

Daniel came back into the kitchen, holding a handkerchief to his face. 'I'm afraid he got me with one of his wild swings. Do you have any antiseptic?'

'Sit down.' She got out the medical kit and dabbed at the cut on his cheek. 'Thanks for coming to my rescue.'

'I wasn't quite sure who I was rescuing.' He looked at the mallet.

She could feel herself blushing. 'I wouldn't have hit him too hard.'

She was so close she could smell his cologne and see each dark eyelash fringing his vivid blue eyes. His chin was smooth and freshly shaven, with a dimple just to the right of his mouth.

He sucked in his breath as she dabbed at the cut.

'Sorry.' It was an effort to speak. She wrapped some ice in a tea towel and thrust it towards him. 'Here. If you hold this against your face, it should stop any swelling.'

'Thanks.'

As she moved away, reaction hit her and she stumbled. He dropped the package of ice on the table and reached out to steady her. Everything seemed to happen in slow motion as he swung her into his arms.

As his arms tightened around her shoulders, she couldn't speak. When he placed the softest of kisses on her mouth, she sighed and leaned against him.

One fingertip raised her chin slightly and his face hovered a few tantalizing inches away from hers. 'You taste of honey and you smell like flowers, Tacie Johnson.' This time his kiss was more insistent. This time, her lips parted under his and his tongue invaded her mouth, making her body melt against him. Before she could stop herself, she was caressing the nape of his neck and pressing herself against him.

When they stopped kissing, they stood close together and let the silence wrap them round. At last she pulled away and he made no move to hold her back. 'I – wasn't expecting that,' she said shakily.

'Nor I.' His voice was quiet and his smile gentle. 'I didn't mean to take advantage of you being upset, but I must admit I was attracted to you the first time I saw you.' He picked up the tea towel and held the ice against his cheek, but his eyes, his beautiful eyes, didn't leave her face for a second.

She was relieved when the timer pinged. 'There!' She managed a more normal tone. 'The meal's nearly ready, if you'd like to come through into the dining room, Mr Gregory.'

'Daniel, surely, after that kiss.' He eyed the table, set for one. 'Aren't you eating with me?'

'Well, I–I . . .'

'Please join me, Tacie. Can't we forget business for tonight and just enjoy each other's company?'

She stood there, as embarrassed as a teenager on her first date. She was afraid to appear to be encouraging more intimacy, and she didn't want to upset the man who might decide her future. But most of all, she was afraid of missing the opportunity to get to know him better, afraid of never kissing him again. Oh, she was a fool!

'Whatever is going on between us has no connection with

business and I don't expect you to fall into my bed to get that mortgage.' His gaze was warm, understanding.

She took a deep breath. 'Well – I don't usually eat with guests, but – all right. For you I'll make an exception.'

After the meal, they lingered at the table, sipping her best cooking port in a companionable silence as they watched the moon rise over the lake. The long enclosed veranda was shadowed, apart from their small oasis, and when he went to switch the light off, she made no protest. She often sat here in the dark in the evenings, enjoying the reflection of the moon in the water.

At his prompting, she told him how she and Richard had set up this small tourist development when her grandfather left her the farm, and how much, how very much, she loved living here.

He was, he explained in return, between jobs but financially independent, so was only taking on short-term projects until he could see his way clear.

'This place is incredibly beautiful,' he said after a while. 'Have you ever thought of expanding it into a large-scale operation?'

'No. I've got as much on my plate as I can manage. And, as must be obvious, I don't have the capital.'

The talk drifted on to travel and the places he'd seen.

'I'd love to travel. I've never been further than Sydney.'

'You can get tired of living out of suitcases, however exotic the location.'

They even found that they shared similar tastes in books and music. In fact, it was a long time since she'd enjoyed a man's company this much. Since her marriage broke up, she hadn't even wanted to date, and anyway, she'd been too busy.

When Daniel left her for the night, he squeezed her shoulder. 'You will lock up carefully, Tacie?'

She didn't allow herself to lean towards him. 'Yes. And, um – just come up to the house for breakfast tomorrow whenever you want.'

As she cleared up, she told herself she was glad he hadn't kissed her again, but deep down she knew that was a lie.

In the morning she had everything ready by seven o'clock, but he didn't turn up for breakfast until nine. By that time she was very much on edge, not knowing whether he was now regretting their evening together.

'Am I too late for breakfast?'

She was furious with herself for blushing. 'Of course not. What would you like? Cereal? Bacon and eggs? Toast?'

'Sounds wonderful. I haven't been this hungry for ages. Must be the country air.'

'I saw you walking round the lake.'

'Yes. I couldn't resist it.'

When he'd eaten, he brought his dishes into the kitchen.

'I don't expect guests to clear away.'

'No trouble. Look, are you busy today, Tacie?'

'Um—'

'Would you have time to show me round your property?'

'Well—'

'I need to get an insight into its potential, for the bank. Your brochure talks about bush walks.'

'They're all clearly signposted.' She wasn't going to throw herself at him!

'I'm sure they are, but it's always nicer when you have someone to talk to. Please?'

She looked across into his smiling eyes and was lost.

She put up a sign saying 'Back in an hour', in case someone came looking for accommodation, and took him along her favourite walks, showing him the tracks of kangaroos and emus, laughing with him at the shrieking squabbles of the cockatoos, and stopping to admire the wild flowers, which were just beginning to bloom. It was one of those early spring days, when the sun lit the world delicately, without its summer harshness, and she was proud that her little kingdom was showing to its best advantage.

'It's a far cry from London and Melbourne,' he said at last.

'Yes, I suppose it is.'

'I hadn't realized how attractive the West Australian bush can be.' His eyes were on her as he spoke, though, not the scenery.

He helped her over a fallen log, which she could perfectly well have jumped over herself, and she let him, just as she let him keep hold of her hand afterwards.

'May I kiss you again?' he asked abruptly, just as she had convinced herself that nothing was going to happen today.

She didn't know what to say and he smiled. 'That was silly of me, wasn't it, Tacie? I should just have taken hold of your shoulders – like this – swung you round to face me – like this – and raised your chin – like this.'

The kiss went on for so long that she panicked and tried to push away from him, but he kept his arms firmly round her.

'Tacie Johnson, you're delicious! How can you do this to me when we've only just met?'

'Hey!' Her voice was shaky. 'That was my line. It's you who's doing it to me!'

His eyes glinted at her in the filtered sunlight beneath the trees. 'Let's agree that we do it to each other, then. Will you dine out somewhere with me tonight?'

'I'd rather dine here.' She was finding it hard to breathe evenly with him so close. 'There's only the hotel in town, and you've already tried that.'

He grimaced. 'Point made. I'll buy us some good champagne, then.'

She gave a sudden gurgle of laughter. 'Not in Marybrook, you won't!'

'I have to drive into Bunbury this afternoon, on business. I'm sure I'll find a liquor store there.'

They walked back hand in hand, then at the house she pulled away, suddenly nervous.

'It's all right,' he said softly. 'I shan't try to push you into anything.'

What did he mean by that? she wondered, as she watched his car pull away.

The place felt empty without him. It was ridiculous. They'd only just met.

She attacked the housework like a madwoman to keep her mind off him. It didn't work.

Later, she went to his cabin to take clean towels and clear up. She'd just straightened the corner of his bed, when she noticed a piece of paper on the floor. As she bent to retrieve it, her own name leaped out at her.

She couldn't resist reading it and what she saw made her sparkling new happiness turn to bitter ashes, and tears well in her eyes.

Daniel didn't return until six thirty, by which time Tacie had calmed down enough to prepare a meal and set a table for two. You're going to deal with this in a very mature, businesslike manner, she had told herself. No losing your temper, my girl. Cool disdain. That's what you'll radiate as you tell him you know what his little game is.

She was grateful that no one else had turned up wanting accommodation, grateful when Daniel only returned in time to put the champagne in the fridge and greet her briefly, before he went to his cabin to change out of his dark suit.

She forced herself to chat calmly to him as they ate their starters of locally raised yabbies and rice salad.

'I've never eaten these before,' he said. 'They're better than crayfish, sweeter.'

'They're a regional speciality. Farmers are starting to breed them commercially in their dams.' Anger rose suddenly in her that he could pretend to be so open and friendly. If we were standing near a dam at this moment, she thought, I'd push you in, you liar!

'You're very quiet,' he said, as they went on to the tender local beef, pot-roasted with fresh herbs. 'Is something wrong, Tacie?'

'I'm a little – er – on edge. You haven't given me any clues about how the bank has reacted to my request.'

'Do we have to talk business tonight? I'm not on duty twenty-four hours a day, you know.'

Oh, aren't you! she thought, and jerked out of her seat to take away their dirty plates before she gave herself away.

It was when she was carrying the desserts in that he said, 'Will you let me stay and get to know you better, Tacie darling?' And gave her a loving look as he said it!

That was the final straw. 'You cheating, scheming worm!' she yelled, and tipped the bowl of fruit salad over the top of his head. She turned to flee, tears rolling down her face.

Before she could reach the door, he had caught her, his fingers digging hard into her shoulders.

'Let me go, you . . . you rotten, sneaking . . .'

He swung her round to pin her against the wall. 'I haven't the faintest idea what's upset you, you stupid wild-woman! Just calm down for a moment and tell me!'

She struggled against him and was horrified when the anger faded from his face, to be replaced by something else, and she felt herself soften against him.

'Whatever it is that's upset you, you're wrong to think I'd cheat you,' he growled. 'But before we discuss it, you're going to help me clean this mess out of my hair.'

She glared at him and pulled away, but he kept hold of her arm and dragged her into the kitchen. As they passed the serving bench, she had visions of pouring the jug of iced water over him, of emptying the bowl of cream over him, of . . .

'Don't even think about it!' he snarled, before releasing her near the sink.

For a moment, anger flickered hotly within her, then she pressed her lips together and grabbed a clean tea towel. I've blown it now, she thought, beginning to calm down. How could I have been so stupid! When will I ever learn to control my temper?

He stood quietly as she dampened the towel and tried to clean his hair and face, but she could see that he was still angry. Well, so was she!

When she'd finished, she tried to move away, but he caught her shoulders again, shaking her slightly. 'I thought we were getting on well, really well. What happened today, Tacie?'

'You were just using me, you – you unscrupulous, conniving mole!'

'Why on earth should you think that?'

Her hands felt sticky as she clenched them into fists. 'When I cleaned your room today, I saw a letter—' She saw his eyes narrow and shouted, 'It was on the floor – I wasn't prying!' She sniffed away a tear.

'Go on!'

'It was from Richard – to you – describing me and my h–home. Suggesting how to approach me.' Tears welled in her eyes and rolled down her cheeks. It was all too much. From anxiety to love to betrayal in two short days. She blinked in shock. Love! She didn't love him! And he certainly didn't love her!

He closed his eyes for a moment. 'Aaah!' Then he opened them again and said more gently, 'Come and sit down, you crazy redhead. We need to talk.'

But he kept hold of her arm still, and his touch stopped her thinking clearly.

'Let go of me, then.'

'Not till this is sorted out.' He grinned. 'I might not be safe. You might have more fruit salad in the fridge.'

She nearly smiled, but held back in time. People like him didn't deserve to be safe.

On the couch, he took both her hands in his. 'Tacie, I'm not here on your ex-husband's behalf. I'm here purely as a representative of the bank. But,' a wry smile crept across his face, 'I am here under false pretences.'

Pain lanced through her and her hands jerked in his.

'The bank only asked me to have a quick look over your property on my way to Bunbury, not to stay and do a thorough analysis.'

'But that letter said—'

'The letter from your ex-husband came out of the blue just before I left Perth. How he found out about my visit, I don't know. I certainly haven't replied to the letter, nor have I agreed to help him and his backers to acquire this property. I don't operate that way, Tacie.'

He sounded sincere. She looked at him through a haze of tears.

He brushed one wet trail away from her cheek with a fingertip. 'It's the truth, Tacie!'

She sagged against him. 'But Daniel, I—'

'I'm coming off duty this very second,' he breathed in her ear, his hands molding her body to his. 'I'm sticky, I smell of that damned fruit salad, but I'm about to kiss you until you beg for mercy. Then we're going to discuss our future plans. You have a dreadful temper, woman, but I'm afraid I've fallen in love with you.'

'What?' It came out as a whisper, but she could feel happiness surge through her.

He smiled and nuzzled her neck. 'When I go back on duty tomorrow, Tacie, I'll go over your accounts, but I expect to present an extremely favourable report on you to the bank.' He feathered a series of kisses along her eyelids and down her cheek to her lips. 'Even without feeling this way about you.'

She gasped aloud as she clung to him.

'Though you won't need the mortgage now, will you, with a rich backer of your own?' He nipped delicately at the lobe of her ear.

'A rich backer?' She was finding it increasingly hard to concentrate.

'Yes. Me.'

'But – why would a man like you—'

His eyes gleamed in the moonlight. 'I'm absolutely crazy about fruit salad – however it's served.'

A long time later, she murmured in his ear, as she brushed a sticky strand of hair from his forehead. 'I think I'm going off fruit salad, personally. If you'll come along to my bathroom, Daniel Gregory, I'll help you to wash the fruit juice off.'

A Summer Romance

Anna's Notes

This story is based on how a lot of people I've met have started trying to write novels. They read a bad book and feel sure they can do better. And some of them can. Even if they can't, it doesn't matter, because it's such fun trying.

People don't feel intimidated by the thought of writing a shorter book, a modern romance, so it's what a lot of people start with. I was one of them. I tried to write Mills & Boon romances and soon found it wasn't at all my cup of tea. It's a lot harder than it looks and I put in too many characters and my stories are too long. I learned a lot trying, though, which I carried over to other sorts of books I've had published.

You learn a lot from writing just by doing it, so I'd encourage anyone to have a try. After all, you don't have to show your work to anyone unless you want to. But be warned: writing/storytelling is addictive. I confess to being totally addicted. Keep me from writing for a few days and I become a grouch.

Like my heroine, I've been to quite a few romance writers' conferences and they're great fun, with very friendly people who welcome newcomers. It was at one of them that I got the original idea for this story.

This is a fairy tale, really − but well, sometimes fantasies do come true.

Katie closed the novel with a sigh of sheer delight. There was nothing she enjoyed as much as a good romance. The heroines always led such interesting lives, nothing like hers. Since her mother's death last year, it was just work, TV and reading − spiced up with a good bit of daydreaming.

The next day on the way home from the office, she picked up a romance novel from the supermarket, her favourite form of reading. But the new book was so awful, she tossed it aside after a couple of chapters. 'I could do better than that myself!' she muttered.

There was nothing interesting on TV that night, either. She felt cheated, and found herself imagining ways to improve the romance she had tossed aside. This led to another dream, of a man – and he didn't have to be tall, dark and handsome – coming into the office, paying his account, smiling at her. She sighed. Dream on, Katie! You're thirty-eight, unmarried and past your prime. Who's going to fall in love with you now?

If she hadn't been so shy, maybe she might have tried Internet introduction sites or speed dating. But the one time she'd gone to a singles gathering, she'd left early because one of the men, who must have been at least sixty and wore his hair in a comb-over, kept pestering her. She wasn't that desperate.

On an impulse, she got out her pad and began to scribble down her own ideas, telling the story as she wished it would happen. It was such fun designing her own romance and a hero so luscious he made her toes curl that she was startled to realize it was eleven o'clock. Where had the evening gone?

After that, things fell into place as if they were meant to be. She found a book on line called, *How to Write a Romance*. That helped a lot. She hadn't realized there was so much to it.

The evenings had never passed so quickly. She simply had to finish telling her story. Something seemed to be driving her.

She no longer watched much television or read as many novels. But she enjoyed a whole range of wonderful dreams, each about the same dark-haired hero. Every day she longed for evening to come, so that she could get home and follow the adventures of Brett and the lovely Helen.

Her heroine was all Katie had ever wanted to be – confident, tall, with a cloud of dark hair. Not short with reddish hair and rather ordinary blue eyes. And Helen didn't have to watch every penny she spent, either. Oh, no! She wore designer clothes and ate in the very best restaurants.

In her lunch break, Katie went and read the menus in the windows of fancy restaurants to find out what sort of meals they served. Some of them didn't even show prices. Imagine buying something without asking how much it cost?

'What have you been doing with yourself lately?' her boss asked her one day. 'You look much happier. Met a fellow?'

But at that moment he saw his wife arriving and forgot Katie. Enviously, she watched them kiss and walk out hand in hand.

'Isn't love sweet?' her friend Wendy mocked.

'I think it's wonderful for them to be so happy after twenty years of marriage,' Katie said, still watching them as they crossed the car park and he swung her round into his arms for a quick kiss.

Wendy snorted. 'It doesn't happen to many. You're better off single, Katie, believe me.' She'd caught her husband being unfaithful and was in the process of divorcing him.

A few months later, Katie saw an advertisement for a conference of romance writers in London during the autumn. She hesitated, then tore it out of the newspaper. Her story was nearly finished now and she wasn't quite sure what to do with it. Maybe she could take some of her holiday leave and go to this conference? Only – it was rather expensive and she was just starting to get on her feet again financially after the expenses of her mother's funeral and a move to a new flat.

Then she bought a scratchie and won a thousand pounds. This was meant to be, she decided, and wrote to book a place at the conference. Prudently, she decided to share a room, to save money, and put her name on a list for that.

But she felt so nervous about going to the conference; she went and got her hair restyled at a fancy hairdresser's she'd never tried before.

'What a beautiful red-gold colour!' the stylist enthused. 'Let me just put a few lighter streaks through. You'll not recognize yourself.'

'I don't know . . .' Then she thought of Helen and stiffened her spine. Her heroine would never have been so wimpish. 'All right.'

Afterwards, Katie stared at her face in the mirror and blinked in astonishment and delight. 'Oh, you've done a marvellous job.'

That success encouraged her to take step number two: buying herself some new clothes. Goodness, her mother would have had a fit at the way she was spending the money she'd won. But she couldn't, she definitely couldn't, face a crowd of strangers in her ordinary clothes.

The next day at work, she had lunch with Wendy, who was always ferociously smart. 'Um – where do you get your clothes from? You always look great.'

Wendy turned to stare at her. 'Why do you say that?'

'Well, I've won a bit of money and – and I'm going to this conference in London next month and I need some new outfits.'

'I'll come shopping with you.'

'I can't ask you to do that.'

Wendy gave her a quick hug. 'I'm delighted to help. It's about time you stopped dressing like a mouse in camouflage. You've got a great figure. You should show it off more.'

Katie wound up with a subtle green silky dress for the cocktail party and a snazzy blue outfit for daytime, with two different tops. They went rather well with her new 'sun-gilded' hair. She hung the cocktail dress on her wardrobe door and beamed at it every time she went into her bedroom.

On the train to London, however, Katie grew more and more nervous. What if no one talked to her? What if she made a fool of herself? What if she was just fooling herself about being able to write a novel?

At the hotel, she found herself sharing a room with a woman from Scotland, an extrovert who never stopped talking. When they'd unpacked, Kate decided to get an early night and took out a book.

Jenny took the book out of her hand and tossed it aside. 'You surely aren't going to sit up here alone all evening?'

'Well, I don't know anyone.'

'Neither do I. That's half the fun of it. Anyway, you know me now. Come on, we'll go down and have a drink.'

Talking all the way, Jenny swept her into the bar. 'First shout's on me. Go and grab that empty table in the corner, quick.'

Katie rushed across the room, tripped over someone's foot and landed in the lap of a man at the next table.

'Sorry!' She blushed hotly and for a moment couldn't move.

He smiled down at her. 'You can fall into my lap any time, gorgeous.' He helped her up and stuck out one hand. 'I'm Jake.'

'Katie.' She shook his hand, thinking what a lovely smile he had. In fact, he was so like her hero that she sneaked a few more glances at him after she'd sat down at her own table. Fairly tall, dark, good-looking and with a whimsical expression that made you want to talk to him and find out what he thought about the world.

Jenny plonked two drinks down and nudged her. 'Bit of all right, isn't he?'

'What?'

'You've been staring at Romeo over there ever since you fell into his lap. Nice move, that.'

'I didn't fall on purpose!'

Jenny grinned. 'I suppose not. I wouldn't blame you if you had, though. I'd certainly like to find him under my Christmas tree.'

'He looks exactly like my hero,' Katie confided.

Jenny studied him openly. 'Does he? My hero's blond and six feet three.'

By this time the man was looking rather embarrassed by their scrutiny. 'Please stop staring at him!' Katie begged.

'Spoilsport!'

Luckily a group of women came in at that moment wearing conference badges and Jenny waved to them and pointed to her own badge.

'Do you know them?' Katie whispered.

'Not yet.' Jenny laughed at her expression of shock. 'You have to make the effort to meet people at these conferences. You just walk up to them and say hello.'

Soon there were eight at their table, talking and laughing. They were all so friendly Katie began to relax.

A little later, Jenny nudged her. 'He's not stopped staring at you.'

'What?'

'Romeo. He's been staring at you all night. Give him a wave.'

Katie blushed at the mere idea, but turned for a quick glance and couldn't resist returning his smile. She was relieved when he walked out, though, because Jenny kept up a running commentary on what he was doing and the other women started staring at him, too.

They all watched him leave.

'Wow, gorgeous!' Jenny patted her chest and pretended to faint. 'Be still my beating heart.'

When he turned at the door to glance back at Katie, he waved and she raised her hand in reply. She'd probably never see him again but she'd certainly dream about him.

Katie loved every minute of the conference – the speakers, most of them published novelists whose books she'd read, the other new writers like herself, eager to learn, the air of excitement. When Dyanne Colby, the most successful romance writer in the world, gave her speech, Katie took page after page of notes.

In the afternoon they had workshops in smaller groups. Lost in a dream of what it might be like to get a book published, Katie fronted up to a talk on forensic pathology. She had an idea for another book, one with a murder in it, where the heroine was a detective.

In the doorway she stopped dead. Romeo was standing at the front, shuffling pieces of paper. Was he the speaker, then? Someone bumped into her and she pulled herself together and moved into the room. Well, she was more or less together. She couldn't help staring at him, though. He was so very – gorgeous. And he winked at her again, he definitely did.

She had to stop thinking of him as Romeo, though. What if she forgot and called him that?

All the back seats were taken, so she had to sit near the front, very conscious of the way his eyes settled upon her at regular intervals. It made her breath catch in her throat.

In spite of the distraction of his presence, however, she found the talk fascinating and took more notes.

When it was over, she clapped loudly with the others, then hesitated. She had so wanted to ask him a question, but time had run out. The thought of how Jenny did things gave her the courage to join the small queue waiting to talk to him. After they'd asked their questions, people rushed off to get coffee before the next session and she found herself alone with him.

He offered his hand. 'We meet again, Katie.'

She wondered why her hand tingled when he shook it, why there seemed a sudden lack of oxygen in the room. For a moment, they stared solemnly at one another, then she managed to ask, 'I wonder if you could just spare me a minute to help me with my murder?'

He chuckled. 'Do you commit many murders?'

She smiled back into his deep-blue eyes, feeling exhilaration course through her. 'This will be my very first.'

'Then we must make it a good one.'

When he had finished his explanation of why her first choice of murder weapon would not be suitable, he said abruptly, 'I've been wanting to speak to you ever since last night.'

'Oh.'

'You have the most gorgeous hair and your smile would melt an icicle.'

The world spun around Katie. This sort of thing didn't happen in real life. And certainly not to someone as ordinary as her.

'If you have a minute, maybe we could grab a coffee and talk? I'd be happy to help you with the other details of your murder. There are quite a few other things you'll have to bear in mind.'

'Oh – yes – lovely.'

She missed the next speaker completely, but found out that Jake was divorced, lived in London and adored Italian food. She also agreed to meet him after the conference ended, because she was using the rest of her winnings to take a week's holiday. Well, it'd be silly to go back to Lancashire without having a look round the capital, wouldn't it?

It took far less than a week for Katie to fall in love with Jake. His kisses made the world spin around her. His voice echoed in her dreams. His touch lit her like a flame.

And since they shared the same sense of the ridiculous, he fell about laughing when she did forget and called him 'Romeo'.

When the last day came, he took her out for a meal, held her hand and said quietly, 'I want to go on seeing you, Katie.'

She stared back at him. 'Yes. So do I.' It was like a romance novel come true, only far better.

'If I come to Rochdale, may I see you?'

'Of course. I'd like that.'

She couldn't quite believe he would come, but then, she couldn't believe what had happened during the past week. Surely this thing between them couldn't be merely a summer romance?

No. Quiet certainty filled her. This was the real thing.

On the train back, she didn't read the new book she'd bought at the conference. She simply sat and relived the most glorious week of her whole life. In a romance novel, the heroine would be filled with doubts and something would happen to tear them apart. In real life, she felt quietly certain of Jake and her own love for him. It was as if something inside her recognized him, and she had never felt so comfortable with anyone in her life.

Wendy took one look at her and guessed. 'Who is he?'

Katie told her a little of what had happened.

Wendy frowned. 'Don't – well, bank too much on him contacting you, love.'

'Don't start getting cynical about love,' the new Katie said firmly. 'I'm very happy and I'm sure I'll see him again. Now, how about you? Are things any better at home?'

Wendy blushed. 'Well, Jack and I – we went away for the weekend and – we're trying to make a fresh start.'

Katie hugged her. 'I'm so glad. I always knew you still loved him.'

When she got home that night the phone was ringing. She picked it up to hear, 'Hi, there. Romeo calling.'

She laughed and it was an hour before she put the phone down. They called one another every night that week.

Within three months, she and Jake were married and she'd moved to London to live with him. She didn't try to find a job, because he said she should have a go at writing full-time first, to see if she could get a book published.

She had never been so happy in her life. And Jake was – oh, he was just the most wonderful husband and lover in the whole world. She was quite sure of that.

The first novel wasn't good enough. She knew that. It had been the childlike fantasy of a woman who had never really been in love. The second was much better because now she knew what love was like – and sex – and a sparkling, joyful relationship. But it was still not good enough.

When she finished her third novel, a romantic suspense tale with a very realistic murder in it, she stared at the screen and said, 'I think this one is really good.'

But still, she did as they had advised her at the conference: set it aside for a while, then read it through quickly, as if it were a real novel, not her own manuscript.

She gave it to Jake to read, too, then left him alone.

When he came out of his home office a few hours later, he

stared at her as if he'd never seen her before. 'It's excellent,' he said, and went to kiss her on the forehead. 'I hadn't realized how clever you were.'

'There's a competition – I thought I'd enter it.'

'You do that.'

Two months later she received a phone call. 'I'm from *Her World* magazine,' a voice said. 'I'm delighted to tell you that you've won our writing competition and we have a publisher who wants to publish your novel.'

She couldn't speak for a moment, and she never did remember what she said or even what the person who rang was called.

To her amazement and delight, the novel caught the public attention and began to sell really well.

'Here's how to handle reporters,' Jake told her. 'Treat them like long-lost friends and let them see how happy you are.'

Let them see that! She couldn't hide it. Joy was oozing out of every pore. She felt as if she was tap-dancing on the ceiling every time she thought about her book.

'How could I not succeed?' she told the reporters who interviewed her. 'My own marriage is proof that romance is alive and well.'

She turned to beam at Jake, smiling proudly in the background. She had some equally exciting news for him when they got home. The pregnancy test was positive.

An Interesting Development

Anna's Notes

I had to write a story with a dog in it at some stage because we once had a wonderful dog called Ellie, a golden Labrador, whom we still remember fondly. I wrote this just after we'd lost her. Why do dogs live for such a short time?

'Hey! Is this your dog?'

The voice sounded so angry Mel's heart sank as she stared at Ellie's muddy nose, then looked up and blinked in shock. The most gorgeous man she had ever seen was scowling at her as if she had just committed a major crime. Tall, with brown wavy hair, grey eyes and a lean body. Wow! she thought. Is he real?

'Er – yes.'

'That damned animal has dug a tunnel under my veranda.'

'I didn't know anyone had moved in next door yet.' She held out her hand. 'I'm Mel Gilby.'

'James Carling. And keep your dog under control from now on, if you don't mind.' He ignored the hand and strode off across the grass, which was just turning green again after the first winter rains.

'Pleased to meet you, too!' Mel returned to her painting. She had a commission for three matching landscapes for a hotel foyer, her biggest earner so far. It would pay her rates and enable her to live here a little longer without going back to work for someone else.

Maybe it was because she was so engrossed in the paintings that she didn't quite manage to keep Ellie under control. Or maybe it was because Ellie had taken an enormous fancy to James Carling.

Five times during the next three days Mel's new neighbour stalked across from his block, with poor old Ellie trotting beside him at the end of a rope. By the time she'd wagged him to death and swiped several licks at his hand, he was beginning to see the humour of it and finding it hard to stay angry.

'I am sorry, truly,' Mel said. 'I hope she hasn't dug any more holes.'

'No. She got inside this time and made a nest in my bed.'

'Oh, no! And she's always so muddy.'

'I noticed.'

'I can't afford a fence,' she blurted out. 'And Ellie's second name is Houdini.'

He sighed. 'I'll keep my door locked.'

He strode off. Ellie whined and tugged at the makeshift lead.

'No! You're to stay here.'

But they both watched him till he was out of sight.

What was a man like him doing on a country block in Western Australia, anyway? Mel began to weave a fantasy around him that he was a millionaire hiding from publicity. When she caught herself imagining how it would feel to be taken in his arms and thoroughly kissed, she suppressed all daydreams. Well, almost.

After a week of winter sunshine with only intermittent showers, she woke to the sound of a flock of cockatoos shrieking with laughter and rain sighing against the windows. She could hear the ocean crashing on the nearby beach. The surfers would be out in force today. She loved to sit and watch them. In fact, she loved everything about living here in what had once been her family's beach shack, even the scrimping and making do.

After breakfast, she realized that Ellie was missing again. 'Oh, no!' She glanced at the clock. It was still early. If she were lucky, she would find her dog before her neighbour did.

She was not lucky.

'I'm sorry, James. I don't know how she got out.'

The sky chose that moment to open and pour water all over them as thunder groaned in the distance. Ellie was first to flee to the porch, standing there grinning at them as they dashed for shelter through a solid wall of water.

Of course, Mel had to trip as they arrived at the veranda. Nice one, she thought, as she crashed on to the boards. Impress him, why don't you?

'Are you all right?' He pulled her up and for a moment they stood staring at one another. He reached out to touch a stray curl on her forehead and she was lost − almost paralysed with anticipation. Would he kiss her? Yes. Oh, yes, please do.

His fingers lingered on her hair. His voice was husky. 'I have a thing about auburn curls. At least, I do now.'

His lips were cool and moist with raindrops. But the kiss was warm.

He seemed puzzled and a bit shy as he stared down at her. 'Um, can I persuade you to stay for a cup of coffee?'

'I'd love to. Here on the veranda? I love watching the rain.'

'If you like. Do sit down. It won't take a minute.'

As the door swung to behind him, Mel fell on to the nearest chair and let out her breath in a long whoosh. By the time he returned with the coffee, she was determined not to be silly about this sudden attraction.

'So − what do you do for a living?' she asked brightly.

'I'm a property developer.'

'Oh? Are you going to build a new house here?'

'A tourist complex, actually.'

'What?' The desire to kiss him switched off and she regained full and instant control of her emotions. 'You mean − you're going to put up tourist accommodation *here*?'

'Yes.'

'But you'll spoil everything, the peace, the wildlife!' She glared at him. 'You'll ruin things!'

He looked surprised. 'But the area is zoned for tourist development.'

'What?'

'They changed the zoning a couple of years ago. It's all perfectly legal.'

No one had told her. She'd been working in the Arab Emirates then, earning good money and sending some home to her brother to pay the rates. 'Oh, I'm sure it's legal! They always say that as they ruin our native bush. I'm sorry. I have to go.'

She whistled to Ellie before he could see the tears in her eyes.

Half-blinded by them, she stormed home through the rain and slammed the door shut behind her.

When he followed her, she yelled at him to go away, *go – right – away*, and take his development with him. When he tried to shout something through the door, she turned the volume on the radio to full.

She expressed herself even more forcibly the following morning and evening when he tried again. And kept the radio blasting for several excruciating hours.

After that he stopped coming.

And she missed him.

So did Ellie. But for once, Mel kept her dog under control.

During the next two weeks they could not avoid meeting occasionally at the local store, which sold all the basic necessities and none of the frills of life. The first time James looked across at her he hesitated, as if he wanted to speak to her. She turned away, seeing in the security mirror on the wall how he scowled. But at least he left her alone.

At home, Mel distracted herself by working furiously on her canvases, not stopping until she couldn't see straight at night. They weren't the peaceful rural scenes she had first planned, but a big stormy landscape, a lush rainforest oozing with water, and a scorching panorama of coloured desert that socked you right in the eye.

Day by day she peeped through her window and watched angrily as her neighbour and two helpers surveyed his whole block, setting out stakes here and there. Tears filled her eyes on the day a portable office was set up on the far side of his old beach shack.

The following day, just before noon, someone knocked on the door. When Mel opened it without thinking, she found James standing there, with a bloodstained towel wrapped around his hand.

'I'm sorry to disturb you, I know you don't want to see me, but I've had an accident and—' Blood dripped from the towel.

She gestured him inside. 'Let me see.'

'If you'll just ring for a taxi, I'll go to the doctor's and get it stitched up. I haven't had a phone put in yet and the battery's flat on my mobile.' Both batteries. He'd been thinking of her, damn her! She was getting between him and his work. Not just her hair, but her firm suntanned legs and slumberous green eyes. He drew in a deep breath and concentrated on his hand.

'Let me look at the injury first.' She could see him starting to refuse and added, 'I'm a trained nurse.'

'You are?'

'I'm not working as a nurse at the moment,' she said curtly.

As they stood by the sink, rinsing off the blood, she was conscious of him as a man first and an injury second – a very attractive man, even if he was a louse. She was also suddenly conscious that she hadn't brushed her hair that morning and was wearing a very old paint-spattered sweatshirt and rather tight shorts with frayed edges.

The cut was deep and jagged. She cleaned it carefully. 'Yes, you do need stitches. I'll drive you down to the doctor's.'

'I can get a taxi. You won't want an untouchable like me in your car.'

'Don't be stupid.'

They drove there in complete silence, both breathing deeply and carefully, sitting as far apart as possible. Which wasn't very far in such a small car.

Two hours later, she drove him back, by which time his hand was neatly bandaged and he was looking white and weary. The doctor, assuming that Mel was James's girlfriend, had given strict instructions that James was not to drive or do anything with the hand for a couple of weeks.

'Do you – er – have enough food in the house?' she asked as they bumped along the track to his front door.

'No. I'll get something sent in.'

'Ben at the store doesn't deliver and there's nowhere else close enough. I'll make you up a couple of casseroles and get you some shopping in tomorrow.'

He was still stiff. 'I can't impose on you like that.'

'You don't have much choice.'

'Well – thank you, then. Mel . . .'

'Have to go. I've got a big commission to finish.'

Ten days later, ten very long days fraught with encounters, she drove him to have the stitches removed. He thanked her and sent her some flowers. If he'd brought them in person, she'd have made up the quarrel on the spot, but he didn't. He sent one of his assistants and that annoyed the hell out of her.

When he was no longer dependent upon her, she found she missed him.

'Why did he have to be a land developer?' she asked the moon as she lay awake at night.

It just winked at her and continued to smile knowingly.

'Stop grinning!' she yelled. 'I can forget him. I can!'

She couldn't, but at least he didn't know that.

A few mornings later, Ellie went missing. Mel searched frantically, but couldn't find her.

Hearing her calling, James came out of his shack. 'Something wrong?'

'Have you seen Ellie?'

'No, not since yesterday. Let me help you search.'

They checked all Ellie's old haunts, but there was no sign of her. Then, as they were walking back along a track through the bush, James suddenly stopped. 'Is that something over there?'

It was. Ellie. Lying unconscious with a bloodied head.

Mel's eyes were so flooded with tears she couldn't see straight. Ellie had been her best friend for ten years.

'She's still breathing,' he said softly, bending down. 'Looks like a dead branch fell on her.' He led the way back, carrying the dog carefully. 'We'll take my car.'

Mel sat on the back seat and let him pass her the dog. Within minutes they were at the vet's, by which time Ellie was stirring and trying to raise her head and Mel was in tears again, tears of relief.

When they got back home, leaving Ellie in overnight for observation, Mel turned to James. 'Thank you very much!' She smiled as she added, 'I guess land developers aren't such villains after all.'

He got out of the car, strode round to her side, pulled her out and smothered her with kisses, which somehow she couldn't resist.

When they drew apart, he said fiercely, 'If you'll only let me explain, you'll see that I shan't be spoiling anything – on the contrary! What I'm building is an ecotourism mini-resort where we preserve the bush and teach people to care about it.'

'Oh.' She sagged against him, feeling an utter fool – but a deliriously happy one.

'We won't discuss the details of that just now. I have something else in mind for tonight, and for a lot more nights to come.' He tucked her arm under his and led her inside his shack, locking the door carefully behind them. 'I'm thinking of getting into this interesting development deal – stepfather to a big furry mutt. Now what are you crying for?'

She sniffed. 'Because I'm so happy.' She grabbed his hair and pulled his face towards hers. 'And if you won't stop talking and kiss me again, I'll have to kiss you.'

His voice was muffled. 'I surrender. Totally. Take me – I'm yours.'

Later that year, Mel won a big prize for one of her paintings. Full of passion, said one critic. Naked emotion, wrote another.

'It's because of you,' she told James, 'filling my nights—'

'And an occasional day,' he interrupted, smiling sweetly and taking the brush from her hand.

'—with love and sex,' she sighed, as she drew him into the bedroom, 'wonderful, heavenly sex and . . .'

Outside the door, Ellie sighed and went to sleep. It was time for her dinner, but she knew better than to interrupt when they started playing this silly human game.

One White Rose

Anna's Notes

This is one of my favourite stories, and it's another one that turned into a book.

Actually, it became one of my favourite modern novels (Kirsty's Vineyard). It's another fairy tale come true. Who wouldn't want to inherit a vineyard?

Of course, in the novel, the heroine changed her name to Kirsty, and a whole set of new characters joined the cast, but still, this story is where it all started.

Julia gaped at the solicitor. 'But I don't know any Australians. Who is this Charles Finlay-Jamieson? Why would he leave me a bequest?'

'I believe you knew him simply as Mr James.'

'Oh.' For a few months Mr James had come to the library twice a week, regular as clockwork. Old, gentle, courteous. She had helped him to find books and lingered to chat, because he was clearly lonely. Then he'd stopped coming, and she'd assumed that he'd either died or moved away. Sometimes you didn't know and never found out, which was sad.

'Did you know Mr Finlay-Jamieson well?'

'No. We used to chat sometimes at the library. What has he left me – some books? We shared a very similar taste in novels.' Romances, the soppier the better.

The solicitor cleared his throat. 'No. Not books. Actually, he's left you his whole estate.'

She felt as if the room were spinning round her and clutched the arm of her chair. It was a moment before she could concentrate on what the solicitor was saying.

Later, she told her family the news. Her brother Robert spoke first, as usual. 'I can't believe it.'

She smiled faintly. It made a change to surprise Robert. Usually he knew everything and didn't hesitate to tell you so.

'Mr Finlay-Jamieson left me his house,' she repeated, 'on condition that I look after his books, and lay a white rose on his wife's grave every year on their anniversary.'

'Well, you've fallen lucky. When are we moving in?'

'It's not that easy. The house is in Australia and there's an income to go with it. I have to live there for five years before I can sell anything or return to England.'

'That's ridiculous!' her sister Sue said.

'The old fellow's wits must have been addled,' Robert stated. 'You can't possibly go. We'll contest the conditions of the will.'

For once, she managed to stand up to them. 'I shan't contest the will. It's what Mr Finlay-Jamieson wanted.'

'But you can't go and live in Australia!'

'Um, the estate's worth well over a million pounds.' It was the only argument likely to convince Robert.

There was silence around her, then her brother began making plans to accompany her. And, through the long months of getting permission to live there, nothing she said would deter him from it.

She was always glad that Robert broke his leg just before they left. Always. She was nervous about travelling so far on her own, but Mr Finlay-Jamieson must have had some reason for leaving her everything and making those conditions. She couldn't let him down.

And she'd certainly remember about the rose. He'd spoken very lovingly about his wife.

Western Australia was very hot in February, which was the height of summer in Australia. People at the airport were complaining, but after the English winter she had left behind, Julia welcomed the warmth of the sun on her face. Exhausted by the twenty-hour flight, she went straight to the hotel and fell into bed, forgetting to ring her family as promised.

When the phone woke her up, she felt groggy. 'Why didn't you ring us when you arrived, Julia?'

'Robert?'

'That was very selfish of you. We were worried sick.'

She slammed the phone down on him, then stared at it in dismay. He would be furious. Well, she was furious, too. That anger gave her the courage to call reception. 'Please hold all calls. I need some sleep.'

It was late afternoon, Perth time, when she awoke. She rang for room service. With the tray came an angry note dictated over the phone by her brother Robert. She screwed it up and threw it across the dingy room. She did the same with a later note demanding that she call her sister Sue.

Family! It was ungrateful, she knew, but she was thirty, had been a deputy librarian for the past five years, and wasn't too stupid to manage on her own. She pulled a wry face. No. Not stupid, but cowardly sometimes. She did so hate arguments and fuss.

A smile crept across her face. At this distance she had a way to deal with her family. If she changed hotels, if they couldn't phone her . . . One hand crept up to her mouth. Dare she? Yes. She'd do it. Turn over a new leaf here in Australia. Be her own woman.

As soon as she'd finished breakfast, she packed her things and checked out. The taxi driver took her to a better hotel, where she booked a luxury room with a view of the river. Robert would have had an apoplexy at the thought of her wasting so much money, but just for once she wanted to live elegantly, in the way she'd read of in books.

Her family didn't know about her secret vice, but she adored reading romances. She loved the tall dark heroes and the courageous heroines who deserved to be loved, as they always were in the end. She even quite enjoyed the sexy bits. It was as near as she had ever come to the great mystery of life.

Her one love had been a man as gentle as herself who had died in a car accident. Poor Donald. He'd never have made a hero, but she thought they might have been happy together, in a quiet sort of way.

The next day she went out. There was a terrifyingly large amount of money sitting in her new Australian bank account, and the solicitor had advised her to get a car. 'You do drive, don't you, Miss Mincham?'

'Oh, yes.' She had an elderly car in England, as gentle and hesitant as herself.

'Well, you won't be able to manage without one over there.

The property is in the country and there's no public transport at all.'

'Oh.'

In between sightseeing, she took a couple of driving lessons to get used to the local traffic rules, then she bought a car. A Mercedes coupé. She hadn't been able to resist it. The heroes in her novels drove cars like this. Just for once she would indulge herself, she thought, as she sat behind the wheel and started the engine.

The car was beautiful to drive, comfortable, with excellent brakes. It gave her a feeling of confidence, enough confidence to ring up her family.

'Where the hell have you been, Julia?' roared Robert.

She'd guess he was fretting about his broken leg. Well, too bad. He shouldn't take out his frustration on her. 'I moved to a nicer hotel.'

'We've been worried sick about you. Give me your number this minute!'

'There's no point. I'm going to my new home tomorrow.'

'Then give me the address there. You forgot to do that before you left England. Typical of you! I don't know how you're ever going to manage on your own.'

His voice sounded so scornful. Had he always spoken to her like that? She frowned at the phone. Had she let him? 'I'll write to you when I get there. Bye, Robert.'

For the second time in her life she put the phone down on him and told reception to hold all calls.

It took only three hours to reach her new home. The country roads were empty by English standards and driving the new car was a pleasure. Julia found herself humming along with the radio.

The sign over the gate said 'Rochdale House'. So Mr Finlay-Jamieson had named his Australian home for the English town he'd been born and died in.

'Five years,' she said as she edged the car along a bumpy rutted drive. 'I have to live here for five years.' The thought gave her a sudden sense of freedom.

The house was very Australian. One storey, with a tin roof and verandas all round. Beige sunburnt grass in the fields nearby, trees and a small patch of green lawn near the house. As she got out of the car a kookaburra started shrieking with laughter. She paused to listen, entranced, eyes half-closed in pleasure.

'What're you doing here?' demanded a loud voice. 'This is private property.'

Julia jumped in shock and turned to find a large man glaring at her.

'I asked what you're doing here.'

Something about the man's voice reminded her of Robert. She stiffened. 'Don't you speak to me like that! If it's any of your business, I own this house.' She waved the key in his face.

'Ah.' The look he gave her was not friendly. 'You're the Pom who soft-soaped old Charles. He always was a sucker for a pretty face.'

'And you must be Sam Carden. Thank you for keeping an eye on the house, but if you're going to be rude to me, I think you'd better leave.'

He shrugged and turned to go, tossing over his shoulder. 'I've had everything switched on for you, as your lawyer asked.' Before she could answer, he'd disappeared behind the trees.

She fanned herself with the straw hat she'd bought. How dare he say that! She'd never soft-soaped anyone in her life. But he'd also said that she had a pretty face. It was a long time since anyone had complimented her, even in a left-handed, sarcastic way like this. Not since Donald.

Then she forgot her rude welcome and stared around, sighing with happiness. Her own house and ten acres of land. What more could anyone want? The house was very old and in great need of renovation, but she didn't care. It was hers.

Not only were the phone and electricity switched on, but someone had thought to stock the fridge with a few necessities. Guilt washed through Julia. It must have been the bad-tempered man. She apologized to him mentally.

She examined the loaf and the other foodstuffs, but could find no prices. She owed him money. And gratitude for his help. But he shouldn't have said that to her, she thought, still indignant.

The living room was large and square, the kitchen almost as large, with a table in one corner. Julia's whole flat would have fitted into these two rooms. 'Gingham curtains,' she decided as she left the kitchen, 'and white paintwork.'

There were two more large rooms, one full of bookcases, then a long narrow corridor with bedrooms on either side. 'Six!' she gasped, after exploring them. 'What on earth shall I do with six bedrooms and three bathrooms?' How puzzling that Charles Finlay-Jamieson had chosen to return to England and live simply, when he had a huge house here. Even more puzzling that he had left it all to her.

Dusk was falling as she finished unpacking. She decided to make do with cheese on toast. Bunbury had lots of restaurants. She'd seen them as she drove through, curious to see what her nearest town was like. But it was half an hour's drive away and she was feeling tired now.

As she pulled the loaf out of the fridge, a car drew up outside, a large four-wheel drive. A young woman in shorts and tee shirt jumped out, followed by a rather pregnant dog that was at least partly Labrador. She strode across to the door, carrying something wrapped in a tea towel.

'Hi! You must be Julia Mincham. Sam said you'd arrived.'

'Sam?'

'I think you met him when you arrived.'

'Oh, the bad-tempered man.'

The young woman grinned. 'Yes, that's Sam. But his bark's much worse than his bite. He's an old softie, really. Just don't let him bully you.'

'I won't.' Julia didn't intend to let anyone bully her from now on, not even her own family. It was wonderful the confidence a bank account full of money gave you.

'I'm Penny Braide, one of your neighbours.' She held out the bundle. 'I thought you might like a casserole for tea.'

'Oh, how kind! Do come in!'

Ten minutes later, Julia watched wistfully as Penny drove off. She'd make a lovely heroine. Not shy and quiet, but full of life and vigour. Then she shook off her regrets and went to heat up some of the beef casserole.

Three days later, guilt could no longer be denied. Julia owed Mr Carden money. However rude he was, she had to pay him back. Perhaps he had spoken so sharply because he was still missing his friend, though Mr Carden was nearer her own age than Mr Finlay-Jamieson's.

She rang up Penny, who had called round every day to check that she was all right and who was teaching her about living in Australia, not to mention how to find her way to the nearest shops. 'Er – could you tell me where Sam lives?'

'Are you in the mood for a quarrel, then?'

Penny's voice was teasing, but Julia's heart sank. 'I dislike quarrels, but I owe him some money.'

'What on earth for?'

'He stocked up my fridge with groceries.'

'Oh, there's no need to worry about that. He was just being neighbourly.'

'I prefer to pay my debts.'

Penny grinned. 'Good luck.'

Sam's house was quite small, with a series of outbuildings made of tin and looking as if they were held together with sticky tape. Julia got out of the car and knocked on the front door before she lost her courage.

'I didn't expect to see *you* here,' a voice said behind her.

'Do you always creep up behind people and make them jump!'

'I was working on the garden. Do you want me to go into the house and open the door before we talk?'

'No. But it wouldn't hurt you to be polite.'

Sam's brows rose, and he opened his mouth as if to shout at her, then he clamped his lips together and breathed deeply. 'Right. What can I do for you?'

'I owe you some money, Mr Carden.'

'You owe me nothing.'

'For the groceries.'

'It was only a few dollars. Charles wouldn't have wanted you to come to an empty kitchen.'

She set her hands on her hips. 'I prefer to pay my debts. That's the way I was brought up.'

He was looking at her sideways, with a calculating expression on his face. 'Are you any good at sewing?'

'Pardon?'

'I need some sewing done. That's the way we do things here in the country. We help each other out.'

'Oh. I see. And yes, I can sew.'

'Come inside.' He took her agreement for granted and led the way indoors. He pointed to a piece of canvas. 'That's fraying in one corner. My mother made it. I can't ask Penny to mend it. She just throws things away when they get holes in them, or wears the holes. Can you embroider?'

Julia picked up the embroidered scene. 'This is lovely. Yes, I can mend it for you.'

And that was the start of their friendship. If you could call it friendship, because Sam spoke his mind on every topic and the new Julia gave him back as good as he dished out. Well, mostly. It took time to make such a big change to oneself. He mended her pump. She cooked him a meal. He fixed her side gate. She lent him a few books.

Now that she'd given them her phone number, her family kept ringing her up from England and Robert in particular took it upon himself to harangue her about not wasting her money. After she'd mentioned Sam in a couple of her letters, he started adding warnings about not letting neighbours take advantage of her generosity. She should remember that a rich woman was prey for all sorts of scoundrels.

Sam came round one day when her brother Robert was lecturing her and she was trying in vain to get in a word edgeways. He saw how upset she was, took the phone out of her hand, listened for a moment, then yelled into it, 'Leave her alone, you bully. She's a woman grown.' He slammed it down.

She should have been angry, but the thought of what Robert's expression would be at this moment betrayed her into a giggle, then suddenly the two of them were roaring with laughter. When the phone rang again, they ignored it and went outside to argue amicably about the vegetable garden.

'Don't let them bully you,' Sam said later, as he left. 'You're too soft with your family.'

'It's the way I've been brought up. Robert's a few years older than me, you see.'

'Then change it.'

'I'm trying.'

'Good.'

That week Julia did something she'd been hesitating about, she asked Penny if she could have one of the pups.

'Are you sure?'

'Very sure. I've always wanted a dog, but no one else in my family did, so we never had one. Even when I left home, I lived in a flat, so it just wasn't possible.

Penny beamed at her. 'That's great. Two of them placed now in good homes.'

'I'll try to make it a good home, but you'll have to give me a few hints.'

As the days passed, one thing led to another. Sam took her out for a barbecue near the beach and kissed her when he brought her back. Greatly daring, she took him out in return, choosing the most expensive restaurant in Bunbury. He was very stiff with her.

'What did I do wrong?' she asked, after a miserable evening.

He looked at her, seeing the tears trembling in her eyes. 'Oh, dammit, Julia, I didn't mean to upset you.'

The tears escaped and trickled down her cheeks.

He pulled her into his arms. 'Come here!' He kissed her nose, then wiped the tears away with one rough fingertip. Suddenly he was kissing her again, very thoroughly, just like a hero in a novel. She flung her arms round his neck and kissed him right back. Those lively young heroines would have been proud of her.

A little later, as they sat together on the veranda, she asked softly, 'What made you so angry tonight, Sam?'

'I can't afford to take you to restaurants like that.' His voice was gruff and she could sense the tension in him.

'Oh, is that all?'

'What do you mean, *all*?'

'Who cares about expensive restaurants? I'll cook you a meal myself next time.'

But the money lay between them like a ghost. And he didn't kiss her again.

When the wedding anniversary of Charles and his wife came round, Sam took Julia to the cemetery. Actually, she took him in her lovely new car, because his was giving him a bit of trouble.

She bought a beautiful white rose from a florist in Bunbury, the most beautiful one in the shop, plus a slender vase to put it in. On an impulse, she bought one for herself, too.

They walked over to the grave in silence and stood looking down at it.

'He loved her very much,' Sam said softly. 'He never really got over her death. The lawyer sent his ashes back to Australia with a request that I bury them here with her.' He looked sideways. 'Why the white rose, do you think? It's usually red for love.'

Julia smiled through the tears that misted her eyes. 'He told me once how on their first anniversary the shop had run out of red roses, so he had to buy a white one. She loved it so much he always bought his wife a white one on their wedding anniversary from then on.' She filled the little vase with water from a nearby tap and set it carefully on the grave. 'For you both,' she said aloud.

'I'm still missing you, Charles,' Sam said quietly.

He took Julia's hand as they walked back to the car and for once, they didn't exchange a single cross word on their drive back.

Three months after her arrival, Julia saw a taxi pull into the drive. Her brother Robert got out. 'Oh, no!' She thumped the table in frustration. Why could her family not leave her alone? She gritted her teeth and went to greet him. 'What a surprise! Why didn't you tell me you were coming? How's your leg?'

'Better. We were worried about you, so I decided to see how you were going.'

Before she knew it Robert had taken charge, telling her what to do as usual. She tried to stop him, but her new-found independence was still too fragile. He even took over the driving – after he had given her a lecture on how she had wasted her money buying an expensive convertible like this.

Robert and Sam took an instant dislike to one another.

'He's a fortune hunter,' said Robert scornfully.

'He's a bully,' Sam hissed at her when Robert's back was turned. 'Why do you let him do this to you?'

She didn't know why. Habit, she supposed. She tried to stand up to Robert, but rarely succeeded.

One day Penny called to deliver the puppy she'd promised Julia, which was now old enough to leave its mother.

'She doesn't want a mongrel like that! She can afford to buy a pedigree dog. Here! Take it back.' Robert picked the little creature up by the scruff of its neck, making it yelp in pain.

Penny glared at him, and cuddled the whimpering puppy.

At that moment something snapped inside Julia. 'Don't you dare take her away!' She snatched the pup from Penny and the feel of its warm wriggling body boosted her courage. 'Thanks. She's lovely. Um, would you mind me not inviting you in? My brother and I have something important to discuss.'

'Don't let him bully you,' Penny whispered, and drove away.

Julia turned to Robert, swallowed hard and said, 'You'd better book your flight back.'

'*What?*'

'I need to get on with my own life now, Robert. You can see that I'm very comfortable here. Just – just book your flight and I'll drive you up to Perth. Or else go sightseeing somewhere.' And she would do the driving herself this time, she vowed.

When he started to argue, she snatched up the car keys and the pup, and fled.

Sam was sitting on his veranda. He scowled as she got out of the car. 'Isn't your dear brother with you? Don't you need protection from a fortune hunter like me?'

'Go and put the kettle on and stop talking such rot!' She pushed him into the house, and the puppy wriggled out of her arms and ran round exploring. They faced each other across the kitchen table.

'You kept the pup, then?'

'Yes.'

'Penny rang me. She said he told her to take it away again.'

'It's my pup. And I've told Robert to leave.'

Sam turned to beam at her. 'You have? That's wonderful.'

'It was about time I stood up to him.'

She stared at Sam. She'd missed their times together. As she fingered the tablecloth, a daring idea started forming in her mind. A very daring idea, worthy of the most spirited of romantic heroines.

And another idea followed: she was suddenly sure that this was what Charles had intended to happen when he left her the house. 'Come and sit down for a minute, Sam. Never mind the tea. I have something to ask you.'

He slouched over to a chair, looking at her warily. 'If it's to do with your brother . . .'

'It's not.' She took a deep breath. 'It's to do with us, you and me.'

'Oh?'

'Sam, will you – will you, please – um, will you marry me?'

He goggled at her for a minute, then scowled down at the fists clenched in his lap. 'No.'

'Why not?'

'Because I'm not a fortune hunter.'

It took several deep breaths, but then she marched round the table, shoved him down on the couch and sat on his knee. 'You will marry me, you know,' she said, giving him a big hug.

'Oh?' But his voice was gentle and he was smiling now. 'Why will I?'

'Because I can be as much of a bully as my brother if I really want something – and I do want this, so very much. It's the way we Minchams are.'

'I'm terrified.' He looked at her, a steady serious look, and when she smiled encouragingly, he began to kiss her.

And she didn't have to bully him into marrying her. In fact, Sam seemed quite taken with the idea.

Time

Anna's Notes

Relatives came to stay with us quite often when we first emigrated from England to Australia, but as in this story, it was sometimes for longer than was quite comfortable, however hard both sides tried, however much we loved one another.

I was learning Italian when I wrote this, and had some Italian friends, so their background sort of crept into the story, too, though the characters are not based on real life in any way. I never use real people in my stories. They might not do what I tell them to.

Jenny Reid picked up the phone and smiled when she heard her daughter's voice. Australia was so far away, but they called each other once a month, at least.

When they had chatted for a while, Sarah said firmly, 'Mum, you promised to come out here for a nice, long visit once you'd got over Dad's death. It's been three years now. I think it's time you kept that promise, don't you? And it's summer here, sunshine every day. I remember how cold Edinburgh winters can be.'

'Well, all right. I'll come for a week or two.'

'When you're travelling so far, you should come for longer, two or three months, at least. Get to know your grandchildren.'

And that thought tipped the scales. Jenny had never even met Tim and Pete, though of course she'd seen plenty of photos of her grandsons. They were already five and seven. Where had the years gone?

Three weeks later, she sat in the shade of a big gum tree, wincing as her two small grandsons raced round the garden, screeching at each other, followed by a yapping dog. No wonder the neighbours in the big two-storey house next door were not on good terms with her daughter!

Sarah didn't believe in disciplining children, but letting them grow up free and happy. It made them hard to live with sometimes, though they meant no harm. Jenny sighed. Oh, for the peace and quiet of her own flat! Why had she let them persuade her to come for three whole months? Two weeks would have been enough – more than enough!

'You all right, Mum?' Sarah peered out of the kitchen window. 'You mustn't get yourself sunburnt.'

She said the same thing every day. Suddenly Jenny had had enough. Getting up, she marched into the house and confronted her daughter, hands on hips. 'Do you remember how old I am, Sarah?'

'Er – fifty-two, isn't it?'

'Correct. And do I seem to be getting senile?'

Sarah blinked in shock. 'What?'

'*Do – I – seem – senile?*'

'No. No, of course not, Mum.'

'Then will you please stop treating me like a child! You've been doing it ever since I arrived!' She made for the asylum of her bedroom, resisting the temptation to slam the door behind her.

Once inside she plumped down on the bed and let out her breath in a whoosh, admitting to herself that she was bored! Sarah kept saying it was too hot to trail small children around sightseeing and making excuses to stay at home.

Jenny groaned aloud. Another two and a half months to go. So much time on her hands! She would go mad!

She had grown used to being a widow now, though it had been a shock when Paul died so young. At first the days had dragged and then, gradually, she'd developed new interests, even taken up painting again. She missed the companionship, though, and probably always would.

Her friend Elizabeth had suggested she join an Internet dating site because she was young enough to go out and meet some men. But Jenny hadn't wanted to do that. The very thought of dating made her feel nervous.

She stared at herself in the mirror, pleased with what she saw.

She was still slim enough for her generation's taste, if not for this one's. (Why did the youngsters today want to look like walking skeletons?) Her fair hair was sprinkled with grey now, but she had it styled regularly, and her complexion had always been good. Her daughter was showing sun-wear round her eyes already, from the harsh Australian sun.

Suddenly Jenny grew impatient with herself. What did it matter if she looked good or not? Who was there to care?

She glared round the tiny spare bedroom, rebelling at the thought of spending another afternoon mewed up here 'resting', to avoid those two ill-trained brats! Her glance fell on the novel her daughter had lent her. Such a miserable set of characters! Someone should have shot them at birth.

Then she brightened. That was it! She would go out shopping, buy herself a good novel, a romance or a story about a family. Several books, even! Cheerful books.

She opened the wardrobe and smiled. What's more, she would wear her cream linen suit! She was sick of casual clothes and sticky fingers. The only social life Sarah and her husband seemed to want was Sunday barbecues – in the heat of the day, with dozens of children screaming round the garden of whoever's turn it was to play host. They all made her welcome, but she found it wearing.

When she was ready, Jenny studied herself in the mirror again. What the suit really needed was a hat to set it off. People wore shady, wide-brimmed hats here to protect their skin. She had always loved hats.

There was a knock on the bedroom door. 'Mum? Can I come in?'

'Yes, dear.'

'Oh, I love your suit, but—'

'Thank you, dear.'

'— but isn't it – well – too smart for wearing round the house?'

'I'm not staying round the house today. I'm going out.'

'Oh. Did you change your mind about the Senior Citizens Centre?'

'Certainly not! I've told you before: I'm not old enough to be a Senior Citizen. No, I'm going into Perth shopping.'

'But there isn't a bus until two and—'

'I'm taking a taxi.'

Her daughter's gentle worried face, so like her late husband's, haunted Jenny all the way into town, but once there, she forget everything except the joys of leisurely shopping.

The centre of Perth was very attractive, she decided, standing in Forrest Place and eyeing the overhead walkways and cool verandas full of elegant shops. Just what she needed today.

She bought two novels and, out of guilt, a pretty scarf for Sarah. Then she found it – a shady cream straw hat trimmed with a drift of pale apricot flowers! Expensive, but irresistible. She had to have it. She wore it immediately. You don't look fifty-two, she told her reflection smugly as she paid the bill.

Her feet were starting to ache, but she couldn't face the thought of returning to that dreary box of a bedroom, so she got some brochures from the tourist bureau and sat on a bench to read them. She would come into town regularly, perhaps go for that cruise on the river. There were lots of things to see and do! Rebellion burned brightly within her.

She made her way to the Cultural Centre and found the art gallery. There was a café nearby, where she ordered a pot of tea and chose a table outside.

A silver-haired man passed by, then came back and stopped in front of her. Heavens, was he trying to pick her up? At her age! It must be the hat. It was too flamboyant. She felt her cheeks burning and had a sudden desire to run away.

He raised his hat. '*Scusi, signora*, but – are you not the mother of *Signora* Shilby?'

He looked vaguely familiar and he knew Sarah's name. Who was he? Jenny's first panic started to subside.

He gave a tiny bow. 'Please – excuse me speaking to you, but I am the father of your daughter's neighbour. I've seen you in the garden with the children.'

She relaxed a little, half-recognizing him now. Sarah and John disliked the Rinaldis, for some reason. Well, the neighbours had probably complained about the noise her grandsons made. 'I'm pleased to meet you properly, *Signor* Rinaldi.' She couldn't help thinking what a nice smile he had.

'It is not Rinaldi, *signora* – my name, I mean. My daughter is Rinaldi. I am Parvone, Niccolo Parvone.'

'Oh, well – I'm Jenny Reid.'

Gravely he tendered his hand. She liked the way Europeans always shook hands. You felt they had truly noticed your existence.

'You permit?' He indicated the empty seat next to her.

'Please.'

'You are awaiting your daughter, no doubt?'

'No. I've escaped for the day.'

He laughed aloud. 'Escaped! Ha!'

She felt embarrassed. Would she never learn to watch what she said? 'Sarah's boys are a bit – er – lively.'

His eyes crinkled up at the corners. 'I make a confession, *signora*. I, too, have *escaped* from my daughter for the afternoon.'

She relaxed and they exchanged smiles.

'Have you ordered?' he asked.

'Yes.'

'May I share your table? I, too, am hungry.'

It was pleasant to sit there chatting. Afterwards they went into the art gallery and walked round the permanent collection. She was entranced. What marvellous paintings!

'Silly, isn't it?' he said at one stage. 'I have never been here before. But I shall come again. I want to see the aboriginal collection next.'

'Oh, yes, but I'm getting tired now.' She looked down at her feet, grimacing, and then spied some seats. 'Shall we?'

They sat in comfortable silence for a while. He was a very restful sort of man. 'Are you visiting your family, Signor Parvone?'

'No, *signora*. My wife died – oh, three years ago – and now I live with my eldest daughter.'

'Is that wise?' She could feel herself blushing. 'I'm so sorry! How rude of me! I didn't mean to – it's none of my business.'

He threw back his head and laughed again. 'But you are right, my dear *Signora* Reid, it is not at all wise to live with one's children.'

'Then why did you . . .' Jenny clapped her hand to her mouth. 'I'm sorry. It's none of my business.'

He shrugged and stared into the distance. 'I moved in with Gina because I wasn't thinking clearly after my wife's death.'

She reached out to pat his hand, he looked so unhappy. 'I was exactly the same when my husband died, but luckily for me, Sarah was ten thousand miles away.'

He nodded and gave her a wry smile. 'For women it is much easier to live alone, I think. For men like me, Italian men of my generation, housework and cooking are great mysteries.' He stared down at his hands, spreading them out and turning them over as if he had never seen them before. 'Yet it takes only two hands to do such things and these I have.'

He gave her one of his slow, warm smiles. 'I think I must buy myself a house and move out.' The smile faded and he began to pick at the crease in his trousers. 'Only, this will offend my daughter, who works hard to look after me.'

'Yes, I can see your difficulty.' Jenny caught sight of her watch and gasped. 'Oh, dear, look how late it is! I'll certainly have offended *my* daughter, *Signor* Parvone, by staying out so long. I wonder – could you tell me where I can find a taxi?'

'I have my car. It is no trouble for me to take you home.'

'I couldn't impose!'

'It would be a great pleasure for me to have your company for longer.'

When they stood up, he contemplated her for a minute, then leaned forward. '*Scusi*. Your hat, *signora*.' Very gently he straightened it.

The admiration in his eyes made her flush.

'*Bellissima!*' The word was a caress.

For a moment, their faces were close together. They were the same height. That felt strange in a man. Paul had been tall. She'd always had to look up at him and their steps hadn't matched very well.

Sarah stared at her in horror. 'Mum! Are you absolutely mad? You accepted a lift home with a strange man! I remember all the lectures you used to give me about that sort of thing.'

'You were a young girl then. I'm not. Besides, *Signor* Parvone isn't a stranger! He's a neighbour of yours.'

'And don't we know it! You might have thought of us!'

'I beg your pardon?'

'You know we don't get on with them, Mum.' She scowled in the direction of the house next door.

'That's your business. I like *Signor* Parvone.'

'But . . .'

'I don't choose your friends, dear, and I don't expect you to choose mine.'

Sarah clutched the tea towel to her bosom. 'You haven't – you couldn't have – you aren't going to be seeing him again, are you, Mum?'

Jenny tried to look airy and confident, but wasn't sure she'd succeeded. Then as her daughter started scolding again, she asked sharply, 'Why should I not see him again? He's a charming man.'

'Mum, you *can't*! After father, that lumpy little man! And what will John say? He can't stand them! Why, he had a row with the husband only last week about their sprinkler system. No, no, you'll have to tell him you've changed your mind.'

Jenny could feel herself stiffening. 'It really is no business of yours – or of John's – whom I see or do not see! And as a matter of fact, I've already accepted an invitation to go out to dinner with *Signor* Parvone.'

This time she did slam the bedroom door behind her.

Next morning, Jenny faced herself in the mirror again. You'll just have to go next door and invite him out, she told her reflection. Nothing to it! Women invite men out all the time nowadays. But *she* had never done it, she thought in panic; never in all her life had she invited a man out to dinner. What if he refused? She'd be so embarrassed!

She sagged against the wall, swallowing hard. She couldn't do it. Definitely not.

Only – she straightened up again – that meant she would have to confess everything to Sarah. And that would be worse. Far worse. After the way John had gone on about it last night, she would die before she would admit to him that she'd been lying.

She dressed carefully in a pretty floral dress in soft blues and pinks and that gave her a bit more courage. *Bellissima*, he'd said. Taking a deep breath, she opened the bedroom door, squared her shoulders and set out on her great ordeal.

As she walked out of the front door, she saw Sarah's bedroom curtains twitch and stopped to glare at the window. How dare her daughter spy on her!

The anger carried her up the next drive to the ornate two-storey house with its carved double doors and, before she knew it, she had rung the bell. The butterflies in her stomach were fluttering about wildly, but it was too late to back out now.

Mrs Rinaldi, a plump young woman, answered the door and sniffed when she saw who it was. '*Si?*'

'I would like to see *Signor* Parvone, please.'

A stubborn look came over the woman's face. '*Non capisco.*'

'Oh, dear.' Jenny couldn't think what to do. She didn't speak any Italian.

Then Niccolo came running down the stairs, with his wide smile and his hands reaching out for hers. He bowed her in as if she were a queen. '*Signora* Reid! How lucky that I saw you walking up to the door. This is a great pleasure! Please come in.'

'*Papa, non è*—'

'It is not polite to speak Italian in front of a guest, Gina. And have we no manners, to leave a visitor standing outside the door like this on such a hot day?'

Gina flushed.

'The *signora* would enjoy some refreshments, no doubt.' He didn't wait for an answer, but shepherded Jenny up the stairs to his sitting room.

It was lovely in the shade of the balcony, but Jenny couldn't relax. She decided to get it over with – then if he refused, she would make some excuse and leave. She tried desperately to find the words to ask him out, but couldn't even think how to begin.

'Hey!' His broad capable hand stopped hers from mangling the handkerchief. 'There is something wrong, I think?'

She nodded.

Footsteps approached. '*Momentito.*' He got up to open the door. Gina entered, slammed down a tray and left.

'She – your daughter – she doesn't approve of my visiting you.'

'She has begun to treat me like one of her children. Where am I going? Why do I not stay quietly at home? I shall most definitely buy a house of my own.'

He poured her a cup of coffee, insisted she take a pastry and piled two on to his own plate. 'Now, please, if there is some way I can help you, for me it will be a pleasure. Or if you have just come to visit, that will also be a pleasure.'

There was no easy way to do it! 'I came to ask if you . . .' Her voice faltered, but she took a deep breath and said rapidly, 'Would you like to come out to dinner with me – to a restaurant – one evening?' Oh dear, she could feel herself blushing! She couldn't even meet his eyes.

'I shall be delighted. What about tonight?'

Sighing in relief, she looked up, and his smile was so kindly, she confessed, 'That's the first time I've ever invited a man out.'

'It's the first time a woman has invited me out. I like it. I like it very much.' He took another huge bite of his pastry, waved it in a flourishing gesture and added, 'My daughter made a big fuss that I brought you home yesterday. Yours, too?'

'Yes.'

'They do not like each other, our children.'

She sighed. 'No, I'm afraid not.'

'So we must teach them the lesson, eh? Not to treat us like little children.'

'You're very kind.'

'I enjoy your company, *signora*. We understand one other.'

'Yes, I think we do.' It was often easier to talk to people of your own generation and he was a charming companion.

They sat on the balcony for quite a long time, chatting about this and that. When she rose to leave, he smiled and said softly, 'I'm looking forward to this evening, *Signora* Reid.'

'I am, too. And – and I think it would be better – I mean, I'd like it better, if you called me Jenny.' Oh dear, she was blushing again!

His hand captured hers and he raised it to his lips. 'So. Jenny. Pretty name. And my name is Niccolo.'

He stood at the door, waving, and that gave her the courage to march into the house and say to her daughter, 'I won't be in for dinner. Niccolo is picking me up at seven.'

During the next fortnight, Jenny and Niccolo dined out four times and made several daytime excursions in his huge white car. He'd retired early from his building business and found time hung heavily on his hands.

The atmosphere in each house grew steadily cooler, but they laughed about that and agreed to ignore it. Well, why should they stop enjoying themselves? He had a dry sense of humour that touched a similar chord in her. And not only did he seem to enjoy her impulsiveness; he often matched it with his own.

One evening, Sarah and John put the boys to bed early and took Jenny to sit in the formal lounge room, which they rarely used.

'Mum, we're . . .' Sarah faltered and looked helplessly at John.

'A little concerned,' he filled in smoothly, 'about the amount of time you're spending with *that man*.'

'His name's *Signor* Parvone. It's not hard to say. Try it! Par-vo-ne.'

'Mum, you're avoiding the issue!'

'What issue? It's surely my own business whom I see or do not see. Or are your guests not allowed out on their own?'

John leaned forward earnestly. 'We just don't want you to get hurt, that's all, Mother. These holiday romances . . .'

She could only gape at him. *Romances!* She wasn't in love with Niccolo! He was just a friend – a very comfortable friend of her own age. Romances, indeed!

Then she remembered how his smile crinkled up the corners of his eyes – his fondness for pastries – the way he held her arm as she got out of the car. Her breath caught in her throat and her cheeks began to burn. She saw Sarah exchange a meaningful glance with her husband and anger began to rise inside her.

John went on with what was obviously a prepared speech.

Jenny sat there fuming. When she couldn't bear to listen for one minute longer, she stood up. 'Please excuse me. I'm very tired.'

She heard Sarah burst into tears as she walked swiftly along the corridor to her room. She felt guilty for upsetting her daughter, but she wasn't going to give in about this. She'd been having such a good time with Niccolo.

But she couldn't settle to sleep. At three o'clock in the morning she abandoned the attempt. It was so hot still she put on her blue satin housecoat and tiptoed out into the garden for a breath of fresh air. The moonlight was bright and it was deliciously cool outside.

A figure approached the fence and a voice whispered, 'Hey, Jenny!'

'Niccolo!'

'You can't sleep either, eh?'

It seemed quite natural to clasp the hand he stretched out to her.

'Tonight,' he said, 'they bring my brother and my eldest son to speak seriously to me. About you.'

'Oh.'

'I am making a fool of myself, it seems. An old man's romance.'

'You're not old!' she said hotly.

He raised her hand to kiss it. 'I'm glad you don't think so.'

Her breath caught in her throat at the expression on his face. 'Sarah and John had a talk to me as well, Niccolo. Holiday romance, they called it.'

'I see. They mean well, I suppose. Only, Jenny – when they talk, talk, talk at me, I suddenly thought, hey, I *am* getting fond of her!'

'Oh!'

'Ha! You're blushing. But who asked me out to dinner first?'

'Well! What a thing to say!'

He chuckled and pulled her towards the fence.

I ought not to, she thought. This will only lead to trouble. But his hair shone silver in the moonlight and his eyes were warm and tender. It had been a long time since a man looked at her like that.

Very gently, he kissed her lips, then each eyelid. His large hands were warm on each side of her head. She pressed her cheek against one of them, but after a moment, panicked and pulled away. 'Niccolo, I–I . . .'

He kept hold of one hand. 'I know, Jenny. It is too quick, eh? At our age, we prefer to take our time about such things.'

'Yes.' She couldn't resist reaching out to stroke his hair, gleaming like silver in the moonlight. 'I–I like you very much, Niccolo, but—'

'But we need time – time to get to know each other better. Mmm?'

'Yes. That's it exactly.'

A light went on in the house.

'Oh, damn them!' she said, she who never swore.

John peered out of the family room door, a baseball bat in his raised hand.

When Niccolo squeezed her hand and gave a low chuckle, Jenny couldn't stop a stifled snort of laughter from slipping out.

John let the bat drop. 'Oh! It's only you, Mother! We thought it was burglars.'

Sarah, wearing an ancient, faded dressing gown, glared at *Signor* Parvone, then turned to her mother. 'You'll catch a chill, Mum. Do come inside!'

'Not just yet, dear. *Signor* Parvone and I have a few things to discuss.'

'Surely that can wait until morning? It's three o'clock at night! What will the neighbours think?'

A window opened in the next house and a flood of Italian poured out.

'She says I'll catch a chill,' whispered Niccolo. 'It's three o'clock at night. What will the neighbours think?'

They stared at each other, then burst out laughing again, leaning helplessly against the fence, holding hands.

They were still chuckling when Gina stormed out into the garden, magnificent in a purple satin housecoat. Ignoring the others, she began to scold Niccolo loudly in Italian.

Sarah took the opportunity to tiptoe across the patio and hiss at Jenny. 'Mum, for heaven's sake come inside!'

Jenny glanced sideways at Niccolo.

He rolled his eyes at her, then turned back to his daughter and snapped, '*Basta!*' in a very sharp tone.

His daughter's tirade stopped mid-sentence and she took a step backwards, looking uncertain.

He turned to Jenny and his expression softened. 'We won't get the time we need here, *cara*.'

'No.'

He winked and breathed the word 'Courage!' Then added loudly, 'How soon can you pack your things? I think this would be a good time to take that little trip down south we were talking about.'

She did not hesitate. 'Half an hour.'

'Mum, you can't! John, stop her!'

Jenny smiled at Niccolo. 'No promises about what this may lead to, my friend?'

'Not yet. Later, perhaps.' He let go of her hand.

She hurried back to the house, fending Sarah off, trying desperately to look calm and collected. Her hands were shaking, though, as she packed her suitcase. I'm not used to being a rebel, she thought, then raised her chin. But it's my life, after all! And Niccolo is – is such a dear, gentle man.

When everything was ready, she took a deep breath and opened the bedroom door.

John was outside, barring her way. 'Mother, please don't go off like this! We'll talk about it in the morning.' He tried to take her suitcase away and she clung to it tightly.

'Let go of it.'

'No. I'm sorry, Mum, but we can't let you do this.'

The spark of rebellion became a fire in her veins. 'If you don't get out of my way, John, I'll scream for help as loudly as I can. The window's open. Not only will Niccolo hear me, but so will all the other neighbours.'

He let go of her case and jumped aside, looking shocked.

When Sarah peered out of the kitchen doorway, head jerking to and fro like a nervous hen, laughter began to well up in Jenny again. 'I'll be back in a few days.' She opened the front door, then turned to add, 'Perhaps.'

Niccolo was waiting for her outside, standing by his car. He looked rumpled and extremely angry. He kissed her cheek with a loud, defiant smack and helped her into the car, then went to put her case in the boot. He glared at his daughter's house before settling into the driving seat.

When he didn't start the engine up, Jenny asked softly, 'What's wrong, Niccolo?'

He fiddled with the ignition key. 'Are we mad? Gina says so.'

'Oh, yes. Quite mad.' Jenny leaned forward to kiss his cheek.

He turned and kissed her lips, stroking her hair tenderly afterwards with his hand. When he pulled away, his smile echoed hers. 'So – we're mad, then. Let's go and have some fun.'

She felt quite breathless as she fastened her seat belt – breathless and young and full of hope. 'Where are we actually going, Niccolo?'

He shrugged and turned the ignition key, giving her another of his thoughtful glances. 'Who knows? Only time will tell.'

Show, Don't Tell

Anna's Notes

It's one of the rules you're taught early on when you start to write: show, don't tell. In other words, show your characters in action, show what happens, don't just talk about it and miss the excitement.

One day, someone mentioned the good old rule yet again and the idea for this story hit me. I enjoyed writing it. I love stories about women who get their act together and make necessary changes in their lives. Some people call these 'coming of age' stories.

It's what happened to me. I got published as my second career, when the children were teenagers. And my goodness, I've enjoyed it so much more than my first career. I'm now utterly addicted to storytelling.

'But Mum, I was counting on you to babysit Ben!'

Jenny steeled herself. 'You didn't ask me early enough. Sorry, but I'm going out tonight.'

'But you never go out at night since Dad died!'

She moved to hold the door open before Helen could ask any more awkward questions. 'See you soon.'

Once her daughter's car had pulled away, she sagged against the wall. She'd done it. Stood her ground. Just.

It wasn't that she objected to looking after her grandchildren occasionally, but her daughters had been taking her babysitting services for granted since her husband died. Especially Helen, who had recently got divorced.

At eight o'clock that evening the phone rang.

'I thought you were going out, Mum.'

'Oh. Well – um, yes I was. But my friend had to cancel at the last minute.'

'Oh, good. I mean, I'm sorry about your night out, but I still haven't found a babysitter, so I'll just bring Ben round.'

Before Jenny could say a word, her daughter had put the phone down.

The doorbell rang a few minutes later and Helen dumped four-year-old Ben then rushed off. 'See you in the morning, Mum!'

As soon as his mother left, Ben started to cry and wanted to be cuddled. It was one o'clock before Jenny got to bed and even then she lay awake for ages, annoyed at herself.

She'd worked out a campaign to gain more independence from her family – and what had happened? She'd failed to carry it through, that's what. Why, oh why had she picked up that phone?

Helen phoned first thing, waking Jenny after only three hours' sleep. 'Look, Mum, I'm running late. Will you please keep Ben till I get home from work? Sorry to dump on you, but it's the first good night out I've had since the Rat left me.'

'But I—'

The phone clicked down. Jenny looked at herself in the mirror opposite. 'If you don't do something drastic, my girl, you'll turn into the family drudge.'

By mid-morning she was so tired of being shut up with a fretful toddler she took him out for a walk. When it began to rain, they took shelter in the nearby shopping centre. She bought Ben a comic and herself a magazine.

It wasn't till she sat down with a cup of coffee at home that she realized she'd picked up the wrong magazine. Ben sat happily turning the pages of his comic. Maybe he would be a reader like his grandmother one day. The rest of her family weren't interested in books.

'"*Writing Australia*",' she read the title of her magazine aloud. 'Well, that'll make a change.'

It was more than a change. It was fascinating. She'd never realized how much went into writing a book, though she'd dabbled with writing short stories a few years ago – had even had a couple published – but in those days there had always been someone calling, 'Mum, can you just . . .' and she'd given up.

She was about to close the magazine when she noticed the advertisement.

SUMMER SCHOOL. *Learn to write in peace
and privacy. Beginners welcome.*

'Ah,' she sighed. 'It must be wonderful to—' She stopped and
read the advertisement again: '*Beginners welcome.*'

After Helen had collected Ben, Jenny went on line and found
out more about the Summer School. Did she dare? Would the
other people all be younger than her? Was she making a fool of
herself?

First thing in the morning she went on line again to apply, then
went out to buy a new computer. She'd hardly touched their old
one since John died and it was a bit elderly; took ages to down-
load anything.

She went up to a woman her own age who was straightening
a display. 'I need a new computer, a good one.' The company's
insurance policy on John's life had been so huge that Jenny would
never want again. It was no compensation for losing him with
shocking abruptness in an accident, but there was no denying it
helped you to get on with life if you had money.

By the time the two women had spent an hour together deciding
what was needed, they'd also discovered they were both widows
and had exchanged phone numbers. As an afterthought, Jenny
bought a fancy new telephone that told you the callers' numbers.

That evening she heard the phone, tiptoed up to the new
machine and forced herself to let it ring.

When she picked up the message from the answering service
she heard it was Liz. 'Tom and I are going out on Saturday night
and wondered if you'd have the twins for us.'

Jenny immediately rang up her new friend and invited Rose
to go out for a meal on Saturday evening.

Then she rang her daughter and said she was going out, so
couldn't help them.

She set up the new computer in John's old office and kept the door
locked when her family visited.

They made encouraging noises about how nice it was that she
was developing new interests, but they didn't like it when
she wasn't always available for babysitting.

She did it sometimes, of course she did. She loved her grand-children. But she did want a life of her own – and that included weekends.

She still hadn't worked out what to do about Christmas. Liz and Helen were hinting about spending it here in the house where they'd grown up. They assured her they'd help with the catering, but she'd been taken in by that last year and had run herself ragged trying to make it just like their old family Christmases without John's help.

It was Rose who found the solution: a Christmas holiday on the other side of the country in Western Australia. It was for over-55s and included all sorts of group activities. Jenny was only fifty-two but Rose said no one would notice or ask.

Jenny invited the whole family round for a drink the following Sunday afternoon and announced her plans then. There was instant uproar.

'But Mum, it won't be Christmas if we don't come here.'

'No one else has a big enough table, or the time to do things *properly*.'

She took a deep breath. 'Well, if you want to come round here and use my table, that's fine by me – as long as you clear up after yourselves.'

Dead silence.

It was broken by the arrival of young Matt, who was eight and precocious with it. 'You didn't tell me you'd got a new computer, Gran! I can't get into it. What's the password?'

Jenny frowned at him. 'How did you get into my study, Matt? I locked that door.'

'I knew where the key was. I wanted to play on Grandpop's computer.'

Tom swooped on his son. 'Well, you can just tell your grandmother you're sorry then we'll lock up Grandpop's office again.'

'Sorry, Gran.'

Jenny nodded, took a deep breath and said firmly, 'And it isn't Grandpop's office any more. It's *my* office.'

Another dead silence.

When Tom came back he said, 'I didn't know you were into computers, Ma. That's a good one.'

'Oh, they're part of modern life, aren't they?' Did he think she was still living in the dark ages?

Helen smiled at her. 'No need to be ashamed, Mum. It's the age of adult toys. Everyone plays computer games and goes surfing the Net nowadays.'

Jenny didn't contradict her. Writing was too new a dream to share with others.

She came home from Summer School so enthused she signed up for a correspondence course on romance writing and spent a lot of time during the next few months learning how to write. On her tutor's advice she became a member of the Romance Writers of Australia, joined their on-line chat list and started entering their competitions.

Her family assumed she was going out with Rose and the 'oldies', as they called the new friends she'd made. How patronizingly they said it – 'oldies'. Well, she'd show them!

Eighteen months later she sat back and stared in wonderment at the pile of paper she'd just printed out. Her second novel. The first one had taught her a lot but it hadn't been good enough. This one had gone well from the start, however, and now – well, it was ready. She hoped.

Only Rose knew what she'd been doing. She was going to read the novel for Jenny and had promised to be totally honest about her reactions. Which led to a few days of nail biting.

'I love it,' Rose said when she brought the manuscript back.

'Do you really? You're not just saying that?'

'Didn't I promise to be honest? I can see your heroine as clearly as I see you. And I was half in love with the hero.' She patted Jenny's arm. 'You're better at writing than I thought you'd be.'

'But what do I do with it now?' Jenny wondered aloud as she stared at the final draft. She was terrified of submitting it to a publisher. It was one thing to be rejected. Most novelists got rejected at first. But what if they said she couldn't write for toffee? That'd ruin her bright new life.

The next day she saw an advert for a competition run by a popular women's magazine and in a fit of what-the-hells, she sent off her story.

Then she started writing another. She was utterly determined to get published, however long it took.

Ten weeks later the phone rang and a man's voice said, 'Jenny Foster?'

'I don't want to buy anything.' she began automatically.

He chuckled. 'I'm from Janson Grey publishers. I'm Matt Perney, calling to say you've won our "Write a Bestseller" competition.'

Jenny gasped and clutched at the desk. 'I don't believe it.'

Another chuckle. 'It was a great story. Look, we want you to come to the presentation night next month. It'll be a big occasion, with a very elegant dinner. What about your family? Do you want to invite them?'

'I'll . . . let you know.'

Jenny picked up the phone to ring her family, then put it down again, smiling as a much better idea occurred to her.

She made all the arrangements then rang them next evening. 'I've got a surprise for you. I'm taking you all out for a very special dinner, yes, your new guy as well, Helen. Oh, and my friend Rose is coming too. I've booked the babysitters, it's all arranged. You just have to be ready when the limo arrives to pick you up.'

'When are you going to tell them?' Rose whispered as they sat in the limo.

'I'm not. When you're writing, you're taught "Show, don't tell" and that's what I'm doing tonight. *Showing* them I'm a success.'

The evening was dazzling. Matt, who was in on the secret, winked at her as she led her family into the spacious function room. She was relieved that the presentations were before the meal, because it would have been hard to keep the secret otherwise.

When the speeches began, Jenny exchanged glances with Rose and tried to calm her pounding pulse.

'. . . and now, I'll stop talking and announce the winner of the competition, who is . . . Jenny Foster.'

There was dead silence at the table as Jenny stood up and walked to the dais. She accepted the congratulations of the speaker, a novelist whose books she read avidly, then delivered the short speech she'd prepared.

When she got back to the table, her daughters were still looking stunned. Liz said, 'Why didn't you tell us you were into writing, Mum?'

'You never asked what I was doing with my computer, just expected it to be a plaything.'

Silence. Then Liz said slowly, 'No, we didn't ask, did we?' Her voice sounded awed. 'I can't believe it. My mother's a novelist!' She got up to hug her mother and Helen hugged her from the other side.

'We let you down, didn't we?' Helen said.

'No, you spurred me on. If things had gone smoothly between us, I might never have given writing the effort it needed.'

Helen picked up her glass. 'To Mum.' Then she let out a blood-curdling yell and danced her mother round the table.

The Group Settler's Wife

Anna's Notes

The first version of this novella was commissioned by the tiny town of Northcliffe, Western Australia, as part of its collection for a Forest Arts Walk. This was a project to draw tourists to the area, where the timber industry was in decline, with sculptures and paintings and stories.

I loved learning about the history of Northcliffe and working with the various other artists.

After this story was finished, I just had to write a longer novel for my UK publisher, with the same background. Freedom's Land was born, which my old agent considered one of my best novels. Group Settlement is an iconic part of Australia's history and the people who settled the land in groups were for the most part brave and hard-working. I admire them very much. I couldn't have done what they did.

The following story has been published in several formats, including as a serial for an English women's magazine. There are slight variations to each version, but the story is basically the same, and is as true to the early settlers' lives as I could make it.

Part One

Australia, January 1924

The ship bringing the migrants to Australia docked in Fremantle on a hot summer's day in January, seven weeks after leaving England. The settlers crowded by the rails to see their new country and Bill gave Maggie a quick hug, then hugged eight-year-old Jenny too. Peter stepped back hastily. At ten he considered himself too old to cuddle.

'I'm glad that's over,' Bill said. 'I'm never making such a long journey again.'

'I enjoyed it.' She'd made friends, played deck games and benefited from a good long rest. She would definitely be travelling on a ship again one day to go back and see her family, she was determined about that.

It was hours before they were allowed to disembark because they had to undergo medical and customs checks.

Bill muttered about being treated like a flock of sheep as they were herded into a battered old charabanc and driven to the Immigrants' Home in South Fremantle, but cheered up as they saw parrots flying about freely.

As on the ship, they had to sleep separately, with women and girls in dormitories, and men and boys outside on the enclosed veranda. Food was plain but plentiful, and the women were expected to help with chores like washing up.

Maggie felt a bit shy because there were other women who hadn't been on the ship. But she soon realized they were just as eager to make friends. Bill was soon deep in conversation with some of the men and her children had never had trouble making friends.

Jenny bounced out of bed the first morning, rushing to the window to stare out. 'Look, Mum, it's sunny again.'

'Shh. Speak quietly.'

'Dad said it was too hot yesterday, but I liked it.'

'So did I.'

'Can we get dressed and go downstairs?'

'Who wants to stay in bed on a beautiful morning like this?'

After their weeks on the ship, the children looked brown and healthy as they ran about in the gardens with the other children. The Spencers weren't the only ones wanting to give their families a better chance in life, Maggie had found.

Fair-skinned Bill suffered from the heat, getting a rash on his neck, but Maggie and the children revelled in it.

What with the sunny weather and blue skies, it seemed as if they really had come to a land of milk and honey. Perhaps Bill had been right to insist on coming here.

But oh, she missed her mother and sisters so much!

A few days later Bill came rushing into the kitchen to find Maggie. 'We're leaving by train tomorrow for the south-west!'

All the women working there gathered round him to listen to the details.

'We go in our groups and stay somewhere called Pemberton the first night, then we go on to our farms by motor vehicle the next day.'

'I wonder what Northcliffe is like,' Maggie said. 'I hope it's a pretty town.'

'It's our *farm* I'm interested in.'

'I hope we manage all right. We don't really know anything about farming, even if you did read a book on it.'

He waved his fork dismissively in the air. 'That's why they're sending families in groups, with a foreman to show us how to go on.'

She sighed. Bill was a clever man and had never had trouble learning anything from a book, but farming was such a different life. Still, they weren't the only townies in the group. The West Australian government must know what it was doing.

The next day they set off early, full of excitement. But this faded a little as the journey seemed to go on for ever. The children were as good as you could expect, tumbling out of the train and running round whenever it stopped, which it did quite often. They wolfed down the pies and cakes she bought at the stations and drank the tepid water from dripping station taps because the hot weather made you thirsty.

Bill grew very quiet, frowning out of the window at the beige, sunburnt landscape.

'You all right?' she asked.

'What? Oh yes, fine. Just thinking. It's not very pretty, is it?'

It was very different from Lancashire, that was sure. 'It doesn't matter, not really. We still have one another.'

But he didn't smile at her and he continued to look worried.

They didn't arrive at Pemberton until after eleven o'clock at night, by which time Bill had one of the headaches that were a result of a head wound during the war. It wasn't the only legacy of war. He hadn't wanted to make love to her since he'd first fought in France.

She missed the closeness dreadfully. Would he never touch her in that way again?

It was terrible what war did to people's lives.

They were greeted by members of the Citizens' Voluntary Committee, who offered them sandwiches and drinks. The tea had been made in a big square tin labelled 'Laurel Kerosene' on the outside and was dipped out by jug.

She sipped the dark liquid gratefully.

Bill yawned and eased his shoulders. 'Where do we sleep?' he asked the man in charge.

'In the railway carriages, mate.'

'What? You must be joking.'

'There isn't anywhere else *to* sleep.'

Bill continued to grumble and fuss as they settled down.

'Why is Daddy so grumpy?' Jenny asked when she and her mother went to the ladies.

'He has one of his headaches.'

'He's always having them.'

Maggie pretended to fall asleep quickly, as the children did. She didn't have the energy to jolly Bill along tonight.

And although he'd been happier since they left England, reminding her sometimes of the cheerful young man she'd married, there were still days like today. She closed her eyes. Her last thought was: they'd reach their destination tomorrow.

Surely things would get better after that?

Five hours later they were woken by a man with a hand bell, to face a cool, misty morning. Tea and bacon sandwiches were provided for breakfast, and they were given other sandwiches in brown paper bags for later in the day.

Maggie went to thank the tired-looking woman serving them from the huge tin of steaming tea, then stayed to chat. 'Have you had many group settlers through here?'

'A few, but it's only just starting.' She hesitated then added, 'I'd better warn you: they've not got all the temporary huts built yet, let alone the permanent houses. You might find yourselves sleeping in tents for a while. But nights aren't cold at this time of year and it doesn't rain much in summer, so you'll be all right.'

'Oh.'

The woman gave her a wry look. 'You're the one with the complaining husband.'

Maggie could feel herself blushing.

'It takes time to build huts – which the government should have realized. It's not our fault they sent you here too soon. Everyone's doing their best to make you welcome. We want more people in the south-west of this state.'

Maggie nodded. 'We appreciate your help. Bill was – um – a bit tired yesterday.'

As she walked away, she heard the woman say, 'She seems a nice woman, pretty too. I don't envy her with *that* husband, though.'

Maggie refused to let that comment get her down. No one was perfect. And Bill was getting better. She knew he cared about them, would work his fingers to the bone to give the children this chance.

He greeted her with a smile, then helped her up into the flat, open back of a vehicle people here called a 'truck'. It had rails round the back but no roof. 'We'll have to sit on our trunks or else the floor.'

'I don't mind.'

The roads were the worst Maggie had ever seen in her life and they were bumped about like dried peas in a baby's rattle. Several times a truck would get trapped in one of the deep ruts and then everyone had to get out while the men and older boys pushed the vehicle out of the hole.

Peter was always by his father's side, helping the men. He was growing up fast, too fast for Maggie.

'We always get these hold-ups,' one of the drivers said. 'One day we'll have proper roads through these forests.' He laughed and added, 'But *we* might not live long enough to see it!'

It was the trees which lifted Maggie's spirits, so tall and beautiful were they, shedding a pleasant dappled light over everything. Some had been felled and six people could easily have stood on one huge stump. She wished she'd seen that tree when it was growing. It must have been magnificent.

She got talking to the woman sitting next to her, who'd come here with her husband and six children, the oldest a lad of sixteen, the youngest only three years old.

'It's for them I came,' Elsie looked down fondly at the little girl sleeping on her lap. 'I don't mind what *I* have to do, but Mick and me want to give them a better start in life than we had.'

They all wanted that, Maggie thought.

Peter and Jenny were leaning on the rail of the truck now, talking away excitedly to the children next to them.

'Keep an eye on your sister, Peter,' Maggie called.

'I'm all right!' Jenny protested.

Peter gave his mother a wink and she knew he'd do it. He was a responsible lad.

Bill was sitting quietly, staring into space. His skin had gone red and he kept rubbing his right temple. She left him to his thoughts and continued to chat with Elsie.

The trucks slowed down. 'We're here!' called their driver.

'This can't be Northcliffe!' someone exclaimed.

'It is, mate.'

'This isn't a town,' Mick protested.

'It will be one day,' the driver said. 'That's why you lot are here, to build it.'

The settlers stared round in shock at the bare patch of cleared land in the middle of a forest. There was only one building, with a sign proclaiming it a general store. It was little more than a tin shed. Next to it was a tent. To one side of the open land were some rough fences covered in hessian.

Disappointment seared through Maggie and she clutched Bill's hand. She'd expected a church, one or two shops, people to talk to.

Jenny pressed against her. 'Is this really it, Mum?'

She forced a smile, for the children's sake. 'Yes. Fancy seeing a town before it's built. We'll remember today, won't we, when this is a proper street?'

The children looked at her doubtfully.

Bill scowled and opened his mouth, but when she frowned at him, he contented himself with muttering something under his breath.

'If you folk want to go to the lavatory, that's it over there!' the driver called.

Peter went with his father to the side of the cloth-covered fences labelled 'Men'.

Jenny and her mother went to the women's side. Behind the rough fence, they found a trench with a pole across it to sit on. Beside it was a shovel and some sand.

Maggie and her daughter both did what they had to. Out of courtesy she avoided looking at the other women.

One young, newly-married lass stood there sobbing, saying she couldn't go in a place like this. Maggie didn't try to comfort her. She needed all her strength for herself and her family at the moment.

'Bit rough, isn't it?' Elsie whispered as they walked back. 'Why didn't they put two poles, one to lean back against?'

'Because it's easier for men and I don't suppose they think what it's like for women and children,' Maggie replied.

By the time they got back to the truck, a man from the store had provided a bucket of cold water to wash their hands in, an enamel bucket of hot, black tea and some thick chunks of bread spread with jam but no butter.

'Can't stop for long, so eat up quickly,' their driver called. 'Have to get you settled in by nightfall. We'll leave again in half an hour. Food will be provided for the first few weeks, but you ladies might want to buy a few extras. Your group's land is nearly three miles from town.'

Maggie turned to Bill. 'I'll need some money.'

'I don't want you wasting it on luxuries.'

She held back her anger – just. Ever since the war, he'd been very parsimonious, doling out money from his wages when she needed something. During the war she'd worked and had her own money. It had been hard to stay at home again and be dependent on someone else, so she'd done a little sewing to earn pin money, just alterations for friends and neighbours.

She bought a pound of fresh figs and a melon, both cheap at this time of year. Fruit was good for children and she loved it too. She'd never even seen fresh figs before, or tasted a melon.

Then they set off again, jolting along an even rougher track. Everyone commented excitedly when they saw three kangaroos hopping through the trees. They were bigger than Maggie had expected.

'Don't get too near the big males,' the driver called. 'They can rip you apart with those front claws.'

Jenny was tired and had come to sit by her mother.

'I'm longing to get to our new house, aren't you?' Maggie said to Bill, threading her arm in his.

'Yes. There's nowhere like home. Look at that lad of ours.'

Peter was still standing by the rail, his face lit up by excitement. Maggie wished she could stand with him.

The trucks stopped at a clearing which was surrounded by what looked like waste land. Many huge trees had been felled, their trunks and branches still lying on the ground. Everyone stared round in puzzlement.

'Why are we stopping here?' Mick asked.

'This is it,' the driver replied. 'The land your group has been allocated. The government's cleared some of it, to start you off, and you'll be paid by the acre to clear the rest. That's how you earn your living at the beginning.'

'They didn't tell us how big some of the trees would be or how thickly the forest grew,' another man said.

'You don't have to fell them if they're above a certain circumference, just the smaller ones.'

A man strode towards them from behind a pile of crates to one side, waving and smiling. He was tall, about forty, looking strong and capable. 'I'm Ted Riley, your group's foreman. Welcome to your new home.'

Bill jumped down from the truck. 'This can't be it. Where are we supposed to live? They said there would be houses provided.'

'We build temporary huts ourselves first, then later teams of carpenters come round and build proper houses. For now, there are tents.' Ted moved over to the truck. 'Can I help you down, ladies?'

Maggie scrambled down into Bill's arms and he clung to her for a minute.

'I'm sorry,' he whispered. 'I didn't think you'd have to rough it like this.'

'I'll be fine.'

Most of the children jumped down without anyone's help. Peter came to stand by his father, who absent-mindedly laid a hand on his shoulder as they waited. Jenny pressed close to her mother. She'd been very clingy for the whole trip.

When they were all standing in a circle, Ted said, 'We'll need to work quickly to erect the tents before nightfall. We'll start building the temporary huts after we've set up camp.' He jerked his head towards a pile of corrugated iron sheets and timber. 'They sent the materials for the huts before the tents. Stupid, but that's the authorities in Perth for you!'

'You men will be paid a daily rate for your labour,' he went on, 'and tomorrow morning we'll draw lots for which block of land each family gets. That's the fairest way. We'll all eat together at first, and the ladies can do the lighter work and the cooking.' He looked round the silent group. 'Things will get done more quickly if the older children pitch in, too.'

'What about school?' one woman asked.

'Can't build schools till you've got houses. It won't hurt the kids to miss a few months' schooling.'

A few youngsters cheered and were shushed by their parents.

'We also need to build two sets of latrines today, one for men, one for women. We want to keep the place clean, don't we? We'll put hessian fences round them for privacy, but we can't take time for a roof just now. Anyone have any experience of digging latrines and putting up tents?'

That made Bill and the other men chuckle. Most of them were ex-soldiers.

'Just a little experience,' one man said. 'Four years' worth during the war.'

'There you are then, they sent me some real experts.'

Ted's joking had lifted the mood, but as people worked under his direction, Maggie saw how they kept glancing at the surrounding forest, which dwarfed everything. Could they really clear that? It'd be hard going.

By nightfall the Spencers were in their own tent, and for once the children didn't protest about being sent to bed as soon as it grew dark. Stretcher beds had been supplied and set up on the bare earth. For bedding, they each had a heavy bush rug known as a 'bluey' and were using rolled towels as pillows.

All the basic items supplied were to be paid for gradually, Ted said, including the horse and cart, the six cows and necessary equipment like cream separators, which would all be sent later, after they'd cleared the land and built cow and dairy sheds.

So much work lay ahead, Maggie thought as she snuggled down on her narrow canvas bed. Well, you could only take one day at a time.

It was surprisingly cold at night, considering how warm the day had been. She could hear animal noises outside, frogs croaking in a nearby stream, which Ted called 'the creek', and all sorts of rustling sounds and calls, though she couldn't have said what sort of animals were making them.

'Goodnight,' she said into the darkness, but got no answer, even though she could tell Bill wasn't asleep by the way he was breathing.

Her last thought was that the following morning they were to draw lots for the blocks of land and then start building the temporary huts out of corrugated iron. She hoped theirs would be a pretty block, hoped they'd be happy there, hoped the children would thrive in Australia – and that her Bill would continue to get better.

It wouldn't be her fault if they failed.

Part Two

Maggie was woken early by birds calling and twittering nearby. It took her a few moments to remember they were in Australia now. Excitement ran through her. Today the foreman would give each settler family in the group the land the government had assigned for setting up dairy farms.

In the dim light inside the tent she could see her sleeping husband and children on their narrow stretcher beds. Bill's face was hidden beneath his forearm, Peter lay on his back, one hand dangling over the edge, and Jenny was on her side, a smile on her face.

Maggie went to use the women's latrine, nodding to their foreman as she passed. Ted was already tending the communal fire, which had a huge blackened kettle hanging over the flames. She was dying for a cup of tea.

Once dressed, she helped the other women prepare breakfast, dividing up the remaining bread carefully and spreading jam thinly on it.

'They'll be delivering more bread from the shop today,' Ted said cheerfully, 'and for the first week. After that you ladies must learn to make your own.'

When they'd cleared up, everyone assembled in a circle round him without needing to be told, families standing together, ready to draw lots for the blocks of land.

After they'd done that, the foreman walked them up and down the track, showing each family which land belonged to them. It took all morning.

Maggie was delighted to see a couple of tall karri trees on their block as they turned off the track, so huge she couldn't even put her arms round their smooth grey trunks.

'They're a couple of hundred years old at least,' Ted said.

'They'll look pretty guarding the gates,' Maggie said.

Ted shook his head. 'You can't put the entrance under them. They're not called widowmakers for nothing. They drop branches without warning and the bigger ones weigh a ton.'

'This is a farm not a park,' Bill said. 'I'm clearing the lot.'

She was fed up of him making all the decisions. 'Not these two beauties, you aren't. It'll look horrible without some trees and anyway, the cows will need shade in hot weather.'

Ted clapped Bill on the shoulder. 'She's right, mate. Anyway, trees like these are a bugger to knock down. You have to dynamite the stumps to get rid of them and that costs extra.' He winked at Maggie.

She changed the subject quickly. 'Where shall we put the hut?'

'Has to be close to the next block, because you'll be sharing. Only big families get both rooms to themselves.'

In the evening they drew lots again, this time for whose hut would be built first. The Spencers came last of all, which was a big disappointment.

The next day, two men brought a milking cow in the back of a truck, provided by the authorities to help feed the group. They led it carefully down a ramp, gave Ted some food for it and left.

'You women will have to feed and milk her,' he said. 'I'll show you how. Now, who wants to take charge of it?'

There was dead silence.

He laughed. 'She doesn't bite, you know. Mrs Spencer, how about giving it a go?'

Maggie swallowed hard. 'Oh. Well, all right, then.'

'Come and meet Dolly.' He slapped the cow on the rump. 'The main thing is to keep everything to do with milking clean.'

'Of course.' As if she wouldn't do that automatically!

When they'd finished milking, he dipped a clean cup into the bucket of foaming, creamy liquid and solemnly handed it to Maggie. 'You first. You've earned it. You made a good fist of that milking, for a beginner.'

She drank the whole cupful. 'It's lovely.'

'Now, you'll need to milk her morning and night, then share the milk out between the families every day. Make sure she always has water and don't let her roam too far. Oh, and clean up after her as well.' He raised his voice to make sure the other women heard him. 'The cow pats make good fertilizer and they'll be your reward for doing this job, Mrs Spencer. Get your kids to pile them up on your block and cover them with branches to keep the flies down.'

Maggie was left alone with her new charge. Dolly had lovely eyes and seemed placid enough. Timidly she patted her.

Bill joined her, but made no attempt to touch Dolly. 'She's bigger than I expected, but I suppose the manure will come in useful.'

'Everything's bigger in Australia.'

For the next few days everyone worked from dawn to dusk, even the older children doing their share, mostly fetching and carrying for the men.

One or two of the women did the minimum they could get away with, leaving someone else to do the dirty chores, so Maggie and her new friend, Elsie, took it upon themselves to organize a roster sharing out all the jobs. Wood had to be fetched for the communal fire, water lugged in buckets from the creek and the group's food prepared from giant tins of corned beef or fruit or jam. And the women decided to do the washing together as well, in big tin baths.

'We need an outside table to prepare the food on,' Elsie told the foreman. He gave her a mock salute and beckoned to two men.

They dug holes and stood the ends of some logs in the ground, then nailed rough planks across the top.

'There you are, ladies. Your kitchen table. I'll give you some sandpaper to smooth it down.'

One of the other women asked, 'What do we do about bread? Will the shop keep sending more out if we pay for it?'

He laughed, not unkindly. 'You'll need to make your own in a camp oven. I'll show you how tomorrow, but it'll only be damper bread, made with bicarbonate of soda. Can't make proper bread till we get our wood stoves.'

The man must have the patience of a saint, because 'ask the foreman' rang out all day. How Ted kept smiling, Maggie didn't know, but she reckoned they were lucky to have him. He always had a solution of some sort, even if it wasn't what they were used to.

Ted gave them a quick demonstration of making damper. After the dough was finished he put it in the heavy iron camp oven and pushed it into the ground at the edge of the fire. After sprinkling hot embers on the lid he left it to cook.

Helped by the bigger children, the men worked from daylight to dusk on the huts because everyone was eager to have a proper roof over their heads. The women and smaller children walked out to them at noon with their dinners.

Bill greeted Maggie with a smile, seeming happier now that he had something to do. Peter was working with his father, obviously proud to be with the men.

When the first tin shack was finished, the women inspected it in silence – two rooms each about ten foot square and a bare earth floor. Open gables at each end let in the light and doors were sheets of corrugated iron with wire loops serving as hinges.

Maggie tried to hide her dismay. Her auntie's garden shed had been better built than this!

'I don't call this a *house*,' Bill muttered.

'Well at least we'll have a room to ourselves and a proper roof for the wet season.' She glanced sideways. His moods were up and down since they'd got here. What had he expected? Luxury? He'd known they had to clear the land and set up the farms from scratch. She sighed. He was a dreamer, not a practical man. Why had she thought he'd change?

It rained the next day and Jenny ran her fingers down the condensation on the tent wall, making patterns. This made it leak and Bill slapped her hard.

Maggie pushed between them, grabbing his raised arm. 'How is the child to know about living in tents? She meant no harm.'

Jenny ran outside into the rain, sobbing.

He glared at Maggie. 'Don't you dare contradict me in front of the children.'

'Don't you dare hit them, then. I won't have it.'

She was shaken, had thought the sudden rages he'd brought back from the war had stopped. But she wasn't going to let him take out his feelings on their children.

Everyone cheered when the stoves arrived. Maggie, who enjoyed cooking, set herself to learn about using theirs. She'd never made her own bread, because it could be bought more easily at the bread shop, but she'd helped her mother do it when she was a child. Only how did they get yeast out here? Did the shop have some in stock? If so, someone would have to go into town for it, plus some more flour, because they were running low.

Ted heard them discussing the problem. 'Why don't a couple of you walk over to the next group? They'll show you how to make potato yeast. I'll go into town and bring back whatever's needed. I'll call in at the next group on the way and tell them to expect you tomorrow.'

'Potato yeast? I've never heard of that.'

'Well, you're about to find out what it is. Don't worry. It makes good bread.'

'I'd have enjoyed a walk into town,' Maggie said wistfully.

'You couldn't carry the flour back, though. We usually buy it in one hundred and fifty pound bags.'

The women gaped at him.

He grinned. 'That's how it's sold. And sugar comes in seventy-two pound bags, tinned jam by the case. You've got to keep a good supply of basic stores. You can't be nipping to the shop all the time. It's three miles away and your husband will need to use the horse and cart, which will be arriving soon, by the way.'

Maggie and Betty were chosen to go for a lesson on bread making. As they walked, Betty complained non-stop about the primitive conditions, which were nothing like they'd been led to expect. Maggie bit her tongue. No use complaining. You had to make the best of things.

At the farm an older woman called Jean came out to greet them.

'I've waited to show you how to make the yeast, but it's put me behind in my chores, so let's get on with it. I've usually got my bread in the oven by now. Twice a week I bake.'

She showed them how to pour the water from strained potatoes on to dried hop leaves. Once cool, this was strained again and three dessertspoons each of flour and sugar added to the liquid, together with a starter saved from the previous batch of yeast.

When the bread was cooked, Jean let it cool a little then cut them a thick slice each, spreading it with jam.

Maggie closed her eyes in bliss. 'This is wonderful bread.'

'I've made you a loaf each to take back with you and I've put some starter mixture into a jam jar. Should be enough for you all.'

'Thank you so much. Come across and visit us sometime,' Maggie said. 'I've always got a cup of tea for a friend.'

'I'll do that,' Jean said. 'Good luck.'

The two women started to walk back, carrying their loaves and the precious starter.

At an uncleared stretch of forest Betty stopped to look up, seeming near tears. 'I don't like these big trees, looming over you.'

Maggie stopped too, ignoring the complaints. She could hear birdsong in the forest, several different birds by the sound of it. One was making a crooning noise, another was going 'peep-peep' and there was something which sounded like a crow's cawing. She must ask Ted what the birds were. She enjoyed a few moments listening to the chorus, standing in the dappled light under the high green canopy.

'It gives me the shivers. I don't feel *safe*.'

'It's different here, that's all,' Maggie said at last. 'But I like it much better than grey streets and terraced houses.' She hadn't expected that.

★   ★   ★

At last all the huts were finished and the Spencers moved in. Even Bill was cheerful that day and the children ran round shouting and calling.

Ted gathered everyone together the next day. 'Time to put in your orders for the necessities of life before the winter.' He produced some catalogues. 'I'd advise at least one hurricane lamp to light the way outdoors at night.' He went on to advise other purchases, too.

Maggie and Bill went over their list again and again, trying to keep it to the bare minimum. A tin bathtub and wash basin were essential, a couple of buckets, of course, matches, candles, lamps, but they had a lot of other things in their crate waiting in Fremantle to be delivered.

When she saw the prices, Maggie expected Bill to praise her for bringing so many of their smaller household implements, because otherwise they'd have had a much longer list to buy, but he didn't say a word. In fact, he never praised her, though even Ted said she was coping well 'for a Pommie'.

She was worried about Bill and his moods. They were getting worse again.

The men were clearing trees now, working in teams. Bill came home exhausted every evening, expecting her to wait on him. But she was working just as hard, doing her housekeeping under difficult conditions and looking after the cow, so she refused to do that, even if it meant the occasional row.

In a day or two the horses and carts would be arriving. That would make the job of clearing the trees easier, surely? Perhaps he'd cheer up then.

They wouldn't be given their milking cows until more land was cleared and they'd each built a cowshed and dairy where they could separate the cream.

Cream was all the Sunnywest Dairy in Manjimup wanted to buy from them. She couldn't bear the thought of throwing away the milk from several cows every day, but how could one family use it all?

Nothing seemed to fit here.

It was carpenters they needed at this stage, not farmers. Bill wasn't good at woodwork, but as long as his crooked structures didn't fall down, she didn't mind their appearance too much.

Ted said women settlers usually kept hens for the eggs, but their birds would have to be protected from the dingoes that howled sometimes in the evenings in the forest.

Fortunately Maggie was thriving on the hard work and sunshine. The children were tanned and growing apace.

Only Bill looked pinched and unhappy, was losing weight and was often grumpy. The war had changed him so much. Perhaps he'd feel better when they had their proper farmhouse and everything set up.

She didn't know how she'd cope with a lifetime of bad temper and moods.

Two weeks later Betty and her husband announced they were leaving. Maggie wasn't surprised by their decision. She'd heard Betty weeping many a night because the corrugated iron partition between the two rooms offered little privacy.

The young couple sold all their possessions to pay their fares to England, so Maggie bought their sewing machine, which she got at a bargain price because no one else in the group could afford it.

In England she'd always used her mother's machine, which was very old-fashioned, but this one was modern, with a very efficient foot treadle. She was thrilled with it. She bought one or two other household items as well.

Her purchases caused the worst row she'd ever had with Bill.

'How did you pay for that?' he demanded when she proudly showed him her booty.

'I had a bit of money saved.'

'*Money saved!* You didn't tell me about that! Give it to me at once. I'm not having you wasting any more of it. We need every penny for the farm. The money I get from the government for clearing trees won't cover luxuries like sewing machines. It'll barely cover necessities. We only get so much per acre.'

'A sewing machine's not a luxury. Growing children need clothes and it's cheaper if I make them.'

He thumped the table. 'Did you hear what I said? Give me that money at once!'

She hesitated then shook her head. 'No. It's my money, not yours, so I'm keeping it.'

For the first time ever, he thumped her. They stared at each other in shock, then rage swelled within her and she picked up the frying pan and brandished it at him.

'If you ever hit me again, Bill Spencer, I'll hit you back with this, even if I have to wait till you're asleep to do it.'

He took a step backwards, letting his clenched fists fall. 'I'm sorry. I didn't mean to hit you, Maggie. Give me the money and we'll forget about this.'

Again she hesitated, not wanting to keep arguing, but in the end she shook her head. 'I worked hard while you were away and I've always done odd jobs for neighbours and saved a bit. That money's mine.' She saw his fists bunch up again and kept firm hold of the frying pan. 'I'm not your slave, Bill Spencer; I'm your wife.'

'The husband is head of the household.'

'I managed on my own during the war while you were away, and I kept things going when you were ill after you got back. I'll be an equal partner or nothing.'

Anyway, the women in her family had always managed the family money and managed it well, too. For all his talk of being frugal, Bill sometimes bought things on impulse, justifying the purchase later in his own mind.

He stared at her for a moment longer and when she didn't back down, he turned and walked away without a word.

She put the frying pan back on the stove and folded her arms across her breast to hide the shaking. After he'd vanished from sight, she drew a long, shuddering breath.

He'd try again to get the money off her, she knew he would. He was stubborn when he wanted something. Well, so was she.

After some thought, she sent Jenny to play with Elsie's children and quickly made a hiding place for her money in the lining of her sewing box. She stitched up the seam again, packed the embroidery silks back inside, then got on with her chores, feeling more like weeping.

What had got into him?

Part Three

Life continued to have its ups and down for the Spencer family. They were still living in a temporary shack, all four sharing a room only ten foot square, but when their boxes arrived from England, they had a few comforts at least. The West Australian government might have given land to ex-servicemen and their families from all over the British Isles and settled them in groups to help one another, but they hadn't provided anything for daily living except the barest necessities.

Even Bill perked up a bit as they unpacked and of course the two children, Jenny and Peter, were bouncing with excitement about rediscovering much-loved toys and books. Unfortunately, they had to pack most things away again till they got their proper house, for lack of space.

The next day was fine, so Maggie heated water on the wood-burning stove, which stood under a lean-to outside the shack. She set the tub on the rough wooden bench Bill had built and rubbed the underclothes against the washboard till they were clean.

Hard work, all this, and would be until they'd cleared the land and got their dairy farm going. But she was young and healthy, and she loved the outdoor life. She could see a wonderful future for them when the dairy farm was up and running.

She looked across at her children, tossing a ball to one another. To see them so brown and healthy made it all worthwhile. If only her husband would realize that.

But as the months passed Bill remained moody, one day playing with the children as he had in the old days, the next day suffering one of the black moods he'd brought back from the war.

Apart from the children, it was the few moments she spent in the forest every fine day that helped Maggie cope. She'd walk a little way along the rough track listening to the birds singing and calling. Or she'd watch the beautiful patterns of light and shadow beneath the tall trees and marvel at the delicate native flowers that were so much smaller than garden flowers.

The beauty fed her soul, gave her strength.

One sunny Sunday afternoon, Maggie suggested the whole family go for a walk.

'It's supposed to be a day of rest,' Bill said, scowling. 'I'm not doing anything.'

'But it's beautiful in the forest. We used to go for walks at home on Sunday afternoons. Why not here? We could go to the next settlement, call in on Jean and her family.'

'There's nothing beautiful about those damned trees. The government might be paying me to clear them, but it's back-breaking work.'

Bill was to get four pounds ten shillings per cleared acre, but had to fell every tree under eighteen inches in diameter, clearing the roots and all the scrub to leave the land in a ploughable condition. He got an additional eight shillings for ringbarking every tree over that size.

Peter had gone to play with a friend, so Maggie took Jenny walking. She taught her daughter an old folk song, which they sang together as they strolled along the track.

When a stranger came into sight, she stopped singing and hesitated. He was tall and looked very strong. Who was he?

Then two little boys came running after him and she felt better. Silly to be worried. Who else could he be out here but another groupie?

Smiling, he touched his hat to her. 'Lovely day, isn't it? I'm Daniel Marr.'

She introduced herself and Jenny. 'Yes, it is lovely. We're enjoying walking among the trees.'

'I enjoy that too. Say hello, John and Henry.' He smiled at Maggie. 'I bring these rascals out every fine Sunday afternoon. It gives my wife a rest. She's expecting a baby in two months.'

'That's nice.' Maggie watched him walk on. She wished she was expecting another child, but no chance of that with Bill still not wanting to touch her. She'd always hoped for a large family, like hers had been. She blinked away a tear at the thought of her brothers and sisters back in England. She and her mother wrote regularly but it wasn't the same, and letters took weeks to go to and fro by ship, so by the time you got an answer, you forgot what questions you'd asked.

After that, she and Daniel Marr met quite often on fine Sundays, stopping to chat for a few minutes while the children played or ran races up and down the track. His wife never came with him and Bill never came with her. It was Daniel who told her the name of a pretty pink flower that smelled so sweet, even the leaves having a faint perfume: crowea.

Daniel wasn't there one Sunday and she heard later that Mrs Marr had lost the baby. He didn't come till two weeks later and told her his wife was still weak.

Maggie felt guilty sometimes about how much she looked forward to their meetings. She mentioned the first one to Bill and occasionally said she'd met the man with the two boys again, but didn't tell him that they met most Sundays and stopped to chat.

They'd done nothing wrong and somehow she'd grown to consider Daniel a friend. Bill wouldn't understand that a man could be a woman's friend. Neither would most of her neighbours. But it was so good to have someone to talk to.

At the end of April, the milking cows were sent to their group. The Spencers waited eagerly to see what theirs were like. Bill had built a shelter for milking, crooked like all his constructions, but sturdy enough to keep the rain off. On the other side of it he'd built a dairy out of corrugated iron, where the cream could be separated and the buckets scoured. That would be Maggie's province.

Mid-afternoon they heard someone approaching down the track. Peter ran out to see if it was the cows and yelled that it was, dancing about in excitement. Maggie sent Jenny to tell her father.

The cows looked tired and dusty, milling around when driven through the rough wire and timber gate. They were a mixed bunch; brown, black and white in colour, and all had full udders.

'Which ones do you want, missus?' one of the men asked. 'This one's a good little milker. And that black and brown one has a nice nature.'

'All right. You choose the others for me.' She watched him shoo six cows into the rough enclosure they'd made from the young trees Bill had felled.

Her husband continued chatting to the men, making no attempt to help with the cows.

Maggie kept control of her temper. 'Come on, Jenny. Let's get the poor creatures a drink.'

She sent Peter to lug water up from the creek. He was such a good worker, that boy, a real treasure. They were all looking forward to having a proper rainwater tank when they got their house.

The two men left soon after and Bill walked across to join her. 'They look a miserable bunch of cows.'

'That's because they're dusty and tired. They'll soon settle down.'

'Can I call the little one Alice?' Jenny asked.

'You can call them what you want as long as you learn to milk them properly,' Bill said.

'Talking of milking, they'll be uncomfortable. Come on, children. We all have to learn how to milk them.' Maggie went to get the special buckets.

Strangely enough, it was Bill who wasn't good with the cows. His heart just wasn't in it, though he did the work without complaining. She could milk far more quickly and soon Peter could too. Both children loved working with the animals.

Oh, Bill, she thought sometimes. Will you ever be happy again?

A week after the cows arrived Bill went out one evening 'to see a man' and came back drunk. She was furious with him, not only for getting into that disgusting condition, but for spending good money on booze, but he was unrepentant.

'A man has to have a bit of relaxation, or what's life about? I earn the money. I'll say how it's spent.'

She couldn't think where he'd got hold of the booze, but Elsie said a man in the next group brought it in from Pemberton, selling it at a small profit.

'Well, I wish he wouldn't,' Maggie said.

'You can't stop men drinking,' Elsie said. 'My husband went out too last night.'

'Did he come home drunk?'

'No, he just had a couple of beers.'

'Bill was very drunk.'

'Oh. Does he often do that?'

'Sometimes. Since the war.'

Elsie patted her shoulder. 'He'll settle down when we get proper houses to live in.'

Maggie was beginning to wonder about that. Bill worked hard, even tried to be cheerful and loving some days, but he was nothing like the man she'd married.

For better for worse, she'd vowed as a happy young wife. And they had been happy for a time. Then the war had ruined everything.

At least in England she'd had her family to comfort her. Here she didn't even tell Elsie how bad it was sometimes.

Northcliffe, Western Australia, Summer, 1925

The first year passed quickly. There was so much to do, Maggie fell into bed exhausted each night. She worried about the children missing their schooling so insisted Peter and Jenny read regularly, swapping books with other families. She even bought a few more books second-hand, something which infuriated Bill, who wasn't a reader.

She was delighted when she heard that a one-teacher school was going to be built only two miles down the road for this group and the next.

A highlight of the year was moving out of the tin shack. Their new home had four rooms with verandas front and back. It felt empty at first, they had so little furniture, but she was making more herself.

The big, square kerosene cans came in pairs in wooden crates which could be used for all sorts of purposes. She had one empty crate in the kitchen as a storage cupboard for her household equipment, and as they became available she put others into the bedrooms to store their clothes. She sanded down the wood herself and made little curtains to hide the contents. They looked very nice, considering.

Jenny helped her with the sewing, trying so hard, she ignored the uneven stitches.

Peter turned eleven, already longing to leave school, though he'd have to wait till he was fourteen, like everyone else. He was born to be a farmer, she sometimes thought.

He and his sister would still have to help milk the cows before they went to school, because she couldn't manage without their help. It was the same for all the groupie children.

Maggie tried to give her two a chance to play each day, but Bill got grumpy if he saw them 'wasting time'. He got even more grumpy when she still refused to give him her money. She was able to earn a little extra sewing for other women, or doing washing and mending for men who came into the area to help clear more trees for new groups of settlers, or to make roads.

One day Bill came home for his midday meal looking smug and triumphant. 'I got your money from Mrs Tennerson.' He patted his pocket.

'What do you mean, *you* got my money?'

'I said she could give it to me to pass on to you, and she did.'

Her voice was cool as she held out her hand. 'Pass it on, then.'

'I need some extra this week.'

Maggie glared at him. 'No, you don't. You're *stealing* it.'

And they were off into another row. No hiding it from the children these days. No hiding why he needed the extra money, either: to buy drink.

She hated the smell of his breath the nights he went drinking, and he never washed himself properly when drunk. What was the use, he said if she complained. He'd only get filthy the next day.

When things went wrong, none of it was ever his fault.

When things went well, she occasionally caught a glimpse of the old Bill – but less often these days.

Maggie didn't tell her family in England how badly things were going. There was nothing they could do to help her so why worry them? At least Bill still worked hard, whether he was hung-over or not, but it was with the grim endurance of a man who loathed what he was doing.

What had he expected? Even she had worked out before they came here that cows needed milking twice a day, every day of the year.

And you couldn't even be a few minutes late with the milking because the man who picked up the cream waited for no one, and it was the cream that earned the money.

Like some of the other groupies, they tried raising pigs on the skim milk that was left, but Bill couldn't face killing them. The first time his hand shook and he turned pale, flinging the knife away. 'I can't do it. It was bad enough killing in the war, in self-defence. But these animals haven't hurt me.'

She put her arms round him. 'We can ask Mick to do it. He won't mind.'

But that upset Bill too, because word got out and the other men teased him.

The children loved the new batch of piglets, and played with them, letting one escape by mistake, shouting with laughter as they chased it round the house. Even Bill watched in amusement, his arm going round Maggie's shoulders, like in the old days.

Two days later, however, all the piglets escaped and couldn't be found. She guessed Bill had let them out deliberately or else sold them to get money for drink.

After that he made arrangements to give the skim milk to a man in the next group, in return for some bacon when a pig was killed. They left the milk in old kerosene tins near the gate to be picked up once a day and clean tins were left for the next lot.

The man turned out to be Daniel Marr. He smiled at her, but didn't have time to stop and chat.

She was proud of making every penny do the work of four and ensuring nothing went to waste. Even the sacks the flour and other groceries came in were used for towels and rough work clothes for the children.

There was only one thing that went to waste in their family, and she bitterly resented it: the money Bill spent on booze. He wouldn't tell her how much savings they had left, which worried her greatly.

One day Daniel didn't come to pick up the milk. Bill grumbled. 'It's not worth bothering, just for a bit of bacon. We should pour it away.'

But Maggie knew something must have happened to keep Daniel away.

Sure enough, her friend Elsie came that afternoon with the news that Daniel's wife had died the previous night – just clutched her chest and dropped dead.

'Oh, no! How's he going to manage? Those poor little boys, motherless!'

'The kids have gone to a neighbour's house for the time being.' Elsie looked at her sideways. 'I didn't think you knew the Marrs.'

Maggie could feel her cheeks heating up and turned quickly to check the kettle. 'I've met Mr Marr and the boys a few times on my Sunday walks with Jenny. I didn't realize his wife was that ill.'

'She's not been well since the baby, so their neighbours have been helping out. Daniel's been doing some of the heavy housework, though how he finds the time, I don't know. Unless he can get a relative to come and help him, he'll have to leave. A man can't run a farm without a wife, or look after young children, and if he sends them to live with relatives, he'll still have to pay money to support them.'

Maggie couldn't imagine him sending his sons away. Daniel loved his boys, tossed them in the air, teased them. 'When's the funeral?'

'They're taking her body over to Pemberton on Thursday. It's more than time we got our own cemetery. I don't know why it's taking them so long to arrange it when permission's already been given for one here.'

Maggie would have gone to the service if it had been local, out of respect, but there was no way she could get into Pemberton, fifteen miles away. 'I'd better tell Bill. Maybe he'll drive the skim milk across for a few days till Daniel sorts things out. Those pigs still need to be fed, after all.'

But Bill refused point blank to add another job to his busy days, saying he'd pour away the damned milk rather than do that.

'Mr Marr's just lost his wife! Other neighbours are helping.'

'Well, I'm sorry for him but I've enough on my own plate in this godforsaken hole.'

She took her worries to Elsie, who spoke to her husband. That evening two men turned up at the Spencers' house to make arrangements to pick up the milk for Daniel. They were very stiff with Bill, and Maggie knew they thought less of him for failing to do his bit.

So did she.

When they'd gone he turned on her. 'What have you been saying to people?'

'I only mentioned the milk to Elsie.'

He raised one fist and she darted behind the nearest chair, suddenly afraid of the burning anger in his eyes. 'I'll leave if you touch me, Bill Spencer! I swear it.'

'And go where? If you tattle to your friends again about my business, I'll give you a lesson in how a wife should behave.' He brandished a clenched fist.

Then he was gone and she knew he would come home drunk.

Only this time he didn't come home till morning. He'd slept under a tree, he said. It was more peaceful than sharing a bed with her.

He'd probably been too drunk to find his way home. Serve him right if he felt as bad as he looked!

But the incident upset her deeply. She'd never been afraid of him before. And the children must have heard the quarrel.

Part Four

Northcliffe, Western Australia, 1926

As the days passed, Elsie kept Maggie informed about how Daniel Marr was getting on after his wife's death. 'That man's a battler if ever I met one. Says he's not giving up his farm while he can stand upright. He's paying neighbours to do his baking and washing for him. Me and Mick drove over in the cart to see them and take them a cake. It fair brought tears to my eyes to see those motherless lads doing the housework.'

'I hope Daniel succeeds.'

'I can't see how. A farmer needs a woman to work alongside him.'

There was no sign of her friend on the Sunday walks now and she missed him.

Maggie went to collect the payment for two dresses she'd altered. She did all sorts of little jobs like that to earn her own money. Her husband didn't like it. Bill didn't like farming, either. Oh, he'd settled down after a fashion here, cleared the land and put some to grass for their cows. But he did nothing but complain about his new life.

She loved Australia, though. Having grown up in a mill town in Lancashire, she'd not expected that when they emigrated.

'I gave the money to your husband,' the woman said.

'But you promised not to do that!'

'My husband said I had to. I'm sorry.'

When Bill came back from tree felling that afternoon, they had the worst quarrel ever. She'd worked hard for her ten shillings. After he slammed out of the house, she put her head down on the table and wept – for the man she loved, changed by the war, for the happy family life that was impossible with a drunken father, and for her children, because she didn't know how to protect them if Bill continued to go downhill.

She watched stony-faced when he went out drinking that night on the money meant for new dress material for little Jenny, who was growing fast. They'd have to wait for that now.

When Bill hadn't come home by dawn she was both anxious and annoyed. He knew there were animals to be cared for.

She got the children up earlier than usual and the three of them set to work. Jenny and Peter would have to go to school late. She needed their help to get the cows milked and the cream separated, because it was pickup day. Even though they all worked hard, they only just got the cream to the gate in time.

There was still no sign of Bill and, after some hesitation, she gave in to Peter's pleas to let him stay home and do the farm work.

Just before noon someone knocked on the door. Her neighbour Elsie stood there.

'It's bad news, love,' she said gently. 'Can I come in?'

What next? Maggie thought.

'Tom Lester found Bill's body down one of the side tracks. He'd been killed by one of those huge branches. You know how suddenly they can drop.' Elsie leaned forward to clasp her hand. 'I'm so sorry, love. The men are bringing his body back.'

Maggie sat there feeling utterly numb. It couldn't be true. But when she looked at Elsie's face, she knew it was. 'I should be crying,' she said in surprise. Instead her eyes felt burning and dry.

'Grief affects us all differently.'

'I can't seem to take it in.' And she felt more angry than grief-stricken. How was she to manage the farm without him? 'The children. Can you fetch them in? I need to tell them before they see . . . anything.'

'My Mick's fetching them.'

There were footsteps outside and the children came in.

Elsie stood up. 'I'll leave you alone for a bit.'

Maggie waited till the door had shut then took a deep breath and told them.

Jenny burst into tears and flung herself into her mother's arms.

Peter stared bitterly at the floor. 'I suppose he was drunk again.'

It was shocking that an eleven-year-old boy should say such a thing of his father, even more shocking that it was true.

'What are we going to do now?' he asked in an angry tone. 'Will we lose our farm?'

'I don't know. I haven't had time to think.' She heard voices in the distance and stood up. 'They're bringing him back.'

The men had Bill's body on a gate, covered up by an old blanket.

'It was a heavy branch. Best the kids don't see him,' one man said gruffly. 'We should put him somewhere outside, Mrs Spencer.'

She led them to the storage shed, standing with her arms wrapped round herself as they set down the man-sized bundle.

'Do you want to look at him?'

'No.'

'We've sent for the doctor to certify his death.'

Elsie came to put an arm round her. 'Are you going to be all right?'

'Yes.'

'Send one of the children across to fetch me if you need anything, anything at all.'

Peter remained angry, Jenny tearful. In the end, Maggie said, 'The cows and horse and hens still need looking after. Come on. Best we keep ourselves busy.'

But she couldn't stop her thoughts buzzing round and round like flies on a piece of meat.

How terrible that Bill should survive the war and then die like this. Would she and the children have to leave the farm? Go back to England? To her surprise, she didn't want to do that. Somehow, Australia had become home to her now.

It was four hours before the doctor came and pronounced Bill officially dead, scribbling a death certificate and offering his condolences.

That evening some men came round with a rough coffin they'd made. 'The doc will let them know in Pemberton that we need to bury your husband tomorrow,' one of them said. 'And after-wards, we'll take it in turns to give you a hand for an hour or two each day till you decide what to do. You can't manage on your own.'

'Thank you. I'm grateful.'

But she still couldn't cry, just – couldn't.

It wasn't until the night after they'd buried Bill that Maggie wept, muffling her tears in her pillow. She wished so desperately they hadn't quarrelled the last time they'd been together. She remem-bered their wedding day, how handsome he'd looked, how much hope they'd both had for the future.

It was impossible to sleep with the worry about what she would do now. Her neighbours were right. She couldn't run a farm on her own; wasn't stupid enough to try.

But she couldn't bear the thought of living in a town again, either, and the kids would hate it after the freedom of life here. Nor did she want to go back to England. She loved the warmer climate in Australia. And she'd made so many friends now that she felt she'd put down roots in Northcliffe, just like those big trees.

When Elsie came across to see her the next day, Maggie poured all her worries out to her friend.

'No one will mind if you take a week or two to work out what you want to do.' Elsie hesitated. 'But if you're giving up the farm, could you let us know first, please? I don't want to sound heartless, but my Mick would like to take it over, if that's allowed. The older boys are big enough to do a man's work and we have to think of their future.'

Maggie nodded. She felt numb, as if her head was full of cotton wool and her thoughts couldn't get through it.

Ten days later she realized it was Sunday. She'd done nothing but work since Bill's death, the children too. 'Let's go for a walk.'

'I want to finish mending that hay trough.' Peter stubbornly refused to contemplate leaving the farm, even though she'd tried to prepare him for it.

She and Jenny followed their usual path, though Maggie couldn't help looking ahead to check that no large branches were hanging over the track.

Daniel was out walking at the same time. They stood together while the three children wandered off, chatting.

'I'm sorry about your husband,' he said gently. 'I didn't have time to come and see you before. Been a bit busy. You must be missing him.'

She stared down at the ground, tried to say something suitable and couldn't. The words were out before she could prevent them. 'I'm not.'

There was silence next to her.

She looked up. 'I expect you're disgusted with me, but I can't lie to you, Daniel. I'm not missing Bill at all. He was drinking heavily, wasting my hard-earned money on booze, not being a good father. And the last time I saw him, we quarrelled.' Her voice broke on the words. Would Daniel think her heartless?

'I was sad when Alice died, but relieved as well. She never forgave me for bringing her to Australia, you see, never stopped complaining, on and on.'

Maggie let out her breath in a great whoosh of relief. 'Bill made me come to Australia. I didn't want to. And now, well, I've grown to love it here and he hated it. Strange that, isn't it? But I can't manage the farm on my own.'

'I expect it'll all work out in the end. Give it time.'

They stood in silence, but it was a companionable silence. It had felt good to admit to her true feelings. Strange how easy it was to talk to Daniel.

Then she sighed. 'I'd better get back. There's always something needs doing. I promised myself just half an hour in the forest.'

He nodded. 'I'm glad we met today.'

'Me too.'

A week later Elsie came across, looking full of herself. She sat down, refusing a cup of tea. 'You don't want to go back to England, do you, love?'

'No.'

'And Daniel Marr is struggling to manage without a wife.'

Maggie froze, guessing where this was leading.

'He asked me to sound you out, see what you thought about marrying him.'

'He – did?'

When she didn't say anything else, Elsie cocked her head on one side and prompted, 'Well?'

'I don't know what to say. Marriage isn't something you'd rush into lightly.'

'He's a good man. My Mick thinks well of him. And those two lads of his are nice kids. You'd have no trouble with them.'

'We might have trouble with Peter, though. He's trying to be the man of the house, won't give that up lightly.'

'Then you're thinking about saying "yes"? You are, aren't you?'

Maggie frowned. 'Not exactly. Not yet. I'd need to speak to Daniel first. Could you ask him to come to tea here tomorrow, do you think?'

'I'll send one of my boys with a message. And Maggie love . . . I'd marry him if I was you. He's a fine-looking man, hard-working and kind with it.'

'You would?'

'Yes.'

'But it's so soon. What would people say?'

'They'd say it makes sense and be pleased that you're staying. And so would I. I don't want to lose my best friend.'

After Elsie had gone, Maggie sat lost in thought. Was it too soon? It'd give her and the kids another chance here, the only chance they had. And she liked Daniel. She blushed at the thought of him as a husband. But smiled as well.

After the evening milking and tea were over, Maggie said to the children, 'Don't get your books out yet. I need to talk to you.'

They sat back in their chairs, looking at her anxiously.

'Do you want to go back to England?'

Jenny shook her head. 'I've got lots of friends here.'

Peter spoke without a second's hesitation. 'No. And I won't do it. I'll run away if you try to make me. I like it in Australia and I like being a farmer.'

'I know. But we can't manage the farm on our own.'

'No one would worry if I stayed off school. They'd understand.'

'You've not got a man's strength yet, love.' She hated to see the light die in his eyes. 'And anyway, the bank wouldn't let me take on any more debt. They don't trust women.' The bank had already written to say Mr Spencer's debt to them must be settled when she sold up.

Peter scowled at the floor. 'Well, I'm *not* going back to England.'

'There is one way for us to stay; the only way, I think.'

He looked up eagerly.

She explained what Daniel had offered and they both stared at her open-mouthed.

'But Dad's only just died!' Peter exclaimed.

'I know. It's too soon, really. Only I don't have time to wait. So,' she paused, took a deep breath then said, 'Daniel's coming to tea tomorrow, with his sons. Give them a chance, Peter, meet them, talk to them.'

'I like John and Henry,' Jenny volunteered.

Peter stared at her in surprise. 'How do you know them?'

'Mum and I meet them sometimes when we go for walks.'

Peter began tracing patterns on the wooden floor with the toe of his shoe.

Maggie waited and when he didn't speak, she said, 'If you think you won't get on with Daniel, I'll not marry him.'

'I don't know what to think,' he said.

Nor did she really. She'd liked Daniel Marr instinctively, right from their first meeting. But would she rue a hasty decision for the rest of her life?

I can always say no, she decided. We'll just – see how we go.

When they were finishing the following morning's milking, Peter said suddenly, 'Did you love Dad?'

She hesitated, then decided he was old enough for the truth. 'I did when we got married, but the war changed him. It wasn't his fault.'

'Did he hit you?'

'Once.'

'He hit me sometimes.'

She stared at him in dismay. 'You never said anything.'

He shrugged.

'You should have said.'

'I got a stick and whacked him back a couple of months ago. He stopped hitting me after that.'

'Oh.'

'But if Daniel hits me, I'm not living with him.'

'I don't think he will, but we can tell him that, if you like.'

Jenny spoke up from the other side of the shed. 'Mr Marr doesn't hit John and Henry. I asked them when Dad hit me once.'

Bill had hit a nine-year-old girl too! Maggie felt sick to think of that.

The children began talking about something else.

But she couldn't get the thought of Bill's violence out of her mind.

Daniel turned up at two o'clock driving a small cart and wearing a suit. His face was rosy red, as if he'd scrubbed it. The boys were equally well scrubbed and in their Sunday best, though their shirts needed ironing.

It was a hot day, so they all went to sit in the shade on one side of the house.

As the children fidgeted, Daniel said suddenly, 'Why don't you show me round the farm, Peter?'

The boy nodded and stood up.

'Can I show John and Henry my favourite places, Mum?' Jenny asked.

Daniel looked at Maggie. 'Do you mind us leaving you for a bit? I want to ask Peter something.'

She shook her head and watched the two walk away. She'd be glad of a few minutes' peace and quiet. Her emotions were in turmoil. He looked good, Daniel, strong and manly, and his sons looked at him with love in their eyes.

Could she? Dare she?

In the shed, Daniel said abruptly, 'Would you mind if I married your mother?'

Peter hitched his shoulders up and down.

'It won't work if you're going to hate it.'

'She says it's the only way we can stay here.' The boy gestured around. 'I love the farm. I want it to be mine when I grow up. Can we keep it, manage two farms?'

'Maybe. We could try.'

'I won't have you hitting me and Jenny, or Mum, like my father used to.'

'*He hit your mother?*'

'Once. She threatened to hit him back.'

Daniel chuckled. 'I can imagine her doing it.' He laid one hand on Peter's shoulder. 'I don't hit people.'

'All right. But you'd better treat Mum properly.'

'I shall. I like her a lot.'

From where she was sitting in the shade Maggie watched them come back. They were gesticulating and talking earnestly, and they stopped once as Peter pointed something out. She felt happiness stir in her at the sight as she stood up. 'I'll get the tea ready.'

Daniel moved towards her. 'I'll help you.'

In the kitchen, she felt suddenly shy.

'I asked Peter if it was all right for us to marry and he thinks it is.'

'Oh?'

'You told Elsie you'd consider it seriously. You haven't changed your mind, have you?'

'No.' Maggie realized she was being a coward, so raised her gaze to meet his. 'I'd rather have waited, but there isn't time for that, is there?'

'Not really. Not for either of us.'

'Do you think we could be happy together, Daniel?'

'It won't be my fault if we aren't.'

'I'm a hard worker,' she offered.

He nodded. 'I know. Everyone says you are.'

'They say that about you, too.'

'And I'd look after your children, Daniel. They're grand little lads.'

He smiled and she noticed how one side of his mouth curved up more than the other, giving his face a crooked charm. His smile lit up his eyes and warmed something in her heart, too.

He knelt down suddenly, taking her hand. 'Maggie Spencer, will you marry me?'

She felt flustered. 'I've already said I will.'

'But I didn't think you should be cheated out of a proper proposal. Just as I don't want to be cheated out of a proper answer.' He looked up at her, head on one side, that smile curving his lips again.

Suddenly she knew it was going to be all right. It might not be smooth sailing, life never was, but this man's heart was in the right place. 'I'll be honoured to accept your proposal, Daniel Marr.'